W9-BEV-417

Also by RM Johnson

The Million Dollar Divorce

Dating Games

Love Frustration

The Harris Family

Father Found

The Harris Men

Do You Take This Woman?

a novel

RM Johnson

Simon & Schuster Paperbacks
New York London Toronto Sydney

SIMON & SCHUSTER PAPERBACKS
A Division of Simon & Schuster, Inc.
1230 Avenue of the Americas
New York, NY 10020

This book is a work of fiction. Names, characters, places, and incidents either are products of the author's imagination or are used fictitiously. Any resemblance to actual events or locales or persons, living or dead, is entirely coincidental.

First Simon & Schuster trade paperback edition February 2008

SIMON & SCHUSTER PAPERBACKS and colophon are registered trademarks of Simon & Schuster, Inc.

For information about special discounts for bulk purchases, please contact Simon & Schuster Special Sales at 1-800-456-6798 or business@simonandschuster.com.

DESIGNED BY PAUL DIPPOLITO

Manufactured in the United States of America

10 9 8 7 6 5 4 3 2 1

The Library of Congress has cataloged the hardcover edition as follows:

Johnson, R. M. (Rodney Marcus)
Do you take this woman? : a novel / R.M. Johnson
p. cm.
1. Male friendship—Fiction. 2. Triangles (Interpersonal relations)—Fiction. I. Title.

PS3560.O3834D68 2006
813'.54—dc22 2006045016

ISBN-13: 978-0-7432-8519-3
ISBN-10: 0-7432-8519-0
ISBN-13: 978-0-7432-8520-9 (Pbk)
ISBN-10: 0-7432-8520-4 (Pbk)

To all those brave and loving enough to marry,
and even more to those strong enough
to make it last

Do You Take This Woman?

1

Last night, after walking into her house from work, Carla Barnes found her husband, Pete, bent over in a chair, his face buried in his hands.

She stood in the doorway, afraid to go in. She was worried that he might have found out some way.

She ventured in, stepped beside him, placed a hand on his shoulder.

"Pete," she said, her voice soft.

He did not look up, did not take his face from his hands.

"Pete," Carla said again, shaking him a little. "Are you okay?"

Pete raised his face. He looked anguished. Carla's heart started to beat faster, something inside telling herself that he did know.

"Just tell me what's going on," Pete said.

"With what?"

"With us."

"What are you talking about?" Carla said, feigning ignorance. She knew he was referring to Carla walking in late every evening, some times after 9 P.M. when she got off work at 4:30 P.M. He was talking about the distance that had been between them, her reluctance to talk to him, show him affection, touch him, make love to him. "I don't know what you're talking about," Carla repeated, turning away.

Her husband got out of his chair and stood there behind her. "Is it someone else?" he asked. "I don't believe you'd do that to me, but I have to ask you. Is it?"

Carla breathed a short sigh of relief. He really did not know. He was guessing, and although he was close to the truth, he wasn't certain of anything. "No," Carla said, turning to him. "I'm not seeing anyone else. It's work, like I told you. Things have been just a little crazy, that's all." She was lying.

She wasn't seeing anyone in the way that Pete was thinking. She wasn't sleeping with another man, wasn't meeting in hotel rooms, wasn't supplementing the sex life she and her husband shared, although there was someone that she had been talking to.

He was an ex-friend, an ex-lover, an ex-fiancé.

When Wayne had pulled Carla aside two months ago, at a barbecue her husband was throwing, and whispered to her that he wanted to see her again, Carla could not deny that she was interested. But that was as far as she wanted it to go.

She knew that she could not be alone with Wayne because of how much she had loved him those two years ago, and how much she feared that she might still feel for him.

"I can't do that," Carla had said to him then, pouring herself some punch, staring directly at her husband standing across the lawn. He was smiling back at her as he grilled hotdogs and hamburgers for the twenty or so people that stood about the yard.

"I'm not asking you to cheat on him," Wayne said. "I just want to see you, talk to you, spend time with you. I miss you. It'll be innocent. I promise."

Carla turned to look at Wayne, and she knew that it could not be that.

The man was beautiful. His chiseled facial features, square jaw, breadcrust complexion, and that dimpled smile, always made her just want to lean over and kiss him.

She felt that urge then, but she suppressed it when her husband smiled again and waved at her.

Carla smiled and waved back, blew a kiss at him. Wayne waved as well.

"You'd do that to him, your best friend?" Carla asked.

"I wouldn't be doing anything. I would be just talking to you, like I said. That wouldn't be nearly as bad as what he did to me."

"So that's what this is, get back for what Pete did," Carla said, sipping some of her punch, keeping an eye on her husband, making sure he did not suspect anything. "You brought that on yourself."

"I don't want to talk about that," Wayne said.

"I bet you don't."

"Will you see me?"

"No," Carla said.

"I'm not accepting that answer. We'll talk some more later," Wayne said, walking away from Carla, through the thin crowd of people and over to Carla's husband. He said something to Pete to get him laughing, slapped the man on the back, then took over the cooking duties. He did not once look back up at Carla, but like he said, she knew he did not accept her answer.

After that, he called Carla at work every morning, sent her flowers, candy, cards. He would meet her outside her office building, his car running, telling her he just wanted to share a meal with her.

Although some mornings she would talk to him on the phone, she would always turn him down for those meals.

And then he started meeting her after work.

She told him how dangerous his actions were.

"What if Pete rolls up right now, sees us out here?"

"Then get in. We'll drive somewhere, and he won't see us," Wayne said, after two weeks of chasing her.

That was the beginning, the first time they sat and had a drink, listened to music, talked. They had a wonderful time.

Carla could not help but think about how things had been with Wayne back when they were together, when they were planning their marriage, how the rest of their lives would've been together.

After the third consecutive after-work outing with Wayne, it seemed she fell right back into a groove with him. She felt so comfortable, and after returning home that night, thoughts start entering her head. They were terrible thoughts, damaging thoughts that had her locked in the bathroom long after her shower was over, hesitant about stepping out, crawling in bed with her husband. These were thoughts that had her rolling on her side, away from Pete, telling him that she wasn't in the mood, had a lot on her mind, that she just needed to sleep.

After spending those few short days with Wayne, Carla was asking herself every day upon waking, had she married the wrong man? Had she been too hasty in her decision to marry Pete?

She needed to stop seeing Wayne. She told herself over and over again that the last phone call would be the final one, the last outing would be the last time she would see him without Pete being somewhere nearby.

"But we aren't doing anything," Carla rationalized to her best friend Laci King, an assistant editor who had the office next to hers. "All we do is talk."

"But the talk is driving a wedge between you and your husband. Carla, he's going to find out one day. Regardless of how clever we women like to think we are, men aren't stupid. This will catch up to you."

And as Carla stood in the den with her husband last night, she realized Laci might be right.

"I'm afraid," Pete had said, "that if this distance between us continues too much longer, it'll be the end of our marriage."

"What are you talking about, Pete? It's a rough patch at work."

"It's not just that!" Pete said, raising his voice, standing up and grabbing her by the shoulders. "I know there's something else. What can I do?"

"We'll be fine," Carla said, stepping away from the hold Pete had on her. She turned and walked out of the room, not answering the question, because she knew there was nothing he could do.

Only she could change things. That was why the next evening, before Carla left work, she had called Wayne, asked him to meet her at Calypso, a Jamaican restaurant in Hyde Park.

The entire drive there, Carla asked herself whether she was doing the right thing. Did she really want to stop seeing Wayne?

After parking the car, walking in the restaurant, and ordering a drink, she told herself she had no choice.

She sat there for twenty minutes. She had drunk an apple martini and was working on a second. When she saw Wayne walk in the front door, she finished the second martini. He was wearing tan linen pants and a matching jacket that his broad shoulders filled out nicely.

Carla stood up from the table, wobbled just a little on her heels.

Wayne caught her by the waist. "One too many?" he said, kissing her beside her ear.

"No, I'm okay," Carla said, hugging him for a brief moment, then sitting back down.

"I've missed you," Wayne said, sliding over one of the menus that sat on the table in front of him. "Are you hungry?"

"I'm not here to eat tonight," Carla said, already starting to feel sadness.

"Then what, you just want to do drinks? I can do that."

"No, Wayne. I'm here to tell you that we can't see each other anymore."

Wayne looked across at Carla, smiled uncomfortably, then said, "You're joking, right?"

"No."

"But we aren't seeing each other. We meet to talk, hang out. What's wrong with that?"

"Everything," Carla said, reaching across the table, taking Wayne's hands in hers. "These two months have been wonderful, but I can't continue this. I have these feelings for you. I think of you all the time, at work, at home. I'm neglecting my husband because of them. I'm sure while you two were at work, Pete told you that things aren't right between us."

"He's told me," Wayne said. "But he said that you told him things are hectic at the magazine."

"You know that's not the truth. You know it's you, Wayne."

Wayne looked up at her. "You don't miss what we've had?"

"I do, but now I have something else. I'm married now. I have to respect that, and you should, too. He's your best friend."

Wayne lowered his head as though he felt shame. "I know. I shouldn't be doing this. I don't want to ruin things between you and Pete. I missed you. I just wanted to spend some time with you."

"And what did you think would become of that?"

He peered up at her. "Maybe that you would realize that you still had feelings for me, realize that you married Pete because I cheated on you, and come back to me."

"No, Wayne. I left you because you cheated on me, and then I married Pete because I fell in love with him."

Wayne looked away to avoid Carla's eyes.

She knew he was crushed. She saw it, regardless of how hard he was trying to hide it. "Fine," he said, rising quickly from the table and moving to leave.

Carla took his wrist, held him there.

She stood up right in front of him, looking up into his eyes. Tears rested on the rims of his lower lids, waiting to fall.

"I'm sorry this had to happen," Carla said, wrapping her arms around him, hugging him tight, right there in the middle of the restaurant.

He let himself be comforted for a moment, then quickly pulled away from Carla and hurried out.

2

The dinner that Pete made for his wife sat on the dining room table, cold. He sat behind it, staring at a clock on the wall, watching as time slipped by. With each second, Carla became increasingly late.

Pete had to ask himself whether she even cared.

If he were to judge by the last two months, he knew the answer to that question would be no.

He picked up his cell phone, punched in her number for the fifth time this evening, and was not surprised to hear her voice mail answer his call, yet again.

He opened his mouth to speak, but not a word came out. He was sick of it all.

He flipped the phone closed, pushed back from the table, picked up the casserole dish, went to the kitchen, and emptied the casserole into the trash.

He had no certain idea of what was going on, but it was bad, and with each day that went by it had only gotten worse.

"How can I make this up to you?" she said one night a week ago, smiling slyly and kissing his earlobe.

Pete was happy, for they hadn't had sex in more than three weeks.

They ended up in bed, made love, and afterward, Pete lay on his back, Carla on her side.

He was unfulfilled.

Sex had lasted all of five minutes, her goal seeming to be to get him there, make him come, get things over with.

"Come on, baby. Come on!" she had urged him.

"I don't want to. Not yet," he cried.

But her thighs were clamped tight around his middle, her arms roped around his back, pulling him in, and he could not stop himself. He spilled himself inside.

Pete rolled off his wife. Carla turned away from him, something she had never done in the past. She had always liked to cuddle. From her side, he heard her say, "You okay?"

She didn't care what the answer was, Pete told himself, but he said, "Yeah. I'm fine." Even though he wasn't. There was something wrong with them. With their marriage. Not knowing was starting to kill him.

Carla was beautiful. From the day that he had first seen her across that bar more than three years ago, he knew he wanted her for himself. Her skin was a radiant, flawless golden brown, her eyes dark, mesmerizing; her lips full, pink, and pouty.

She was shapely, with large breasts and curvaceous hips, standing five-foot-three, exactly the height Pete liked his women. Her hair was thick, shiny, healthy, and black, her eyebrows perfectly arched. But Pete was scared.

He had spoken to her that night, tried his best to convince her to date him, and she did, but not for long.

She had lost interest in him, and Pete managed to lose the woman that he knew he could've spent his life with to another man. The one man Pete thought would never threaten his happiness.

But he had gotten her back. He wasn't proud of how, but he had, and now he felt that he might be losing her again, and he didn't know why.

The days and nights passed, but they weren't much better. With each one, Carla spoke a little less to him, became a little more distant, sat a little farther from him on the sofa when they watched television.

Pete broached the conversation so many times that Carla told him she was sick of talking about it.

"I told you," she said, becoming annoyed one night, as she pulled the corner of the blanket back and was about to climb into bed. "Can't things be bad for me at work? Can't I have hard days sometimes, when I just don't feel like coming home and talking?"

"Yes, but it's been more than a month. Can't I expect my wife to treat me like her husband and not a fucking stranger?" Pete said, letting his anger get the better of him.

Carla let the blanket fall from her hand, stepped away from the bed and toward the door.

"Where you going?" Pete said, sitting up in bed.

"I'll sleep in the guest bedroom tonight. Please don't try to convince me not to."

From that night on, Pete tried to give his wife the space she seemed to need, to allow her to have a few more bad days. But those few days turned into two weeks, then to months, and now Pete was standing angrily in front of the cold dinner he had just dumped into the trash.

Pete went to his bedroom closet, changed his shirt, combed his hair, checked his billfold to see how much money he had, and found himself at the bar of the W Hotel. There, the main room contained a sea of beautiful, scantily dressed people. The music played loud around him as Pete sat in front of his third scotch and soda, trying not to meet the eyes of a woman who seemed intent on getting his attention.

He told himself she was not looking at him, because the woman was striking, chocolate, with piercing eyes, almost as beautiful as his wife, but not quite.

And Pete was, well, fairly ordinary looking, with a broad nose, straight teeth, and a smile that improved his overall appearance when he chose to show it. But that was basically it. He was six-three, in good shape, for he ran five miles daily and got to the gym a few times a week, but with his plain, Crayola brown skin, and just-above-average looks, women weren't in the habit of trampling over people to get to him.

It wasn't the norm for gorgeous women to look his way, laugh, smile, and wave at him, as the woman across the bar just had.

But it was attention, something that he had been lacking for what seemed so damn long. It felt good. Good enough, he thought, to risk making a fool of himself, to try a come-on line or two.

So Pete downed the last of his drink, pulled himself from his seat, and walked over to the woman. He stood before her, not knowing what to say.

But he did not have to think long, for she spoke first. "You want to have a seat, or should I come with you?"

Pete thought of all of the reasons why he shouldn't do what he was about to.

But he also thought of how much he had been recently hurt, how Carla seemed not to care about him anymore. So as the woman that Pete had met at the bar only an hour ago reached down between his legs, stroked him, pulled him forward, he knew this was his last chance to make the so-called right decision.

Pete suddenly realized that the reason this woman had smiled at him was that she recognized him from his practice. She had sprained her ankle three months ago, and he had examined her, wrapped her foot, given her a prescription for painkillers, and sent her on her way.

He also remembered that she had been quite flirtatious during the visit, but things were just fine with him and Carla then, and he would never have considered returning her advances.

But now, as they lay in the hotel bed that Pete had paid for, as he suspended his naked body over hers, the woman trying to guide Pete into her, he knew he was wrong.

But he needed this, he thought, as he gave in.

He had needed it for weeks now, wanted it from his wife. But she would not give it to him, so he had to come here.

As Pete lowered himself and felt the tip of himself slide easily within the warm, wet crease of the woman, he looked down at her.

It was Carla he saw for a moment.

Then it became the woman again, and Pete let all his weight drop upon her, buried his face in the pillow beside her head, held her tight, slowly pushed into her.

An hour later, Pete jumped up from the bed and stumbled into the bathroom, groped blindly for the switch on the wall, clicked it on, and stood in front of the sink, breathing hard, staring at himself in the mirror.

His brown skin was covered with sweat, his lean muscled torso glistened with it.

What the hell had he just done? He yelled at himself as he turned on both water spigots full blast.

Water streamed hard into the sink, and Pete yanked a hand towel from the rack, soaked it into the water. He grabbed the bar of soap, vigorously rubbed it into his crotch hair, then scrubbed the area with the wet wash cloth.

"Fuck, fuck, fuck!" he said to himself, looking over his shoulder, back into the bedroom.

The bed sheets and blanket were strewn over the floor; the woman lay sprawled out across the bed, her arms and legs stretched out toward the four corners.

She slept hard, snoring. He had screwed her into a sound slumber.

Pete threw the damp rag to the floor, snatched a bath towel from another rack, and blotted the area between his legs dry.

He pushed his nose into the towel, testing it for the woman's scent.

He should've jumped in the shower, but it was already after 11 P.M.

He needed to get home. He needed to get back to his wife.

Pete plucked his clothes from the bedroom carpet, slid on his slacks, stepped into his shoes.

He opened the door, looked back at the woman. He thought of waking her, maybe jotting a farewell on the back of a carry-out menu, leaving it for her. He didn't. He closed the door and buttoned his shirt while running toward the elevator.

When he jumped into his car, he picked up his cell phone from the leather passenger seat. There should've been twenty messages from Carla, but when he checked, there wasn't a single missed call.

He punched in the code for his voice mail. Maybe the messages just hadn't registered. There was nothing in his mailbox either.

As Pete slid his key into the ignition, his shirt still mostly unbuttoned, his tie slung around his neck like a scarf, he told himself that maybe his wife really didn't care about him anymore.

When he pulled up in front of the seventy-year-old house he had bought for himself and Carla as a wedding gift, he saw that all the lights were out, save for the single lamp that burned every night in the front window. He imagined Carla was sleeping peacefully without a care about where he was, what he was doing, or what he had done, for that matter.

And look at him, he thought. Not half an hour ago, he had been racked with guilt for the sin he had committed.

Pete stepped out of the car, slammed the door hard, like it was noon, and not almost midnight.

He walked into the huge house, across the hardwood floor of the living room, and navigated his way up the stairs, to the second floor. The bedroom door was pushed partially closed. Pete stepped in.

He stood over the bed, over his wife sleeping peacefully. He could hear her faint breathing sounds.

She had stopped waiting up for him a little less than two months ago, but the least she could've done was woken up when he walked in.

For all she knew, he could've been an intruder standing over her with a razor-sharp knife and bad intentions.

Everything was obviously just fine in Carla's little world.

Pete stripped off his clothes, let them fall in a pile at his feet.

He could still smell the faint scent of the sex he had with the woman, wafting up from his groin, but now it didn't matter.

If his wife no longer cared about what was going on with them, then neither did he.

3

His bedroom was dark as Wayne Mason lay in bed, staring blindly up at the ceiling.

He thought about Carla, about the man that she had left him for, probably in bed making love to him at that very moment.

Pete was like a brother to Wayne. No, he *was* Wayne's brother, had been since they were ten years old.

Pete had lived around the corner, and down the block. They were in the same fourth grade class. On the days that Pete said he forgot his lunch, Wayne shared his.

And when it kept happening, when Wayne thought that maybe Pete wasn't forgetting his lunch, but didn't have a lunch to bring, Wayne started bringing two.

They would sit together, Wayne telling Pete how he always wanted a brother. Pete would tell Wayne the same thing.

"Then let's do it."

"Do what?" Pete said.

"Be brothers."

"How?"

"I don't know. I guess if we just say that we are, then we are. Okay?" Wayne said.

"Okay," Pete said, smiling, seeming not to realize how simple it was.

From that day on, they were officially brothers. And when Wayne didn't see Pete in school for days at a time, he would walk over to his house to check on him. And when Pete asked Wayne if he could stay with him after school, because he didn't know when his mother would be back home, Wayne would stay with him as long as he could.

Then there was the day after school, when they sat in Pete's run-down house, on his mother's secondhand sofa, watching the black-and-white TV.

"Why doesn't your mother buy any food?" Wayne asked, after they had both checked the kitchen cabinets and found them bare.

"She said she's going to when she gets back."

"When she gonna get back?" Wayne asked.

"I don't know."

"How long she been gone?"

Pete turned to Wayne and said, "Only two days this time."

Two days later, Wayne could remember standing just outside Wayne's father's house, Pete beside him, his head down, his face and clothes dirty.

When Wayne's father opened the door, Wayne took Pete's hand, and said, "Pete's mother been gone for four days, and we don't think she's coming back."

"Come on in, Pete," Wayne's father said. He was a doctor, clean shaven, graying just a bit about the temples, and always smiling. Wayne watched as his father wrapped his arm around Pete's shoulder and ushered him into the house. "Don't you worry. We're going to find your mother, and everything's going to be just fine."

The three of them went back to Pete's house, got him enough clothes and whatever else he needed for the next week.

Pete went to school from Wayne's house, ate all his meals there, and was treated as though he was one of the family.

Wayne's mother and father called him son, and asked him to do all the same things they would ask their own son, Wayne, to do, as if there was no difference between the two of them.

Wayne's father had gone to the police. They said they would do all they could to find Pete's mother, and tell him any news they found out.

After Pete had been at the house for two weeks, Wayne's father stepped into Wayne's bedroom.

"Can I borrow Pete for a minute?" he asked.

Wayne watched as Pete rose from his bed, uncertainty on his face, then stepped out of the room. Wayne ran to the door, to watch his father lead Pete down the hallway to his home study.

Wayne imagined his father helping Pete into a chair, then his father sitting before him.

That night after Pete came back to the room, he told Wayne that his father had pulled a letter from his pocket, opened it up, and put his glasses on.

The letter was from Pete's mother, letting him know that she could not handle raising him anymore. She had been battling a drug problem for so long, and it had taken what little money she made, and all of her ability to properly care for him. She wrote that she was sorry, would always love him, and would understand if he could never forgive her.

Wayne's father looked up from the letter and put his hand on Pete's shoulder, a smile again on his face.

"Your mother is entrusting me with you, son. Do you think you'd like to stay here and live with us?" Pete told Wayne that his father had said.

Pete nodded, smiled as though he was happy.

He was ten years old then, but that night, Wayne heard Pete, lying in the twin bed beside him, crying like he was two.

"Damn, damn, damn!" Wayne had said to Pete, two years ago, when they were both thirty-five, "I think I'm going to sleep with Eva."

She was the girl that Wayne had been trying to date all during the years Pete and Wayne were in medical school together, before they met Carla. At the time Eva had always told Wayne that if she had not already been engaged, maybe it would've been him she'd be engaged to, or at least they could've had a wonderful sexual relationship. She continued to smile and flirt with Wayne until graduation, when they both had gone their separate ways.

But then, later, after Wayne was about to get married to Carla, he ran into Eva at a restaurant. She told him she was no longer engaged and was very interested in seeing what she had missed in medical school with him.

"I got to do it," Wayne said, excited.

They were at Pete's North Side condo. Pete was lacing up his basketball shoes. "Did you tell Eva that you were engaged?" Pete said.

"Yeah. That's what's so cool. She just wants to have sex one time. She doesn't care that I'm engaged."

"Then I guess that makes two of you. And I guess you already got permission from Carla."

"Who?" Wayne said, joking.

"Your fiancée."

"I know this sounds like the most ridiculous thing in the world," Wayne said, spinning the basketball in his hands, "but I don't think I'm going to tell her."

Pete stood, looked Wayne right in the face. "If you want to fuck around, why marry Carla?"

"Because I love her. Because I want to spend the rest of my life with her."

"But . . ." Pete said.

"All right. You want to hear that I'm scared? Then I'm scared.

Or maybe I just feel like this will be my last hurrah. You know. Men do it all the time at their bachelor parties. I'm not even having a bachelor party, so I'll just do it now."

"And if she finds out?" Pete said.

"That's not going to happen. You and I are the only ones who will know about this. She won't find out."

"This is wrong. Carla's cool. She loves you," Pete said. "I really think you need to consider what you stand to lose."

"Pete," Wayne said, resting a hand on his friend's shoulder, "this is one of those moments that every person has when consideration is the last thing they should give, because they know what they're about to do makes no sense at all. Just support me on this, or at the very least, say that you can halfway understand why I'm doing it."

Pete shook his head. "Sorry, man. I can't do it."

Wayne slept with her, and for what it was worth, he would've enjoyed himself more with a porno flick and a handful of Vaseline.

Afterward, he stripped off the rubber, smiled at Eva, kissed her on the cheek, and said, "At least now we know what we missed."

Before he went home, Wayne stopped off at Pete's place.

"So?" Pete said. "Did you come to your senses, or did you behave like the typical man, be a dog and fuck her?"

"I fucked her. It wasn't worth the time it took me to drive over there, but it's over," Wayne said, smiling.

"You seem particularly happy about that. You don't think you made the wrong decision?"

"I don't necessarily think it was the right one, but it's done now. I still have Carla, who I love, who I'm going to marry, and never cheat on once that's done. So everything is everything. No harm, no foul, right?"

"Right," Pete said.

Later that evening, it was strange, but when Wayne saw Carla, he felt that sleeping with Eva only made him realize just how much he loved the woman that he was engaged to.

Maybe it was the comparison that let him know how much more he had than what he had just been with. Or maybe it allowed him to remember what it was like to have sex with a woman that he cared nothing for, versus actually making love to a woman.

Whatever the reason, that night, Wayne could not stop professing his love and happiness for Carla.

"You're acting weird," Carla said.

"If telling you how much I love you, and actually meaning it means that I'm weird," Wayne said, holding Carla tight and kissing her on the cheek, "then I'm the weirdest man alive."

When Wayne made love to Carla that night, he kept his eyes open the entire time, for he wanted to see the pleasure he gave her. When they finally fell asleep, he held her tight to him, knowing that the rest of his life was there within his arms.

The next day, Wayne could not remove the smile from his face. Everything seemed wonderful. He had plans with Carla later to do dinner and go see one of his favorite blues singers. It was odd, when after 6 P.M. he had not spoken to her all day.

He had tried calling her from work once in the morning, just to say hey, like he normally did. And then he called again around lunchtime, which was the ritual. He had left messages both times, but his calls had not been returned.

After Wayne got off work, he had called her three more times on both her cell and home phones and still got no answer.

He had driven by her apartment, knocked on her door, but she was not there.

As he walked back toward the street, he glanced at his watch. It was ten minutes till seven, and their dinner reservations were for seven thirty. Something was definitely wrong, and he really started to worry.

After climbing into his car, he dialed Pete's number.

"What's going on?" Pete answered.

"I'm worried, man. I've been calling Carla all day, and she hasn't called me back. We were supposed to do dinner tonight. This isn't like her."

There was silence for a long moment on Pete's end, so long that Wayne said, "You there?"

"We need to talk."

"What do you mean, we need to talk?"

"Meet me at the old Red Dog bar," Pete said. "I'm right near there."

"Pete, what's going on?" Wayne said, more worried than before.

"Just meet me there, and I'll tell you."

Wayne hurried toward the bar. Pete was there, hunched over an empty mug of beer, looking melancholy.

"What's going on?" Wayne said, running up on him. "Why do you have me meeting you here?"

"Carla is all right," Pete said.

"How the hell do you know that?"

"Because I was with her today."

"You were with her?" Wayne said, confused but starting to anger.

"I met her after work, and then we went back to her place."

"To fucking do what, Pete?" Wayne said, grabbing his best friend tight by his jean jacket.

"So I could tell her what you did. So I could tell her that you slept with Eva."

The words were like a punch, like an actual physical assault that had Wayne stumbling back, throwing his hands to his face. He bent over, Carla's face in his mind, Wayne seeing, knowing how painful that news must have been. After all he had said to her last night, after the love they made, the promises he guaranteed, and then the following day to hear that it was all lies, and from Wayne's best friend no less.

Wayne stood, slowly pulled his hands from his face, glared at Pete with all the anger within him, and said, "Why? Why the fuck did you do it?"

"Because she deserved better, Wayne. She deserves better. I told you not to do it."

Wayne snatched Pete by his collar, reared back, punched him hard across the jaw, knocking Pete from the barstool onto the floor.

He fell on his side, scurried to protect his stomach when Wayne rushed up on him, about to kick him. Wayne held the blow, a tear sliding from his eye, as he looked down at Pete.

"I'm sorry things had to turn out this way," Pete said, holding his jaw, wincing in pain.

Wayne looked down at him pathetically, shook his head, then ran out.

That was two years ago, and now as Wayne lay in bed, he could not shake the thought of Carla from his mind. Her telling him that he could no longer see her hurt him more than he ever imagined it would. But Wayne had to ask himself if that was because he was just trying to win Carla back, because of how Pete had stolen her from him, or did he still have feelings for the woman?

None of that mattered. Carla had made her decision.

Wayne shifted his weight in bed a little, a question coming to his mind: What would he do now?

Carla said her marriage was beginning to suffer because she was seeing Wayne. That was the last thing he wanted to happen. Yes, he knew that if Carla did decide to leave Pete and come back to him, it would mean the destruction of his brother's marriage—but that would be because Carla alone made the decision. Wayne told himself he would not try to persuade her or force her hand in any manner. She would make her decision on her own, and last night she had done just that.

Wayne had to respect that decision, he thought sadly. He would have to forget her and move on.

Wayne turned a little in bed, then made an effort to still himself, but it was too late.

An arm was thrown over his bare chest, and a beautiful, mocha-skinned woman with thick curly black hair placed her face in the crook of his neck and kissed him on the jaw.

"I love you," Me'Shell said, her voice groggy.

It took him a moment to dump all that he had been thinking out of his head, and then Wayne finally said, wrapping an arm around her, pulling her closer, kissing her forehead, "I love you, too."

4

When Carla returned home around 10 P.M., after leaving Wayne, she expected to see her husband the moment she had walked in the door, Pete sitting in the living room, the TV off, his legs crossed, just waiting.

But to Carla's relief, he wasn't there.

She walked into the house, feeling numb, as though what she had just done to Wayne wasn't real.

She had managed to keep herself from crying too hard on the way home. She didn't want Pete to see her that way when she stepped into the house.

She was hungry, but as she walked into the kitchen, she knew she couldn't eat, wouldn't be able to keep the food down.

When she felt for the light and clicked it on, she saw the pile of dirty pots and pans, dishes, and glasses stacked in the sink and the discarded meal in the trash.

She had forgotten: Pete had promised to make dinner tonight. Another attempt at fixing things between them after he had been so upset the night before.

How wrong she had been to him, Carla thought later while pulling on her nightgown. For so long he had tried to remedy a situation he had no idea how to fix. In typical Pete fashion, he assumed everything was his fault—and Carla had let him go on thinking that.

Pete's attempts to fix things would give her more time to decide just what she wanted to do with Wayne, she thought then. But as she lay down in bed and pulled the covers up to her chest, she knew she had been wrong. That was the reason Pete had trashed the dinner, why he was probably out that very moment—because he was just fed up, she thought.

But she would make it up to him, she told herself.

At eleven, Carla clicked off her bedside lamp, but she wasn't able to sleep. Sometime near twelve she heard Pete's car door slam. She heard him come in, make his way up the stairs, and walk into the bedroom. She lay on her side, facing the windows, pretending to be asleep. She didn't exactly know why—maybe because she felt so guilty, felt that if she even said a word to him, a torrent of incomprehensible gobble would spill from her mouth, and in that mess would come her confession.

Carla didn't need that, not at that moment.

So as she heard her husband disrobing, she told herself that in the morning, she would discuss the situation with him, work on making things better.

When the morning came, Pete was not there.

After putting on her robe, walking through the house, checking the garage for his car, Carla realized that he had left. It wasn't even seven yet, a full hour and a half before he normally left for work, but he was gone.

An hour later, after driving to the building that housed the magazine where she worked, Carla walked through the parking garage and climbed onto an elevator peopled with attractive-looking employees of some of the other businesses in the building.

She spoke to no one. Her mind was on Pete, and . . . still on Wayne.

Last night at the restaurant, he'd said he had made a mistake a year and a half ago, and asked her if she could just get past it. If he had only known the pain she felt that day after she answered the door and found Pete standing there, looking as though he needed to confess some horrible crime. She could tell there was something terribly wrong just by the look on his face, the sweat on his brow.

"Come in," she said.

She walked him over to her sofa, where she had been looking at seating arrangements for her wedding reception.

"Is everything all right?" Carla asked him, worried.

Pete looked down at the papers on the table, picked up one of the seating charts, but did not answer her.

Carla grabbed the sheet, set it back on the table. "Pete, why are you here? Is everything okay?"

At first Pete didn't respond, then finally said, "How much do you love Wayne?"

"I'm about to marry him. I love him a lot. Why are you asking me that?" Carla said with increasing anxiety.

Pete shifted on the sofa, turned to face her. "I don't know how to tell you this."

"Just tell me, Pete!" Carla said, her voice rising.

"Wayne . . . he slept with another woman."

The elevator opened on the floor of the *Verge* magazine office, and Carla snapped back to the present, putting Wayne out of her mind.

Verge wasn't only a fashion magazine, nor a social, celebrity-driven, or women's magazine—but all of the above.

She walked across purple carpeting, past glass-topped workstations, where writers, fashion editors, graphic designers, and other support staff tapped away on keyboards and glared at flat-screen computer monitors.

The ceilings were high, the walls were lime green and pink, and a fusion of neo-soul and jazz music played softly from tiny hidden speakers.

Carla's office was at the back of the huge open area where all the magazine's employees worked.

When she got to Laci's office, she stopped just at the door and stuck her head in. "Need to talk to you," Carla said, then continued on to her office.

Once inside, she walked through the huge space with its back wall of floor-to-ceiling windows looking out over Chicago's Grant Park.

She slid open one of the drawers of her glass-topped desk, dropped in her purse, then leaned back in her executive chair, crossed her legs, and covered her face with her hands.

Carla's attention was drawn to the door when Laci knocked lightly on the frame, then entered closing the door behind her.

Laci and Carla had worked together at the magazine for more than five years. In that time she and Carla had become best friends, even though at twenty-nine, Laci was six years younger.

Laci sat in one of the two green leather chairs in front of Carla's desk.

The younger woman was attractive, brown skinned, and always very well manicured. Her hair was cut short, shiny black, straightened, and parted on one side. She wore narrow-framed glasses on the tip of her pierced nose, which made her look studious, and she always wore slacks that clung just a little tighter than Carla thought appropriate for the office setting. But Laci was Carla's girl.

"You feeling all right?" Laci said.

"I did it. I told Wayne I couldn't see him anymore," Carla said, standing up from her chair and turning to look out the windows.

"Is that what you wanted? I thought you said you were trying to decide if—"

"That's the thing," Carla said, turning back and cutting Laci off. “Decide what? I have no right to decide anything. I’m married, and whether or not I still feel I may love Wayne, or moved too fast in marrying Pete, that doesn’t discount the fact that I did.” Carla sat back into her chair. “I took those vows and I need to stay true to them.”

“And that’s it?” Laci said.

“That’s it.”

“I imagine Wayne took it hard,” Laci said.

“Probably not harder than me,” Carla said, lowering her face into her hands again. She heard her friend rise from her chair, felt Laci’s hand on her head, smoothing her hair.

“Don’t worry about it. That part of your life is over. Now you can concentrate on you and Pete. You know that man really loves you, don’t you?”

Carla looked up. “I know he did. But I don’t know about that anymore. I’ve been spending so much time trying to decide what I was going to do with the man I had, that I may have messed up things with the man I’m with.”

“So what are you going to do?”

“I have to do my best to fix it.”

5

When Wayne rolled over in bed that morning, he thought that he might have had a very bad dream. That was until he took a moment, lay there, and remembered what had happened the night before.

Sleep was awful for him, tossing and turning, knowing that the chance for him and Carla ever being together again had passed.

Some hours ago, he was gently awoken by Me'Shell.

As he slowly opened his eyes, her beautiful brown face came into focus.

"You're going to be late for work," she said softly. "I'll run your shower water. Come down after and I'll make you some breakfast."

"Don't worry about it," Wayne said, his voice raspy from sleep. "I got up, called in, and canceled my appointments."

"You sure?"

"Yeah, but thanks," Wayne said, raising up in bed to give Me'Shell a kiss.

He rolled onto his stomach, pulled a pillow over his head, and tried to stop the painful news Carla had given him from entering his dreams again.

When Wayne woke for the second time, he glanced at his alarm clock.

It was ten minutes to ten.

He pulled himself up to a sitting position and remained in bed, bare chested, for a moment, deciding what he should do.

Carla had always been the first thing Wayne thought of upon waking, but now things were different. He had to admit, regardless of how strongly he felt about getting Carla back, what he was doing to Me'Shell was wrong. And although she hadn't known what he had been doing over the past two months, he had warned her.

He had met Me'Shell six months ago.

It had been almost that long since Carla left him, and although Wayne still felt as though he was not over her and wasn't willing to entertain another relationship, he noticed when he bumped into Me'Shell standing in line at Starbucks.

He felt an attraction for her, which surprised him.

She was beautiful. Rich, smooth skin, big, vivid, black eyes, a button nose, and full, kissable lips. Her spring dress clung nicely to her hips and exposed her shapely legs. He stared down at the fine curls on the back of her neck, feeling the urge to brush them aside, kiss her there.

She walked past Wayne, sat down at a corner table, glanced at a newspaper.

He pulled money out his pocket to pay for his coffee and a muffin. He glanced over his shoulder at her, took his change.

Standing at the door, ready to leave, he eyed her again.

His intention was to just go, thinking of Carla. But he asked himself, was she still thinking of him?

No.

She had just gotten married. He was there to witness that, up close, as Pete's best man.

It had killed him, but now it was time to move on.

Wayne found himself standing over the woman's table, coffee and small white bag in his hand.

She looked up at him, seeming intrigued.

"My name is Wayne," he said. "Would you like to share my muffin?"

The woman looked at him oddly; then a sudden smile lit her face.

"Have a seat, Wayne."

They spent the rest of the day together, and they saw each other for the next six days straight.

They bonded quickly, had wonderful times together. Got close in a hurry—and after another week, found themselves on her floor in the dark, the TV going, kissing and pulling at each other's clothes.

"Hold it," Wayne said. He sat up, inched away from her. "I think this is turning into something that could be really good for us."

Me'Shell looked at him, flustered, hair all messed up, lipstick long ago kissed from her lips. "Yeah, me, too. So what's the problem?"

What he was about to say was foolish, Wayne thought. But he had to say it.

"There's another woman."

Me'Shell's eyes widened.

"No, no. Not now. That I used to see. We broke up more than six months ago." He hesitated. "But I still have feelings for her. She's moved on, told me there will never be a chance of us getting back together, but . . ."

"But, what?" Me'Shell said.

"There's nothing more that I want than that."

"And me?"

Wayne sighed. "We've known each other for all of two weeks, and I'm crazy about you. I would love to see where this could go."

"But what? If ever there's a chance that you can get back with this woman, you'd do it?" Me'Shell said.

Wayne nodded.

"You'd leave me?"

"If it were to ever happen down the line, I can't say for certain. But right now . . . yes, I would leave you."

Me'Shell stood, fastened the few buttons on her shirt that Wayne had undone.

Without a word, she walked to the front door, opened it.

Wayne took the hint. "I'm sorry, Me'Shell."

"Whatever you say."

Wayne walked to his big Audi A8, looked up at her before he climbed in. She was still there, the door open, looking down on him, as though there was something she wanted to say.

He waited.

Nothing.

He drove off, rolling down the street, feeling as though he might have made the biggest mistake of his life by not being willing to commit to Me'Shell.

His cell phone rang.

"Hello."

"You said she moved on." It was Me'Shell.

Wayne was happy to hear her voice. "Yes."

"What are the chances that she would want you back?"

"Slim. She's happily married. Actually it's a pipe dream."

"But you're dreaming it?"

"For the moment. Yes."

There was silence on her end of the phone.

Wayne's brake lights flashed as he stopped his car in the middle of the street. He hoped she would say the words he wanted to hear.

"Come back."

Wayne smiled, whipped a U-turn, and headed back.

They'd been together ever since.

Wayne pulled himself from bed, and wearing nothing but pajama bottoms, stepped through the room and out the bedroom door.

He walked to the stairs, and stopped there, listening.

Me'Shell taught music at a local elementary school, but now she was on summer vacation.

She had her own apartment, not twenty minutes from Wayne's house, but the better part of the week she preferred to stay with him, which was what he preferred as well.

As he stood at the top of the stairs, Wayne heard that Me'Shell was watching *Oprah*. *The View* would come on after that, so he knew she would be occupied for the next hour, that was, if she didn't feel the need to come up and check on him.

Wayne had a thought but told himself to resist it. He needed to just go downstairs, sit beside the woman who loved him, who didn't have indecision in her heart, who didn't have a choice to make between Wayne and another man, but just loved him.

He should take those steps down there, sit down, wrap himself around her, and tell her that he loved her, too. The problem was, he could not get Carla out of his head.

And because of that, Wayne found himself walking back into his bedroom, where he closed the door.

He took his cell phone off the dresser, walked around to the side of the bed farthest from the door, and sat with his back against it on the floor.

Wayne punched in a number, and when it was answered, said, "Carla Ellis, will you marry me?"

"You aren't supposed to be calling me. We discussed this, Wayne," Carla said.

"Carla Ellis, will you marry me?" he repeated, ignoring what she had said.

"My name is Carla Barnes, because I'm already married, Wayne," she whispered loudly.

"Marry me, Carla. I'm ready now. I'm ready to do this."

"Then do it with someone else," Carla said.

"You don't mean that."

"What don't you understand? I'm married to Pete. I love him, not you. So just move on."

"But Carla—"

"Move on, Wayne. Good-bye!"

Wayne tried to get another word in but realized the line was dead. She had hung up on him.

What did that mean, he asked himself?

It meant that she wanted nothing else to do with him, and even if she still loved him, which he suspected she did, that didn't matter, because she was trying to deny it.

So it was over, and now he would have to do what Carla said—move on.

That moment, Wayne heard Me'Shell coming upstairs.

He quickly slid his cell phone under the bed, stood up and leaped into the blankets, just as Me'Shell was opening the bedroom door.

"You all right?" she said, eyeing Wayne with slight skepticism.

"Yeah."

"You sure?"

Wayne sat up, extended his arms to her. "Come here."

Me'Shell smiled. She always smiled, bright and beautiful, a smile that lit her face, sometimes for no reason at all, and that was one of the reasons he loved her.

"Why?" she said.

"Because."

"Because, why?"

"Because birds can fly—now come over here."

Me'Shell laughed, went to Wayne, and slid between the sheets with him, letting him spoon her.

He rested his head on the side of her face, feeling the soft, big curls of her hair tickling his nose.

"You having a good morning?" he asked.

She nodded, smiling even wider. "I ate a doughnut for breakfast, watched *Oprah*, don't have to go to work, and now I'm in your arms. What you do you think?"

"Do you love me?"

"You know I do."

"How much," Wayne asked.

"Take all the love that all the women feel for all the men in the world, double it, and that's how much I love you."

"Wow. That's a bunch."

"Well, you're a great guy."

Wayne didn't respond to that, feeling guilty. He just lay there a moment behind her, holding her, telling himself that the decision he was about to make was the right one. He pulled her a little closer, placed his lips to her ear, and whispered, "Me'Shell Jacobs, will you marry me?"

6

Carla had called Pete before she left work, not knowing what if anything he would say to her.

She asked him if he was coming home straight from work.

"Yes," was all Pete said.

"I'm going to make dinner for you. What would you like?" Her tone was chipper, cheery. It did not rub off on him.

It had taken him so long to answer, while Carla sat on the phone, that she thought he had hung up on her.

"Are you still there?" she asked.

"Yeah," Pete said. Then, "I don't know what I want for dinner. Make whatever you like."

"But, I wanted something special—"

"I have a patient waiting. I have to go," Pete interrupted, hanging up before Carla could say another word.

Carla came home with grocery bags filled with all of Pete's favorite food.

This was her first attempt at fixing things. She had kind of made him dinner over the last two months, thrown together this and that, warmed up some leftovers, but she had not really cooked for him like she used to.

Pete used to love that, always complimented her on her cooking, and she hoped he would tonight.

She prepared his favorite meal of steak and shrimp, cooking the meat medium rare, and stir-frying the jumbo shrimps in butter, then dusting them with a combination of special seasonings.

She did all this wearing a simple, but beautiful, low-cut, red spring dress she had bought at the mall before going to the supermarket.

She watched the clock as she took the meal from the kitchen into the dining room, knowing exactly what time he usually came in after work.

Just as she set the last piece of silverware down, and had lit the two candles in the center of the table, Pete walked in the front door.

Carla looked up at her husband, a huge smile on her face. "Come in, baby. Just in time," she said, walking up to him, taking his briefcase from his hand, and leading him in the direction of the dining room.

She pulled out his chair at the head of the table.

"Can I at least wash my hands first?" Pete said, sounding irritated.

"Oh, sure, honey."

He stepped around her.

Carla waited by the chair till Pete returned. She pulled it out for him again, then pushed the chair in after he had sat down.

Carla served him his food, then placed some on her own plate. She poured them each a half glass of red wine, then sat in the chair adjacent to his, took his hand, and bowed her head.

There was silence for a moment, then Carla said, "Will you say grace, please?"

"Thank you for this food. Amen," Pete said without ceremony, releasing his wife's hand and picking up his utensils.

He cut into his steak, put a chunk into his mouth and chewed.

He stabbed a shrimp, ate that, all the while staring down at his plate, never once looking up at Carla.

She sat there, looking up at him occasionally, wondering how to start the conversation or whether she should just leave him alone. She knew that he was mad at her, knew that letting him continue to sit there and stew in his anger would only make things worse.

"So do you like the food? I know it's your favorite."

"If it's my favorite, then you already know I like it, Carla," Pete said, paying her little attention.

Yes, he was angry, she thought, feeling the sting of his comment, but she persisted.

"Do you like my dress?"

Pete looked up long enough to take a passing glance.

"I haven't seen that before."

"That's because it's new." Carla smiled. "I bought it special for dinner."

"Oh," Pete said, cutting into his steak again.

Carla lifted her glass, took a sip of wine, then lowered her head and told herself that she was the one who had done the damage to their marriage. It was her responsibility to repair it.

She lifted her head, smiled again, and asked how his day at work went.

"If you don't mind, can we not talk," Pete said, looking up at her, holding his knife in one fist, his fork in the other. "Can we just eat?"

"Yes," Carla said, feeling very much like a child. She picked up her utensils and dug into her food. "Yes we can."

The rest of the night, Pete did not say a word to Carla if she didn't ask him a question first.

"I went to the store and got a DVD. Do you want to watch it?" Carla asked him an hour after dinner. Pete looked as though the question was the most difficult one he had ever been asked, as though lives depended on the correct answer. He finally said yes. The movie was quite good, but Carla could not really enjoy it. Unlike the last two months when they watched TV, Carla sat very close to Pete tonight, pushed up against him. She had pulled his arm around her, for she didn't think he would've placed it there on his own.

But although their bodies were practically intertwined, she felt very far away from him, as though he really didn't want to be there. She looked up at him every now and then, knowing he felt her stare, but he would not acknowledge it. Carla didn't know if that was because he didn't care to, or if he was just so far off into his thoughts, that he didn't even notice the attention she was giving him.

And now she understood how he must've felt for all that time she had been neglecting him.

Later that night, at bedtime, Carla came out of the bathroom after showering, a towel wrapped around her, smelling of flowers and fruit-scented lotion.

Pete had already crawled into bed. He lay awake, on his back, his half of the bed in shadows.

Carla pulled the towel from around her, and slid naked under the blanket and sheets with her husband. She lay on her back, too, her hands behind her head.

There they remained silent, in darkness, until Carla said, "Will you kiss me?"

"What?" Pete said.

"Please, Pete."

"I don't want to."

"Okay. Then can I kiss you?"

Again he deliberated over the question for much longer than Carla thought he had to, but finally said, without much enthusiasm, "Sure." She rolled over on top of her husband, feeling her nipples starting to harden as they pressed against his bare chest.

Although she could hardly see him in the dark room, she looked him in the eyes, kissed him lightly on the cheek, then more passionately on the mouth.

He was tight lipped at first, then slowly he opened his mouth and received her tongue.

She felt him growing beneath her, pressing into her thigh. She started to gyrate, grind against him. Carla grabbed his hand, placed it on her bare behind.

He seemed apprehensive at first, and she worried Pete would move his hand away when she let go, but he didn't.

Their kissing became more heated, Pete became more excited; she felt him pressing even harder against her leg.

She reached down, tried to push down the waist of his pajama bottoms.

"I want you," Carla whispered, sweetly. "I want you inside me."

"No," Pete said, still kissing her.

"Yes. Please. I need you, now."

"No," Pete said, turning his head away from her kiss, then pushing her off of him, rolling from under her.

He sat up in bed, clicked on his lamp. "You need me?"

Carla didn't answer.

"That was a question," Pete said. "Did you say you needed me?"

"Yes."

"Over the last two months, did you know that I needed *you?* Didn't I tell you that? Didn't every single one of my damn actions point to that fact?"

"Yes," Carla said, her head lowered.

"And what did you do?"

"I ignored you."

"Look up at me when you talk to me."

Carla raised her head. "I ignored you."

"Busy at the magazine," Pete said. "Is the magazine—a damn job, more important than us?"

"No."

"But you acted that way," Pete said, out of bed now, looking angrily at Carla. "And now, I walk in this evening, and you have dinner prepared, you're seating me, pushing in my chair. You're all up under me while we're watching the movie, like nothing ever happened. And now you want to make love, you say you need me. Part of me is happy that you made whatever change you did, but another part is asking, why the fuck now? After all the begging I did just to get your attention, you just didn't care. Why is it that today, this very day, of all days, you decide you want to start acting right?"

"Because I finally realized that neglecting you was wrong," Carla said, her voice soft. "I love you, but I haven't been showing it. And I felt that if I kept on doing you that way, that I might lose you."

Pete chuckled sadly, shaking his head. He grabbed his pillow from the bed, and then, before walking out of the room, said, "You might have already done that."

7

The timing sucked, Pete thought, as he carried his pillow into the guest room down the hall to sleep.

If she had only changed her behavior one day earlier, or if Pete had only waited one night longer, then everything would've been fine.

But no, just last night, he had slept with that woman, and he could not imagine entering his wife a single day after sliding out from between the other woman's thighs.

When Pete had walked in earlier to see the dinner that Carla had prepared, to see how beautiful she looked in that dress, he was touched.

During the movie they watched, he wanted nothing more than to hold her closer, tell her how much he loved her, and that she didn't have to worry, that everything was going to be just fine. But he couldn't.

His mind was elsewhere, on the intense guilt he was feeling for being weak, questioning whether his wife still cared for him, and stepping out on her.

That was the reason he was cold to Carla, barely spoke to her, and turned her down when she tried to make love to him.

He was mad as hell at himself, and felt he did not deserve the attention his wife was giving him. Yes, Carla's affection was still long overdue, but the infidelity that Pete had committed erased any penalty she needed to pay. He climbed into the guest bed and wondered what he would do about their situation, as he fell off to sleep.

Hours later, when Pete opened his eyes, the room was still somewhat dark around him, but he was awakened by a sensation, by a feeling that had him moaning, squirming.

When his senses came to him fully, he realized his wife was in the guest bed with him, had straddled his legs, had his pajama bottoms pulled down, was sucking him, stroking him.

The pleasure was immense, as he lifted his dizzy head to look up at her.

She rose up, still sliding her fist up and down him. "Is this okay?" she asked.

"Yeah," Pete said, barely able to get the word out.

She went back to work, then a minute later, said, "Do you want to feel me? Do you want to be inside me?"

"Yeah," Pete said again.

Carla rose up off of Pete's legs, climbed out of bed, and walked across the room, naked, till she got to the dresser, where she leaned against it. She looked over her shoulder with wanting eyes, and said, "Then come and get me."

Pete got out of bed, let his pajama bottoms fall off his feet, and walked to her, fully erect.

He stood behind his wife, took hold of her ass, and gently inserted himself into her. She was wet, but somewhat tight. He slid in easily, but with enough resistance to almost make him explode in her that moment.

Carla moaned, arched her back, tightened around him, as he slid further into her. He pulled himself out, long, hard, dripping, then pushed himself back in.

The pleasure was exquisite, Pete thought, as he started to lose himself in the moment. He reached out, grabbed Carla's hair, pulled. She moaned louder, just like the woman in the hotel had the other night.

The other night, Pete had that woman in this same position. She clamped herself around his dick the same way, called his name, "Pete, Pete, fuck me, Pete!" just like Carla was doing that moment.

He continued to fuck his wife, holding tight to her round ass, banging into her now, causing the mirror atop the dresser to rhythmically strike the wall.

Get out of my head, he commanded the thoughts that tormented him. But they continued—the woman lying on her back, her legs thrown over Pete's shoulders, dangling behind him. Images of her on top of him, Pete holding handfuls of her large breasts, squeezing her dark nipples as she leaned over him, giving him wild kisses. And the thought of her pushed up against the hotel's dresser, just like Carla was now, that woman's arms extended, palms pressing against the front edge of it, using it for leverage to slam her ass into Pete each time he thrust his dick into her.

The pleasure was so damn intense that they both, he and that woman, had been crying out, moaning, shaking, trembling, cursing, until they came simultaneously.

And that's when Pete could not take it anymore, yanked himself out of his wife and stumbled away, sweating and breathing hard.

"What's wrong?" Carla said, turning, shocked.

"I can't," Pete said.

She came to him. "I said I was sorry for—"

"No. It's not that."

"Then what is it?"

"I just can't."

They ended up back in their bedroom, in each other's arms.

They had talked; Pete had said he'd forgiven her treatment of him and that he was sorry he couldn't make love to her tonight, but he would make it up to her.

Carla had apologized profusely, to the point that Pete was wiping tears from her cheeks.

"It'll never happen again. I swear, Pete."

They promised that from this moment on, things would be better, be the way they used to be. And that's what Pete went to bed thinking about, that, and the nagging guilt he felt for betraying his wife.

In the morning, as Carla sat at the dining room table with Pete after serving their breakfast, he told himself that it was truly a brand-new day. That he would stop dwelling on the mistake that he made, and be happy, be fucking thrilled with the fact that things were back on track for them.

"Baby," Carla said, pulling Pete out of his thoughts.

"Yeah?"

"Are you okay?"

Pete leaned over, gave Carla a kiss on the lips. "I'm fine, sweetheart. Just fine."

8

Wayne walked through the glass double doors of the orthopedic practice that used to belong to his father, but that he now co-owned with his partner Pete.

It was just after 8 A.M., but the waiting room was already filled with patients, most of them older and graying, wearing casts, holding crutches, or sitting in wheelchairs.

He proceeded through the corridors of the brightly painted office, past exam rooms, past a nurse's station, and past an x-ray procedure room, saying good morning to his employees, medical staff, as well as the two older, grinning ladies in clerical.

Wayne did not stop to chat, as he often would, for something was on his mind, and he wanted to be alone for a moment. All last night, and all during the day today, he kept telling himself he had made the right decision. He had to believe that, for when he and Me'Shell were in the jewelry store, standing over the glass case, Me'Shell wearing the three-carat ring she wanted, Wayne knew this was his last chance to pull out.

He could've ended it all right there, told her to take off the ring for a moment. He could've taken her by the arm, led her just out of earshot of the aging saleswoman, and said, "I'm sorry, Me'Shell, but I was a little hasty in asking you to marry me. I've changed my mind. Get your things and let's go."

But Wayne didn't do that.

When Me'Shell looked up at him, a tear in her eye, saying she had chosen the ring, Wayne simply said, "Are you sure?" pulling out his credit card and handing it to the smiling saleslady.

While the saleslady was charging the ten-thousand-dollar cost to Wayne's card, Me'Shell hugged him tight, looking over her shoulder at her new ring, whispering to him how much she truly loved him, and how much of a surprise this was.

Yeah, it was kind of a surprise to him, too, Wayne thought now, standing in the middle of the break room, wearing slacks, a collared pale pink shirt, a print tie, and his white lab coat. He sipped from a rapidly cooling cup of weak coffee he had just poured from the coffee machine, thinking about something Me'Shell had said last night.

They were lying in bed after they had just finished making love. A candle burned by the bedside, casting long shadows in the dark room. As Wayne lay over Me'Shell, he saw the sweat glistening on her brown skin, and then saw a tear roll from her eye, down the side of her face.

"What's wrong?" he asked.

Me'Shell looked at Wayne. "I love you, and ever since I met you, I've always dreamed of this day when you would ask me to marry you. I looked forward to it, but now that it's happened . . ." She brought her hand up, admired her ring again, and couldn't help but smile through the tears. ". . . It's just that it's only been six months for us, and the decision seemed kind of quick in coming. I know I'm sure about us. There is no place I'd rather be, and no man I'd rather be with. But you? And trust me, Wayne," Me'Shell said. "The last thing I'm trying to do is talk you out of this, but are you certain? Because I don't think I can take you telling me one day this isn't really going to happen."

Wayne had yet another opportunity to wriggle out of the lifelong commitment he was offering. All he had to do was say that he didn't want it, that he was only marrying her because Carla wouldn't marry him, and that he never even loved Me'Shell.

But that wouldn't have been true, for he did love her. And he actually did want to get married. As he had told Carla, he was ready.

Yes, he would've preferred it to have been with Carla, or at least that's what he had thought, but he could be happy with Me'Shell.

He lay down beside her, pulled Me'Shell close, and looked directly in her eyes.

"Listen to me, okay?" he said. "I love you, and so what that it's only been six months. I felt the same way at six weeks. I thought about this longer than you know. You and I are supposed to be together, and we'll be happier than anyone ever has been. I'll never hurt you, okay?"

Me'Shell displayed the brightest smile he had ever seen her give, and that alone made his proposal worth it. She threw her arms around his neck and said, "I'm going to be such a good wife to you. Just wait and see."

"I know, baby," Wayne said. "I know."

And now, back in the break room at work, a slight smile came to Wayne's face, as he poured his cold cup of coffee into the sink.

He was going to get married, and there were worse things that could happen. He would be happy about it from now on, he told himself.

Just then Pete walked in. He looked overjoyed.

"Wayne, good to see you in the office today. Thought you might have abandoned me when Mary said you rescheduled all your patients yesterday. Thought I'd never see you again."

"I was feeling a little under the weather."

Pete shook Wayne's hand, clapped him hard on the shoulder. "Well, I'm glad you're feeling better."

"It seems that I'm not the only one. You're looking happier than you have in a while. Things improve at home?"

"As a matter of fact, they have. When I came in from work last night, Carla had made me dinner. She apologized for treating me the way she had, and we said we'd work on getting back on track. We even made love."

Wayne didn't care to hear that part. He turned away from Pete and poured himself another cup of coffee, so his friend could not see the look of disgust on his face.

Then Wayne turned back and said, "That's great news. I have a little of that myself."

"Spit it out," Pete said.

"I'm getting married."

At first Pete didn't say a word, just looked at Wayne with wide eyes, then exclaimed, "You're bullshittin'!"

"Nope."

"To who?"

"Who do you think? The woman I've been dating for the last six months. Me'Shell."

Pete walked over to him, grabbed him by the hand again, gave him a hug, patted him several times on the back. "I can't believe it. Welcome to the land of the married." Pete released Wayne from the hug. "We have to celebrate. Tomorrow night. Come by, bring Me'Shell, and the four of us will do it the right way."

"I don't think so, Pete. Maybe another—"

"Why not? You haven't been by the house in over two months. I know Carla will be happy to see you—she's probably forgotten what you look like, it's been so long. I won't even tell her. It'll be a surprise. It'll be good. You're coming, right?"

Wayne didn't answer.

"Wayne, you're coming, even if I have to drive over and get you guys. Okay?"

"Yeah," Wayne finally relented. "I'll guess we'll make it."

9

Wayne took Lake Shore Drive home from work, exiting at Thirty-first Street.

His cell phone rang.

He answered it when he saw it was Carla.

"I thought you couldn't talk to me," Wayne said.

"I have to."

"But you said no more."

"Wayne, it's important."

He agreed to see her.

When Wayne walked into the same restaurant he was just in two days ago, the same one where Carla broke his heart for the last time, she wasn't sitting at their table, but at the bar. He was sure she sat there on purpose, not wanting him to reminisce about the times they used to have.

Carla looked beautiful as always, wearing a pale orange business skirt suit, her hair pinned in a bun, two long strands falling to either side of her face. She acknowledged him with a nod when he took the stool beside her, but she did not speak.

She wasn't drinking.

"What are you having?" Wayne asked.

"I'm not," Carla said.

"I see. The other night you weren't here to eat, today, not here to drink. Tell me, then, why have our last two meetings been in a restaurant?"

Wayne waved down the bartender and ordered a scotch and soda.

"I'm sure Pete told you that we're trying to put things back together."

Wayne received his drink, gave the man a ten, told him to keep the change. "Yeah, he was doing back flips all up and down the halls today," Wayne said sarcastically, taking a sip of his stiff drink. "And giving all the patients high fives. He's definitely excited."

"So am I. But I still feel guilty about what I was doing, seeing you behind his back."

"We weren't seeing each other. All we were doing was talking."

"I'm still feeling guilty."

"I'm sorry that you're having trouble dealing with that."

"I am, and I want to be free of it."

"Really," Wayne said, not looking at Carla, but facing straight ahead. "And how do you plan on doing that?"

"I want to tell him what's been going on."

Wayne spun on his stool. "Are you . . ." he stammered. "You can't do that. Pete would never forgive me."

"Funny, you weren't saying that when you were trying to convince me to leave him."

"I know that was wrong. But since it's over now, it doesn't make sense to tell him about it."

"It does," Carla said. "I'm trying to be honest with him from now on."

"No, what you're being is selfish. You're only willing to tell him because you know he'll forgive you. That won't be the case with me."

"You forgave him for telling me that you cheated."

"Pete is not like me. We don't think the same. If you have to do this, just tell him that you were seeing someone, but don't say it was me."

"I can try that, but he'll want to know who it was. He has that right."

"So that's it?" Wayne said. "No other options?"

"You can go to him first. Tell him your part in this. I'll wait for you to do that."

Wayne shook his head, chuckled pathetically as he grabbed his drink and took a sip.

"Just because you're insane, doesn't mean I am. That'll never happen, Carla."

"If that's how you feel," Carla said, standing up from her stool and getting ready to leave. "Take care, Wayne."

"Carla," Wayne called to her as she walked away. "When are you going to tell him?"

"I don't know. Whenever hiding the truth becomes too much."

10

That evening, after Pete and Carla had finished dinner, they sat out on their huge front porch, sipping coffee. The night was beautiful, warm with an occasional breeze.

They weren't talking, hadn't said anything for the last ten minutes or so. Pete's mind was deep into his thoughts. The guilt was bothering him again, and all during dinner, really from the moment he had stepped into the house and set down his briefcase, he had thought about going to his wife and just spilling it all.

But Pete had held his tongue.

And now he thought again about relieving himself of this burden. He looked over at his wife, bringing the cup of coffee to her lips, sipping from it, looking out on the neighborhood. She looked peaceful, serene.

So unlike that time when Pete had told her Wayne had cheated on her. He could remember her crying, trembling. "It's not true!" she had said, standing up from the sofa.

Pete had stood up too. "Why would I lie about something like that?"

"I have to see him," Carla said, grabbing her keys from the table and rushing to the front door.

Pete beat her there, blocked her way out. "I'm not lying to you, and you're in no condition to drive."

"Move, goddammit!" she screamed. "Please!" She started crying again, looked weak, as though she might crumple to the floor at any moment.

Pete took hold of her, walked her back to the sofa, held her in his arms, comforting her. "Everything will be all right. Everything."

After Carla had finally spoken to Wayne and found out firsthand what he had done was true, she was distraught. She had stopped going to work for a week, would not leave her apartment, and never seemed to stop crying.

Pete would bring her groceries, sit with her, watch TV, or just listen to her painful stories.

"We were going to get married in two months," she would say, puffy eyed, her nose swollen.

"I know," Pete would say, sitting beside her, his arm around her, comforting her. He was the only one she was really speaking to at that time. Pete was her shoulder to cry on, and that was fine with him.

Things were rough at the practice with Wayne. For the first week, Pete wouldn't say a word to Wayne, outside of what was necessary to treat their patients and take care of the day-to-day requirements of the business.

Pete had always been worried that Wayne would one day step into his office and tell him that he wanted to end their partnership. But Wayne never did, and Pete was thankful for that.

After two months, one evening when Pete had stayed late, after most of the lights had been turned out and he thought everyone had left, he was searching for a file in the records room when he was startled by a noise. He spun around to find Wayne standing in the shadows.

"You scared me," Pete said, his heart pounding in his chest.

"How is she?" Wayne said.

"Carla?"

"Yeah."

"She's hurting, but she's getting better," Pete said.

Wayne turned, was about to walk out of the room, but stopped, turned back, and said, "I'm glad you're there for her."

That was thoughtful of Wayne, Pete decided. Wanting someone to be there for Carla to help her through this, even if it was the man who had told on him, brought all this business out in the open.

Pete knew it wasn't exactly that, but he took it as a go-ahead sign from Wayne. He spent more time with Carla and they became closer. Carla was getting over Wayne, or at least it seemed that way to Pete. She had been back at work for some time, and they were going out, getting dinner, doing movies.

She had even said to him a few times that, if it weren't for him, she probably would've slit her wrists or something. She would hug him, kiss him on the cheek, showing him gratitude. "You're a true friend," she would often say to Pete.

But Pete wanted more. He was falling in love with Carla once again, and he did everything short of actually saying it, to show her that.

But either she did not get the picture or she was just ignoring it, so one day, about four months into their new friendship, Pete asked if they could take the relationship to the next level. They had just come in from partying with a few friends. They had both had a little too much to drink and were standing in the open doorway of Carla's apartment.

"I want to ask you something," Pete said, standing very close to Carla. "Do you think of me in that way?"

"What way, Pete?"

"In the way that makes you want to be closer to me. In the way that makes you want to physically express your feelings for me. Because that's how I think of you."

Carla smiled a little, as though she thought this might be a joke. When Pete didn't smile with her, she became more serious and said, "Pete, what is it you're trying to ask me?"

"I want us to have an intimate relationship. I want to make love to you."

Carla looked astonished, like that thought had never once crossed her mind. "Pete, we're friends, and I love you, but just as a friend. Why would you want to ruin that?"

"Because I feel more for you than that. I've tried to deny it, but I can't. I just can't."

"I'm sorry," Carla said. "I like what we have here, but if you don't think you can put those feelings aside, then maybe we should reevaluate this friendship." Carla stepped farther behind her door. "Let me know, Pete," she said, before closing it.

Pete decided that he didn't want to sacrifice what he had with Carla for sex, so he left the issue alone.

But one night, as Pete helped Carla paint her kitchen, Carla was angry, even though she was trying to deny it. She had happened to see Wayne out with a woman. "The girl was clinging to him like she was drowning. It was disgusting."

"Did they see you?" Pete asked.

"No. I ducked behind a car."

That entire night she could talk of nothing else but Wayne and the woman. It got to the point where Pete just didn't want to hear Carla's jealous ranting anymore, and he said, "I better be going. It's getting late."

Carla turned to Pete from across the room, paint on the tip of her nose, on her cheek, and said, "Why don't you stay tonight. You're covered in paint. You can shower, and I'll fix you breakfast in the morning. It's the least I can do."

That night, Pete found himself in Carla's bed. He had been prepared to sleep on the couch, but when he asked for a blanket, she said she wanted him to sleep with her.

He lay in bed beside her in his T-shirt and boxers, not knowing what to think or how to behave. Carla rolled over onto him, suddenly pressing her lips against his, rubbing her hand under his T-shirt.

Pete pulled away, not because he didn't like it, but because he had no idea what was going on. "What are you doing?" Pete said, up on his elbows.

"You said you wanted to take things to the next level," Carla said. "I've decided to let you do that." She scooted a little closer to him, as if wanting to resume their kiss.

"Hold it," Pete said, raising a hand. "Are you doing this because you care about me, because you want to express your feelings for me, or because you saw Wayne with another woman, you're mad, and in your mind, this is a way to get back at him?"

Carla looked as though she gave the question some serious thought, then said, "Does it make a difference? I want to have sex."

Later Carla sat on top of Pete, riding him, giving herself to him. Pete stared, light-headed, up at her. She was breathtaking to him, closing her eyes, as she made soft moans and grunts, bringing him closer to giving himself over to her.

Pete was not a fool, realized her eyes could've been closed because she wanted to see Wayne with her mind, rather than Pete with her eyes. Or she could've been moaning instead of speaking, just to stop herself from calling Wayne's name. But at that moment none of that mattered to Pete. Carla was with him that night, and if he had his way, one day she'd be with him forever.

They continued seeing each other. When Pete would tell Carla that he loved her, Carla would not respond, or she'd say something like "That's sweet," or "I appreciate that."

Pete accepted her replies for the moment, but he was growing impatient with her unwillingness to reciprocate his feelings. He had given her everything that he could, the things that she would accept. Three times she'd had him return jewelry he'd bought for her, saying it was too expensive. He had mentioned trips he wanted to take with her, too, but Carla said she just did not have the time.

After six months, Pete was becoming weary. He told himself that he was a better man than one who had to beg and plead for a woman's attention, even though she made it quite plain that she didn't want to give it. So he decided to make one final attempt.

That evening after work, Pete bought the engagement ring he would present to Carla. That night, without ceremony, no dinner, no candlelight, no special location, he proposed to her. In the middle of her living room, five minutes after arriving, Pete said, "Carla, you know I love you. I've tried to give you all I have, but you don't seem to want any of it. But even though you try to deny it, I know you have feelings for me. I know you love me, I can feel it when we're together, when we sleep, when we make love. At one time I worried that you were showing me affection because you were still in love with Wayne. But you got rid of him because he cheated on you. So now I'm here, and I would never cheat like he did. I'm a good man, and I want you to marry me," Pete said, digging into his jeans pocket and pulling out the ring box. He opened it to display the huge solitaire diamond.

Carla gasped, said, "I don't know what to say."

She stood there, a few feet away, looking at him and then at the diamond ring, but not approaching. She was about to speak, but before she could, Pete said, "Before you say anything, I want you to know, this just requires a yes or no answer, and that's all I'm willing to accept. I won't wait, and I won't be your friend anymore. The decision is yours to make."

Carla looked up at Pete for a long moment, seeming to give what he said serious thought. Then she stepped closer to Pete and said, "Okay."

"Pete," Carla said.

Pete snapped out of his thoughts, the coffee cup still in his hand, and looked over at his wife, there on the porch of their home beside him.

She was smiling. "You still with us?" She held out her hand to him.

Pete reached out, grabbed it. "Yeah. Just thinking, is all." And again, he wondered if telling her about his infidelity was the right thing to do. They were starting over. They had agreed to that. Didn't that mean starting with a clean slate?

"Carla," Pete said. "Are you happy you married me?"

She smiled again. "Of course I am."

"Do you think we have a good marriage, a strong marriage?"

A bit of concern crept into her expression, but she continued to smile. "Yes. Why do you ask me that?"

It took Pete a long moment to answer, then he said, "I just wanted to know."

11

The next day, Wayne sat in his office at his desk, his head in his hands, thinking. Everything was wonderful at home. Me'Shell was "walking on clouds," as she put it, but Wayne still could not get Carla out of his head.

He thought about how he and Carla had first met.

It was more than two years ago at a North Side bar, crammed with people standing and sucking down beers.

Pete spotted her first, across the bar, yanked on Wayne's arm like he was witnessing a murder.

He pointed the woman out to Wayne, and at that moment Wayne knew he was looking at the girl he would marry.

"Just give me a minute. I'm going to talk to her," Pete said.

But he was too scared to approach her.

Instead, Wayne took a step in her direction.

Pete grabbed his arm, "No, I can do this," he said, then headed off himself.

Pete sealed the deal that night, but after his second date with Carla, he asked Wayne to accompany them. "Just bring a girl. We'll double. It'll make me feel more relaxed."

They did that on the next four of Pete's dates with Carla. Wayne was with a different girl each time.

They had good times. Wayne was his usual self, open, cracking jokes, confident. That allowed Pete to relax some, it seemed. He was able to come out of his shell with Wayne there to back him up.

The dates were going well for Pete, but Wayne could not keep his eyes off Carla.

Once, when Pete went for more beer, and Wayne's date had gone to the restroom, Carla eyed Wayne.

"What?" Wayne said.

"I'm waiting to see how many double dates we have to go on before you run out of women."

"It's easy to find women. The hard part is finding the right one," Wayne said. "I thought you were it."

"What are you talking about?" Carla asked, leaning closer over the table.

"Yeah, I thought that about you, but Pete saw you first. He insisted he talk to you."

Just then, Pete popped up behind Carla with the beers.

Wayne didn't know if that encounter between him and Carla that night had anything to do with it, but a month later, Pete came to Wayne distraught. "Carla let me go. She said she thought we'd have a better friendship than relationship."

A week after that, Wayne was having a beer at the same bar, with some of his old medical school friends. He felt a tap on his shoulder. He turned around to find Carla in worn jeans and a T-shirt, looking gorgeous.

"How many times did you have to come to this bar before you found me?" he asked.

"Every damn day."

"I hope I'll be worth the effort," Wayne said.

"You better be."

For the first two months, Wayne kept Carla a secret from Pete. He knew he would take the news hard.

But things were progressing well for the two of them.

Wayne was falling in love. Carla said she already had fallen.

"Pete," Wayne said, soon afterward.

They had finished playing a little basketball and were sitting on the outside cement court.

"I know you're going to think I'm wrong for this, but I've been seeing Carla."

"Who? My Carla?" Pete said.

"Yeah. That's the one."

Pete gave Wayne a long look. He let out a pathetic chuckle.

He rose from the court, picked up his ball. "Why am I not surprised. Did she come to you?"

"That's not important, Pete."

"Did she come to you?" he said again.

"Yeah."

"Good old Wayne. Can never turn down what someone else is interested in." Pete started to walk off.

Wayne stood. "This isn't Susie Taylor. This isn't a high school crush."

Pete stopped. Turned. "I know it isn't."

"I love her, Pete. Are we okay with this?"

"We have to be," Pete said, walking again. "We have a pact, right?"

In his office, Wayne looked up from his thoughts when he heard a tapping at his door.

"Come in," he said.

The door opened. It was Pete. "Done for the day?"

"Yeah," Wayne said.

"Me too. Can I talk to you?"

"Sure."

Pete lowered himself into one of the two chairs in front of Wayne's desk. He appeared troubled.

"What's going on?" Wayne asked.

Pete dropped his face in his hands, shook his head, then looked up at Wayne. "I did something I'm not proud of, something disgraceful."

Wayne sat up some in his chair. "Pete, what are you talking about?"

"It was because of how she was treating me. I needed . . . I need to know what I should do about this."

Wayne came out of his chair, walked around his desk, stood just before Pete, concerned. "About what?"

"A few nights ago," Pete said, his voice soft, regretful. "At the W Hotel, I slept with this woman."

Wayne took a moment before saying, "I don't think I understand what you just told me."

"I slept with another woman. I stepped out on Carla."

Wayne stared angrily at Pete. "You son of a bitch!" he spat, as a patient walked by his office door.

Wayne went to the door, slammed it shut, then said it again: "You son of a bitch!" This time louder. He paced angrily around his office, pulling off his lab coat, balling it up, and slinging it at the wall.

"I made that mistake and slept around, and you ended what could've been the rest of my life with that woman."

"I know," Pete said.

"I loved her," Wayne said.

"I know."

"And now you do it, and what? You think you're just going to fucking get away with it. No way," Wayne said, bending over, pointing a finger in Pete's face. "You're going to tell Carla exactly what you did, or I'll do it for you."

"I know," Pete said. "I can't expect to subject you to rules I can't follow myself. I'm going to tell her, I was just coming to you to ask you how."

Wayne stood over Pete, his pulse racing. He wanted to reach

out, strangle him for what he had done those two years ago, for what he had just done now. Wayne wanted to punish him, but Pete would surely get that when he told Carla about what he did.

"Pete," Wayne said, sitting down in the chair next to his friend, feeling himself calm just the slightest bit. "I hate you for this, you know."

"I know."

"What do you think she'll do?" Wayne said.

"I don't know."

"You think she'll leave you?"

"I don't know," Pete said, glancing at Wayne for only a second, then back to the floor. "I don't think so. I believe what we have is pretty good. I don't think so."

If Pete told Carla about this, like he was planning on doing, she would surely leave him, Wayne thought quickly. She would be alone, and then that would leave nothing standing in the way of his getting back with her.

But Wayne had spent time with her over the last two months, hoping that she would consider leaving Pete.

She didn't. Carla said no. She meant no.

And Wayne didn't want her back by default, just because Pete had screwed up.

Besides, he had to remember, he had proposed to Me'Shell.

And of course, there was the fact that Pete would be torn apart if Carla walked away from him again. Carla had let Wayne know what the deal was. He had moved on, would be with Me'Shell, so what good would it do anyone for Pete to ruin his marriage? If anything, it would just hurt Carla for her to know that once again she had been cheated on, and Wayne didn't want that.

"Pete," Wayne said, placing a hand on his shoulder. "Don't tell her."

Pete looked as though he didn't understand what Wayne was saying.

"Take it from someone who knows firsthand, you tell her this, she'll leave you. Do you want that?"

"I don't believe she will."

"It doesn't matter what you believe. She will be gone. There is no doubt about it."

Wayne picked up his lab coat from the floor, hung it up calmly. He walked back behind his desk and dropped defeatedly into his chair.

Pete stood up, looked around as if he didn't know where he was.

"Pete. Promise me this, will you? That you won't tell Carla. Promise. Yes?"

"Okay, I'll think about it," Pete said. He reached for the door, opened it. "You still coming tonight, right? Bringing Me'Shell to celebrate."

"Considering what we just talked about, I don't think there's much to celebrate," Wayne said.

"Come on. Nothing's changed. I haven't told Carla about dinner, because I want it to be a surprise. I've been looking forward to this. It'll keep my mind off the guilt. I'll see you at my place, eight thirty P.M. All right, Wayne?"

"Yeah," Wayne reluctantly agreed. "Eight thirty, we'll see you there."

12

When Pete stepped out of his best friend's office, he knew that he had hurt him. He knew that Wayne was probably behind his office door, wracking his brains to remember why in the hell they were still friends. Trying to remember how they shared a medical practice, even after Pete had ruined things for Wayne and the woman he was going to marry.

Pete knew he remembered the pact—would never forget the bond he had with Wayne.

When both Wayne and Pete were sophomores in high school, Pete had a crush on this girl, Susie Taylor.

He had admired her from afar, gazed at her from his locker down the hall, followed twenty feet behind her in the crowded corridors between classes, wondering how he would approach her.

He had told Wayne of his crush, that he could not do anything but think about Susie.

"Just go up to her and tell her that," Wayne suggested.

"I can't do that. I'll stutter, look stupid. I'll make a fool of myself."

"You want me to talk to her for you?"

"Will you do that?"

Pete was excited, knew his brother would handle everything for him.

For the next two weeks, Pete asked about Wayne's progress with Susie at least three times a day.

"I'm talking to her, but I don't want to rush things," was always Wayne's reply.

But at the end of those two weeks, Pete had heard rumors around the high school campus. One day Pete was telling one of his friends about Susie, saying that "I'll be dating her soon. You just watch and see." His friend, a tall, red-haired boy, turned to him and said, "What are you talking about? That's Wayne's girlfriend."

"Wayne who?"

"Uh, your best friend. My sister said she saw the two of them kissing at the end of seventh period."

"No," Pete said. "That can't be right. Your sister is wrong."

"Okay. Whatever," the boy said.

Pete continued to believe that Wayne couldn't have screwed him like that until he got home, until he was able to ask Wayne face to face.

"She said she wasn't that interested in you. She likes me," Wayne said, as though it was no big deal.

"Why didn't you tell me?"

"Because I was still working on her. I knew how much you liked her, so I was still trying to convince her to give you a chance."

"By kissing her?"

Wayne was silent and hunched his shoulders, a guilty grimace on his face.

Pete walked out of their room, and for the next two weeks he said nothing to his brother.

They continued to share their bedroom, ate their meals with their parents, passed each other throughout the large house they lived in, but did not speak a word to each other till the day Wayne's father locked them in their bedroom.

"And I'm not letting you two out till you come to some kind of resolution," he had said through the door.

After sitting for twenty minutes in silence, Wayne finally said, "I don't see what the big deal is. She's just some girl."

"Some girl I said I liked. The girl I trusted you to talk to, but instead I hear you're trying to screw her."

"I wasn't. She was talking about giving it to me."

"And you were going to take it."

"No. I told you I knew how you felt about her." Wayne rose from his twin bed, walked over to Pete, who sat on his own bed. "This is crazy, all this over some girl. What do I have to do for us to be cool again?"

"Leave her alone?"

"Done. You want me to try and hook you two up again?"

"No!" Pete said, rising from his bed, standing face to face with Wayne. "We have to make sure this doesn't happen again."

"I know what we can do," Wayne said, turning, and hurrying to his desk drawer. He pushed stuff around in there, then returned to Pete with an open safety pin. "We can make a pact."

"A pact?"

"Yeah. Give me your hand."

Pete held out his hand to Wayne. "We can make a pact that we'll never let a girl come between our friendship, never come before the fact that we're brothers." Wayne stuck Pete's thumb with the pin till it bled.

"Ow!" Pete cried.

Wayne squeezed a drop of his brother's blood onto Pete's opposite palm; then he stuck himself and did the same.

"Do you promise to keep this pact, that we will never let some stupid girl come between us being friends and brothers?" Wayne said, holding out his bloodstained hand.

"I promise," Pete said, taking Wayne's hand in his own.

The boys locked their palms tight and shook.

"Then this pact is sealed as of this day on," Wayne said solemnly.

Pete knew that was the reason Wayne agreed to continue being Pete's friend now, even after Pete had told Carla that Wayne had cheated on her. Carla was still a girl that they would not lose their friendship over. It seemed childish now, but something they both believed in.

It had taken Wayne almost four months to speak to Pete again, but with a lot of effort and a lot of apologizing from Pete, he had finally gotten over it.

"So, you're not still mad about what I did?" Pete asked on the first day that Wayne had actually said a kind word to him, more than just about work-related business.

"No," Wayne said. "But even if I was, I have no choice but to continue being your friend, your brother—because of the pact, right?"

"That's right. Because of the pact," Pete said, feeling like shit, because that day just happened to have been the exact day after he had slept with Carla for the first time. Wayne had no idea that Pete had been seeing her, had befriended her, comforted her, after what Wayne had done to her. But Pete knew that he would have to tell his brother everything one day, he just didn't know when.

To Pete's dismay, that day came two months later, after he had asked Carla to marry him, after she had said yes.

Pete tried to pick the right time, the right place, the right words, but there was no right way to tell your best friend such news.

So one day, after a lakefront run, Pete blurted out to Wayne, "I'm getting married."

Wayne stopped in his tracks, looked back at Pete, a smile on his face.

"What? You're joking. You haven't even told me you've been seeing anyone."

"It's no joke. And I have been seeing someone."

"Who?"

"First say you'll be my best man. I need for you to be my best man."

"What the hell are you talking about?" Wayne said, walking over and punching Pete in the shoulder. "Of course I'll be your best man. We always said we'd do that for each other, right?"

"Right."

"Now who's the lucky woman?"

"Carla."

Wayne's face went blank. He looked directly at Pete like he was looking through him, then he chuckled a little. "Not my Carla, right?" His voice was small, unsure, and Pete thought that was the first and only time he heard his brother sound like that.

"Yeah, Wayne. Your Carla."

"Oh," Wayne said, looking like he was trying his best to keep his emotions all in check.

"Are you okay?"

"Sure," he said, turning, starting to walk away. "I'll be fine."

"You'll still be my best man," Pete called to Wayne.

Wayne stopped, turned to look at Pete, and after a thoughtful moment said, "Yeah. I'll still do that."

Only now did Pete realize how underhanded he had been.

His rationale was always that he did it only because he felt Wayne didn't truly love Carla. If he had, he would've never stepped out on her the way he did. But now Pete knew different. He had cheated on his wife, and he still loved her very much.

And as Pete walked away from his brother's office door, he could only imagine how crushed he would be if Wayne were to have gone behind his back and told his wife the horrible thing he had done to her.

That's why, despite what he had told Wayne, Pete was still seriously considering telling Carla of his infidelity. Like he had told Wayne in the office, he should not be above the rules he had set for his own brother.

13

When Wayne and Me'Shell came through the door for dinner that night, Carla immediately gave Me'Shell a hug.

She hugged Wayne, too, but he could feel the distance and chill in her embrace.

Carla stepped back beside Pete, put her arm around his waist, and said, "So my husband told me you two were coming over, but he still didn't tell me what this surprise was all about."

Me'Shell giggled, hiding her hands behind her back. "Should I tell her, baby?"

Wayne looked directly into Carla's eyes. She was looking right back at him.

"Sure. Go ahead and tell her."

Me'Shell showed her hand to Carla.

"We got engaged, girl."

Carla gasped, threw a hand over her mouth, gave her best surprised I'm-so-happy-for-you look when she saw the three-carat diamond Wayne had bought Me'Shell.

Me'Shell and Carla had only hung out a few times. Wayne knew Carla wasn't sincere, had known her long enough to know she was being fake.

Carla gave Me'Shell another hug, but threw Wayne the evil eye from over his fiancée's shoulder.

After two bottles of wine, a half dozen beers, and conversation about everything from how things were going at the orthopedic practice, to what was happening at both Carla's and Me'Shell's jobs, the discussion turned to the engagement.

"So," Carla said, leaning back in her chair, holding her wine-glass with both hands, "did you have any idea Wayne was going to propose?"

"No. It came as a huge shock," Me'Shell said. "We were just lying in bed the other morning, and out he came with it."

"Out he came with it," Carla repeated. "Nothing like a spontaneous man. Have any idea what triggered it?"

"Doesn't matter," Wayne said. "Fact is, twenty years from now, this will still be my wife." Wayne put his arm around Me'Shell.

"You must be so surprised," Carla said to Me'Shell.

"Not totally. We had started talking a little bit about marriage at one time, but then two months or so ago, it just stopped. I would bring it up, but Wayne just didn't want to speak about it anymore."

"I wonder why," Carla said.

"Doesn't matter," Wayne said.

"You think it'll work?" Carla asked. "Marriage can put you through some pretty rough times."

"Why don't you speak on that, Carla," Wayne said. "Considering you and Pete have been having a pretty rough time of it lately. At least that's what Pete has been telling me."

"Everything is fine now," Pete said nervously, looking back and forth between Wayne and Carla, sensing the tension.

"That's right, everything is fine," Carla echoed. "But, Me'Shell, you haven't even known Wayne for a full year. He used to be a flirt back in the day. You sure he doesn't have any women that he's still seeing on occasion?"

"No, Wayne's not like that now," Me'Shell said, rubbing a hand over his thigh. "He's as loyal as they come."

"I'm just checking. I believe you need to know everything about a man before you marry him."

"Is that right?" Wayne said.

"That's right. I know everything about my man," Carla said, grabbing Pete's hand and giving it a squeeze.

"Do you?" Wayne said.

"And what is that supposed to mean?" Carla said.

"Okay," Pete said, quickly jumping in. "What is the deal with the two of you tonight, going at each other's throats?"

"Nothing," Wayne said.

"Nothing," Carla said, looking away from Wayne.

"Then, baby, we need another bottle of red. Can you go in the kitchen and get that for us, please?" Pete asked Carla.

"Sure," Carla said, standing, walking around the table and out of the room, giving Wayne a narrow stare.

"I need another beer," Wayne said, standing up from his seat. "Let me get you one, too, Pete."

Wayne followed Carla into the kitchen. When he pushed through the swinging door, Carla was leaning against the counter, her arms crossed over her breasts.

"What the fuck was that in there?" he said.

"You're marrying her. Why?"

"What difference does that make to you?"

"Because I want to know," Carla said, her words slurring.

"You're drunk."

"No. You are. Why are you marrying her?"

"Because I love her," Wayne said.

"No, because I told you there was no hope for us and turned down your last-ditch proposal. Because your feelings were hurt, and you wanted some consolation, so you asked Me'Shell. Don't you think that's pretty damn selfish?"

"Even if that was the case—which it's not—why do you care? Just like you said, you did turn down my proposal. You made it perfectly clear that you wanted nothing else to do with the idea of us getting back together, and now you're acting like the jealous girlfriend. What's up with that?"

Carla lowered her head, then looked back up at Wayne. "I know. You're right. This is wrong of me. I know we can't get back together, but I'll admit, I don't want anyone else to have you either."

Wayne stood there staring at Carla, his head spinning slightly, not knowing just what to say.

"Don't marry that woman," Carla said.

"Why not, Carla?" Wayne said, taking a step toward her. "You can be honest with me." He took another step toward her, placing him right in front of her. "You do want to get back together, don't you?"

Carla looked deep into Wayne's eyes. "No. I told you that can't happen. I love Pete."

"If that's the case, why are you in your kitchen kissing me?"

"I'm not—"

But before Carla could speak another word, Wayne leaned in, pressed his body to hers, his lips to hers.

She did not object, but threw an arm around him, pulling him tighter, sinking her tongue into his mouth.

Just then, the kitchen door swung open.

"What are you guys doing in—" Wayne heard, as he pulled away from Carla, whipped his head toward the door, to see Me'Shell standing there, her eyes wide with shock, her mouth hanging open.

The three of them, now totally sober, stood gaping at each other for a long moment.

Then Me'Shell lowered her eyes. "I'm sorry. I didn't mean to interrupt." She stepped back out of the doorway.

Wayne glanced at Carla, shook his head, then pushed through the door after Me'Shell.

When he came up behind her, she was already at the closet, pulling on her jacket.

Pete was beside her. He turned to Wayne.

"What happened in there?"

"Me'Shell got sick," Wayne lied. "I really need to take her home."

14

Wayne hurried the car home, gripping the steering wheel tight, not knowing what to say.

Me'Shell sat beside him, silent, tears streaming down her face.

"Pull the car over."

Wayne turned to her. "What?"

"Please! Just pull the car over."

Wayne did as he was told, parked on a quiet residential street, lined with darkened houses.

"The woman you told me about when we first started dating," Me'Shell said, not looking at Wayne, but straight ahead. "The one you said you would've left me for. It's Carla, isn't it?"

Wayne let his head fall back on the headrest, closed his eyes, sighed deeply.

"Cut the dramatics, Wayne, and be a man and fucking tell me! Is it her?"

"Yes."

"So for all the time that I've known you, you acting as though you loved me—"

"I do love you."

"—you were actually wanting her?"

"No. We weren't seeing each other then," Wayne slipped up and said.

"What do you mean, then? You've been recently seeing her?"

"Me'Shell, it's not—"

"That's why all of a sudden we stopped talking about getting married, isn't it?" Me'Shell said, beginning to put it all together. "And that's why Pete and Carla had been having problems over the last two months, because she was seeing you. Oh, God," she said, wiping more tears from her face. "Tell me I'm wrong." She turned to Wayne. "Tell me I don't know what I'm talking about!"

Wayne said nothing.

Me'Shell opened her car door and jumped out.

Wayne quickly got out from his side and hurried after her down the dark street.

"Me'Shell," he called.

She quickened her pace, started running as fast as her heels allowed.

Wayne ran behind her, caught up, spun her around, took her by the shoulders. "What are you doing?"

"This ring, this proposal," Me'Shell cried. "It was only because she didn't want you. You don't really love me."

"If you want me to be honest, yes, she said things would not work out between us, but I do love you. I mean that. And I still want us to get married, to have children, to do all the things that married people do," Wayne said. "You don't still want that with me?"

Me'Shell's tears slowed some. She looked to be giving it thought. "And the kiss in the kitchen?"

"We were a little drunk, but that was good-bye. I swear. That was good-bye. She's married to Pete, and I will be married to you. That's it. If you'll still have me."

"I don't know. I can't trust you now, what you say, or what you do." She looked down sadly at her ring. She made an effort to twist it off her finger. Wayne stopped her.

"Don't. I'll earn your trust back. I'll make you know that I love you, that we should be together. But I want you to wear the ring till I do that. I want us to stay engaged. Okay?"

"I'm sorry, Wayne," Me'Shell said, taking off the ring. "I can't do that."

15

After Me'Shell and Wayne left in such a hurry, Pete asked Carla what had happened.

"Just like Wayne said, she pushed through the door, and it looked like she was about to throw up. I guess she had too much to drink."

Pete knew he had told Wayne yesterday that he would not tell his wife that he had slept around on her, but his conscience would not let him hold it in any longer. Especially after the comment Carla made earlier about knowing everything about her man.

When Wayne had challenged her, Pete knew he had been referring to his infidelity.

He knew the man probably had one too many, but Pete wanted to lash out at Wayne for saying that. And even though he knew Wayne would never tell Carla what he had done, he didn't like feeling as though someone held something over his head, even if that someone was his brother.

Telling Carla would get this off of his chest, out in the open, and it would be over with.

Pete grabbed Carla's hand, and led her out of the kitchen, into the dining room, and asked her to have a seat.

"I need to talk to you," he said.

He took the chair directly across from her, so they could be face to face when he admitted his mistake.

She would forgive him, he kept telling himself as he reached across the table and took both her hands in his. She would forgive him, because although he had committed adultery, she would realize that he was an honest man for telling her. She would know that all he wanted for them was for things to work out, or he would never even confess to such a horrible thing.

"Carla," Pete said, swallowing hard. "There's something that I think you should know."

"No. Wait," Carla said, pulling her hands away from Pete's. "I have something to tell you first."

"No, Carla. I need to get this off my chest."

"Pete, I want to go first," Carla said, and she got up out of her chair and stepped away from her husband, turned her back to him. "The reason it felt like I was neglecting you—"

Pete heard his wife begin, but he didn't make out the words. He was ready to confess, he had finally built up the courage, and he knew that if he was sidetracked at all, what he had to tell her might never come out.

"—was because—" Carla continued.

But Pete stopped her, blurted out in a voice much louder than hers, "Carla, I had an affair."

There was an immediate and deafening silence.

Pete stood where he was, watching Carla, for she said nothing, did not move, didn't turn around. Pete began to worry. "Carla, did you hear me? I said that I had an affair."

When Carla turned to face him, tears were running down her cheeks. But she was not hysterical as he thought she might have been. She did not appear angry, not disturbed. She did not even raise her voice, when she said, "I thought you said you would never do that to me."

"I know. I said that, but you were neglecting me, you were—"

"When?"

"What?" Pete asked.

"When did it happen?"

"The night I cooked dinner for you," Pete admitted.

Carla's shoulders slumped, her head dropped; she looked staggered by the information. "Two nights ago."

"Yes."

"And then you come home and sleep with me," Carla said, more tears coming.

"Yes, but I didn't want to."

"But you did. Who was it?"

"That's not important."

"It's important to me!" Carla raised her voice.

"A woman I met in a bar," Pete said, his voice low. He was ashamed. "She was an old patient of mine."

Carla turned her back on her husband again, reached out, placed a hand on the corner of the table for support. Pete saw her raise the other hand to her face. "Did you use protection, or do I have to get tested?"

Pete walked toward her. "I wouldn't put us in jeopardy that way."

"Stop," Carla said, hearing him come up behind her. She chuckled sadly, turned to him, a woeful smile on her face, tears running off her chin. "You'd sleep with another woman, but you wouldn't put us in jeopardy. It's so fucking sad that you don't realize it's the same thing, Pete. It's the same fucking thing."

Carla pushed by her husband.

Pete tried to grab her arm, but she snatched it away and ran upstairs. He followed behind her, stood in the bedroom doorway, watching her go into the closet, pull out a suitcase, and throw it onto the bed.

"What are you doing?" he asked.

Carla did not answer, but she carried an armful of clothes out of the closet, hangers still in the necks, and dumped them into the open luggage.

Pete stepped in front of her. "You don't have to do this. I'm the one that's wrong. I'll leave."

"You're goddamn right you will. But I don't feel like waiting for that, so you'll be gone by the time I come back tomorrow. Your ass will not be here."

16

Carla threw her bag in the trunk of her car. She looked back toward the house, saw her husband looking at her from the bedroom window.

She wanted to scream at him. She wanted to run back in there, gouge his eyes out. She wiped the tears that ran down her face, got in the car, started it, and drove away.

It was summer, a beautiful, warm, sunny day, five years ago, one month before Carla was supposed to have gotten married to her then boyfriend Steve. He was a wonderful man. He worked for a bank. He said he wanted a family. Carla and Steve had dated four years. After three he had proposed. He said he could not live without her, and Carla felt the same way about him.

On this day, the Taste of Chicago was going on, and she walked from her office to grab something light to eat and to get some sun.

She stood at one of the food stands, sampling a chicken and vegetable kabob, thinking about how wonderful her wedding was going to be, when someone caught her eye.

It looked like her fiancé.

It couldn't have been him, he was at work thirty miles from

there, but Carla realized she was moving through the crowd of hundreds of people, trying not to lose track of the back of his head.

He stopped.

She saw that he was not alone but with a woman.

They exchanged words. The woman pointed, and the man who Carla was now sure was Steve went off in that direction.

Carla walked closer but was halted when the woman turned around.

It wasn't the fact that she was beautiful, or that she appeared almost too young to be legal.

It was her obvious pregnancy that made Carla feel faint, her knees threatening to give out.

The kabob dropped from her hand.

She felt tears wanting to fall.

She pushed them back.

Again she was moving, one foot in front of the other, toward the woman, stopping in front of her.

Carla stretched a painful smile across her face.

"Hi," Carla said. "I had to come over here and tell you how well you're carrying. You're just glowing."

The girl smiled. She was older than she first appeared.

She was still beautiful.

"Thank you so much. One month to go," the woman said, smoothing a hand over her belly. "And I'm counting the days."

"It's so hot. Should you be out here by yourself?"

"Oh, no. My fiancé will be back. He just went to the little boy's room."

"Fiancé," Carla said. "Really. When's the wedding?"

"Next week."

And Carla felt those tears wanting to come again.

She fought them once more, but this time they won. One raced down her cheek as she looked in the direction of the bathrooms and saw her fiancé emerge, look around to gain his bearings, then head in their direction.

"Are you all right?" Carla heard the pregnant woman ask.

She couldn't give her any attention. Her eyes were glued to the man she thought she loved. No, the man she did love, more now than she ever realized.

He came closer.

He caught Carla's stare.

He stopped abruptly, almost tripped and fell.

He looked both ways again, like for an escape.

The woman again asked Carla if she was okay.

"Allergies," Carla heard herself say. She wiped the tear away, did not turn her eyes away from her fiancé.

He lowered his head and took the last twenty steps or so to reach them.

He took his place by the side of the pregnant woman.

She looped her arm around his waist. "Oh, here he is. This is . . ."

"Carla," Carla said, extending a trembling hand to her fiancé.

He stared at it, dumbfounded, but finally took it.

He opened his mouth to speak his name.

"No, let me guess. Steve, right?" Carla said.

The woman's eyes brightened. "How did you know?"

Because I loved him so much once. Because he promised his life to me, his children, the days from then till he died, but he obviously lied. He lied, and he ripped my heart out, left me with nothing to love another man with, Carla thought.

"He just looks like a Steve," is what she said, then turned and walked off.

Carla could've lost her mind right there, screamed and cried, tried to hurt Steve for cheating on her, for promising everything he had, and then deceiving her, but all it would've done was cause yet another woman pain.

It wouldn't have erased all that he had done to Carla, wouldn't have won him back. So she walked away, telling herself that he was with the woman that he needed to be with. They were expecting a child, so she would just leave the situation be.

A month later, Carla's phone rang at 2 A.M. She was awake, lying in bed, but still distraught over what Steve had done. She leaned over in the bed to check the caller ID to see a number she did not recognize.

She let the answering machine pick it up.

Immediately she recognized Steve's voice, even though he didn't say much at first. He seemed to be searching for words, and then he said, "Carla, I'm so sorry."

Carla considered snatching up the phone, yelling the words that had been screaming in her head for the past month, but she just lay there, a tear coming to her eye.

Steve went on to say that he really did want to marry her. He said the other woman was an old girlfriend, someone he slipped up and let back in his life. Then, after he had proposed to Carla, he realized that he needed to break things off with her. That's when she had informed him that she was pregnant.

Still Steve said he planned on telling her he could not be there for her, that he loved someone else. But as the days passed, as his child grew inside of her, he knew that he couldn't just leave her.

"I promise, I was going to tell you. I didn't mean for you to find out that way. If you're there, Carla, if you're listening to this right now, please forgive me."

Carla lunged across the bed, snatched the answering machine from the wall and threw it across the room, the tears refusing to stop spilling from her eyes.

That was the first time she had been cheated on, Carla thought, as she opened the door of her car, which she had parked in front of her mother's house.

It had taken her an entire year before she was able to trust a man again. She ended up with Wayne, told him what happened with Steve. Wayne promised that he would never do anything like that to her. He would never hurt her like that. But he did, and just like Pete made that exact same promise, he then turned around and hurt her as well.

Three times, with the last three men she had been with.

She really knew how to pick 'em, Carla thought to herself, as she brushed away tears, opened the trunk of her car, yanked out the suitcase and hauled it toward the house.

It was late, not quite midnight.

Carla could see the shadow of her mother moving around behind the curtains.

She rang the doorbell, smeared the remaining tears from her face as best she could, displayed a fake smile, and waited for her mother to answer.

When she opened the door, her mother smiled at the sight of her daughter. "Girl, what are you doing here so—" And almost immediately her expression changed. She seemed to feel the sorrow that Carla was feeling, seemed to have known, or had a very good idea of what had happened even before Carla landed on her doorstep. She opened her arms, moved to Carla, and took her in an embrace.

"Come on in, baby. Everything's going to be all right."

17

Please don't tell me you told her," Wayne said, after opening the door for Pete.

It was 11:45 P.M.

Pete walked slump shouldered past Wayne, into his house. He landed on the sofa.

"I had to. I couldn't deceive her anymore. I tried to explain why. I thought she'd understand, but now . . ."

"But now you know you should've listened to me, right?" Wayne said, standing just before him.

Pete stood up, placed himself face to face with his best friend.

"I'm worried, man. Something's telling me she's really going to leave me for good," Pete said. "Tell me what I can do to stop that."

"I tried to tell you. Why couldn't you just listen to me? You two were doing fine, you said you were back on track. All you had to do was just forget about what you had done, and—"

"I know all that," Pete said, getting more upset. "But I didn't, all right. I fucked up, and I didn't listen, and now she knows!"

"Keep it down, will you? Me'Shell's upstairs asleep."

Pete turned his back on Wayne a second, then turned back to face him.

"Look, I realize that I should've probably listened to you. But it's a little too late for that now. Just tell me what I need to do, Wayne. You've always been here for me in the past. Just tell me what I need to do."

Pete was concerned by how long it took Wayne to answer.

"There's nothing you can do," Wayne finally said. "If you only knew everything I did to try to get Carla to forgive me when we first broke up."

"Yeah, I do know," Pete said. "She told me."

"The flowers, the cards, the letters, the constant invitations to talk about it, the promises that I'd never do it again. She had none of it."

"So what are you saying?"

"That you're fucked. The only way that you stay with Carla," Wayne said, "is if she allows you to."

Pete lowered his head, fell back onto the sofa. "Mind if I crash here tonight?"

"Sure. Kick your shoes off, make yourself comfortable," Wayne said. "I'll grab you a pillow and a blanket."

18

An hour later, Carla sat at the kitchen table, drinking tea with her mother and her older sister, Camille.

Her mother and sister, like Carla, both had beautiful black hair. Camille's was pinned up now, for she had never cut it and it fell to her midback.

Carla's mother's hair was streaked with gray. Her mother was in great shape, her skin still smooth, looking like a woman ten years younger than her sixty years.

With their big, black eyes, thick arched eyebrows, and brown skin, they looked very much like triplets only at different stages in their lives.

Camille had rushed right over when Carla's mother called her (against Carla's will) and told her what happened.

When Camille had walked in, she immediately went to Carla and gave her a long hug, smoothing her hand across her back.

"Sweetheart, it happens, but you'll be okay. I promise."

They had been discussing Carla's situation for the last twenty minutes until now, when Carla just sat, staring down into her cup of tea, not answering the question that had been long ago posed to her by her sister.

"Carla," Camille said.

Carla looked up, as if awakened from a nap. She looked at her mother and her sister, then said, "I want to leave him."

"No," Carla's mother said. "He's a man. Men do those things. I've never told you girls this, but your father did before he died."

"No!" Camille said, shocked.

"Yes, he did. But that didn't mean that he didn't love me, or love you girls. That act meant nothing to him."

"That's what he told you," Carla said. "If it didn't mean anything, why did he do it?"

"Because we don't give them enough attention, because we give them too much attention, and all the reasons in between," Carla's mother said. "No one knows. They're just men, and that's what they do sometimes. They mess up, but that doesn't mean you should end your marriage, sacrifice the time you have invested and the love you feel for that man—not just because he spent half an hour in bed with another woman. Isn't that right, Camille?"

Carla looked over at her sister, surprised. "John didn't . . . did he?"

"Thanks, Mom," Camille said, "for telling the world my business."

"She's not the world—she's your little sister."

"Did he?" Carla asked again.

"Two years ago, he had this thing with a woman at work."

"He told you about it?"

"No, and that's one of the reasons I think Pete is worth staying with. He came to you with his dirt. I had to get proof of what John was doing, and he still tried to deny it."

"But you guys are so in love. Your marriage is so perfect," Carla said.

"It is now," Carla's mother said. "Because they had to work at it, both of them, and Camille had to learn to forgive. But her marriage is an example to you that things can work out, if you just give them the opportunity."

"And that's it?" Carla said, standing up from the table, her voice rising. "What, I'm just supposed to forgive Pete? Go home and work things out, wait till I feel better about it? I won't ever feel better about it."

"That's what your sister did."

"Well, that . . ." Camille said, taking a sip from her cup of tea. ". . . And I had an affair of my own."

Their mother gasped, throwing her hands over her mouth. "You did not!"

Carla actually laughed.

"Oh yes, I did," Camille said. "There ain't that much forgiveness in the world without a little revenge. He did what he did, and in order for things to be even, I had to do what I had to do. It was only fair."

"Shameful, Camille. That is not the way I raised you girls."

"Ma, it was either that, or leave his ass, which I wasn't doing, because my children need their father, and, bottom line, I love him too much."

"I don't have kids," Carla said. "So that leaves me where?"

"Carla, don't leave him," her mother said.

"Okay. I probably won't, but it's not because I shouldn't. But it's because I really think every man is going to do it. If I continue trading in men because they cheat on me, I will have married the entire South Side before I'm done."

"I think you should do what he did to you," Camille said. "I think you should cheat."

"Camille!" Carla's mother said.

"I think you're right," Carla said, looking up at her sister.

"Carla! Don't do that. I promise, you'll regret it. Do you know how many women have been cheated on by their husbands? This is nothing new. Your case is nothing special."

"I know, Ma. And that's what's so pathetic about it. If those women choose to let their men do what they want, and not have them pay some sort of price for it, then that's their mistake. But I can't allow that."

"You go, baby sister!" Camille said.

"We're in this marriage together. We're equal partners in this. If he gets to cheat, then so do I."

"Fine, Carla," her mother said. "But when this comes back, don't say that I didn't warn you."

"This is awesome," Camille said, standing, seeming a bit overexcited. "Now, listen to me, there's steps you have to take to pull this thing off successfully. I know all of them, so I can guide you through it. The first and most important thing you have to make sure of is that you don't get caught."

"I won't have to worry about that," Carla said.

"What do you mean, you won't have to worry about that?"

"Camille, what's the point in sleeping with another man if Pete doesn't know about it?" Carla said. "In order for him to truly learn his lesson, I'm going to sleep with another man, but I'm going to tell him first."

"Oh, Lord," Carla's mother said, slapping a hand across her forehead. "Here we go."

"Oh, this is really awesome," Camille said.

19

The next day at work, Pete did just enough to get by.

He wasn't his normal, cheery self, sitting, talking and cracking jokes in the exam rooms for a few minutes with his regular patients after their appointments. Today, he spoke only the words that were needed to explain his patient's medical situations.

Afterward, he walked back to his office, shut the door, and sat brooding behind his desk.

He called his wife several times, at home, at work, and on her cell. She had not gone in to the magazine today, he was told by an employee. All his other calls were answered by voice mail and were not returned.

At the end of the day, Wayne stuck his head in Pete's door. "Me and Vince are going for drinks, you ought to come. Do you some good." Vince was an ob-gyn who ran a practice upstairs from theirs.

"Naw, you two go ahead. I think I'm gonna head home. See if my wife will talk to me."

"Maybe you ought to give it a little more time."

"I can't, Wayne. Not knowing is tearing me up. If she's going to leave me, then I'd rather know now."

"Give me a call, let me know how it works out?"

"Yeah. I'll do that. Thanks."

"No problem."

Pete sat quietly alone at home, waiting and sipping from a glass of water at the dining room table, before he heard the front door open.

He got up quickly.

Carla froze upon seeing him there, then after a moment, she closed the door and dropped her purse on the sofa, as if Pete wasn't there.

"I'm sorry for what I did," Pete said.

Carla went to the kitchen, ignoring him.

He followed her, stopped at the doorway. She pulled a can of diet soda from the fridge and took a sip, acting like none of this mattered to her.

"Carla, you were behaving like I was a stranger, you barely paid any attention to me. And sex, on the rare occasion we had it—you would lie there like you were doing me a favor. I couldn't take it anymore. I needed to feel as though someone wanted me."

"So you went to a patient of yours. I'm sure she really made you feel wanted."

"More than you."

Carla shook her head.

"I'm sorry."

"Sorry doesn't make what you did go away."

"Then what will?"

"Nothing will."

"Then what are we going to do?" Pete said. "I can't take another night not knowing what the future is for us, and I'm not trying to sleep on Wayne's couch again. So what is it?"

Carla put her soda can in the sink. She told herself she should not be as mad as she was at Pete. She herself had been cheating by seeing Wayne. But, as Wayne said, all they did was talk. And yes, that was still wrong, but at least she respected their marriage enough not to sleep around on her husband. Carla walked past Pete as though he had not said a word to her.

He grabbed her by the arm before she reached the door, spun her to face him.

"I was wrong, but don't ignore me like I'm not even here!" he said. "That's the reason we're in this situation to begin with. I know you've thought about it, now tell me what's happening with us. Are you leaving me, or what?"

Carla looked at him angrily. "I'm not leaving you."

Pete was relieved, but only partially. He knew there had to be a punishment of some sort.

"But . . ." Pete said.

"If you'd let go of me, I'll tell you."

Pete released her arm. "Sorry."

"I've changed my mind. You don't have to leave the house."

"Thank you," Pete said.

"But I don't want you sleeping with me."

"Then where will I sleep?"

"The guest bedroom, on top of the dining room table, the street for all I care, just not in the same bed with me."

"Okay," Pete said, feeling a little better already. "I can do that. Carla, I really think that we can get through—"

"I'm not finished."

"Whatever. Name it."

"Like you said, I thought through this long and hard, and I've determined that it's my turn now."

"What are you talking about?"

"I won't leave you, Pete. But in order for things to be right with us, I'm going to do what you did. I'm going to find a man I think is attractive and have sex with him," Carla said, as calmly as if she was telling how she was going to go about redecorating the bathroom.

Pete stood frozen. He could not speak, not just because of what his wife had just said, but because of the image that just skirted his mind, which was that of some blank-faced man raising his head up from between Carla's legs.

"Oh, no you won't!"

"Or what?" Carla said, stepping closer, looking him square in the face. "You'll go out and fuck around on me, again? Or will you just leave? Considering what you just did to me, I really think I'd be able to handle that."

"Carla, listen, two wrongs—"

"Don't even think about telling me that two wrongs don't make a right, because in this case it not only makes things right, it makes them even."

"If you think that I'm about to sit around and let you go out and sleep with some man, then you must be crazy."

"I'm not asking for your permission. I'm just letting you know that it's going to happen whether you like it or not," Carla said, walking to the stairs. She turned back to him and continued, "And if you need something out of the bedroom, knock on the door and I'll set it in the hallway for you. Otherwise, goodnight."

20

Me'Shell sat in the passenger seat of Wayne's car, looking up at the house she grew up in, and she knew if she were to ever turn back, this was the time to do it.

Last night, after they had come back from dinner and a movie, she stood behind him as he unlocked the front door to his place. He stepped in, but Me'Shell remained on the porch.

"What's up?" Wayne said, turning around. "You coming in?"

"No."

It was only the second night since Me'Shell had found out that Wayne had been seeing Carla.

They really hadn't spoken too much about it, because Me'Shell was in no mood to talk. She was just too damn shook up. She felt like a fool for being used the way she had, felt like a fool for still talking to Wayne, felt like one for even standing there on his porch that very moment. She didn't have to ask herself what held her there, because she knew it was love. Plain, stupid, make-you-disrespect-the-hell-out-of-yourself love.

And what was worse, she knew before she even lay down to have sex with Wayne six months ago that he had issues. He came right out and told her there was another woman that he was interested in, that he would actually leave her for that woman if she would have him back. But Me'Shell acted as if those words had never been spoken and told herself not to worry. Things would be just fine. And they were for a while.

Wayne had been wonderful, attentive, loving, caring, everything she thought he might be from the first time she had seen him in that Starbucks.

Me'Shell had never told Wayne that she had sensed him standing behind her in line, had first noticed him when he came through the doors. She had been trying to think of something to say to him. When she sat down, she had hoped he'd walk over, but when he didn't, instead made his way to the door, she had actually risen from her chair and was about to try to grab him before he left. Then, as he had turned around, she quickly sat back and picked up the paper, acted like she was caught up in what she was reading. And then he'd come over to her table.

He was a gorgeous doctor, with no kids, no drug habits, no crazy guy friends dragging him out to strip clubs every night. None of that. All there was was this thing he had for an ex-girlfriend, that he was honest enough to tell her about. And that's why she thought she truly had nothing to worry about.

That evening when she allowed Wayne to walk out of her house, to drive away, she sat by the window, thinking about what she would do. She was thirty-six years old, a schoolteacher, no children, and no prospects for getting married.

Her last boyfriend was seven years younger than she was. He'd told her he was just not ready. "I still have too much of my life to live," he'd said. And Me'Shell had to ask herself, what did he think being in a relationship with her meant? Death?

When she lifted the phone and dialed Wayne's number as he drove away that night six months ago, she imagined her previous, unsuccessful relationships. None were as good as the potential one she thought she could have with Wayne.

That night she would've begged Wayne to come back if she had to. She told herself she would take the chance and hope that things worked out.

But they hadn't.

For two months Wayne had been trying to get back with that woman. He said it was he who had ended things, but Me'Shell didn't know if she believed him. He said the kiss she walked in on meant good-bye.

That night, as she lay in her own bed, after giving her ring back to Wayne and demanding that he take her home, she had cried hard. At the same time she had prayed that what he said was true, that things really were over between him and Carla, because although she told herself she shouldn't give him another chance, she knew she would.

The next day, Wayne sent her two dozen roses, which Me'Shell declined to accept, along with the twenty or so phone calls he made to her.

She was teaching him a lesson, trying to act as though she did not truly love him, as though she couldn't have cared less if they were together or not.

But Me'Shell assumed she had failed in that attempt, when a little after ten that night she stood in front of Wayne's door, hoping that it wasn't too late. That her rejecting his flowers, not answering his phone calls, hadn't made him decide that he no longer wanted anything to do with her.

When Wayne answered the door, he smiled, reached for her, taking her hand and trying to pull her inside.

"Wait!" Me'Shell said. "I'm not here because I forgive you. And I'm not here to have sex with you, have you thinking that's all it'll take to make up for what you did. I'm just here to decide, once and for all, if I'm going to continue things with you. Do you understand?"

"Yes," Wayne said, pulling her in and happily wrapping his arms around her.

When Me'Shell woke up the next morning to Wayne standing beside the bed, holding a tray with breakfast on it and smiling broadly, she thought that maybe she was right for not getting rid of him.

He waited till she sat up, then he placed the tray over her lap. There was juice, sliced fruit, eggs, sausage, grits, and a single flower in a tall vase.

"Thank you," was all she said, for she still wasn't really speaking to him.

"Don't take too long, because we have something very important to do today."

"What's that?" Me'Shell said, picking up her fork.

Wayne smiled even wider. "It was going to be a surprise, but I might as well tell you. We're driving out to your father's, so I can ask for your hand in marriage."

She could've said no that very moment. She could've said no, after breakfast, while she was showering, while she put on the clothes Wayne ironed for her. She could've said no on the silent drive to the house in Wisconsin where her father lived, or she could've even said no while she sat in Wayne's passenger seat, looking up at the house she had lived in so many years ago. Which is what she was doing that very moment.

"You ready?" Wayne said, after getting out of the car and opening her door for her.

"You've already proposed to me, and I already accepted," Me'Shell said, from her seat in the car.

"But you gave me back the ring, voiding that proposal. So I'm going to do it the right way now, the way I should've done it to begin with."

"This is not necessary, Wayne."

"Why not? Because you'll marry me now?"

"No. I didn't say that."

"Then it is. I told you I was going to prove to you that I wanted to be with you, and only you. This is how I'm going to start. Are you coming, or do I have to do this by myself?"

What if she said no, Me'Shell thought. Wayne would be angry, but it would be well within her rights to tell him to turn around now, that she had changed her mind. She would leave him, never call him again, and she wouldn't have to worry if things were truly over between him and Carla.

But she looked at him, down at his hand holding hers, and her mind drifted away. It floated off to the wedding, to their honeymoon, her giving birth to their first child, the second, maybe even a third. They would all grow together, have wonderful times, and awful times, and Me'Shell would thank God for both.

That would be her life—or it wouldn't be, depending on what she said.

"You asking my father, regardless of what his answer is, doesn't mean I'll say yes," Me'Shell said, stepping out of the car.

"Then what will it take? Because I won't stop trying till you have me back."

"That's for you to find out," Me'Shell said, trying to step around him.

Wayne moved in front of her, locked her in the space between his arms and the car. "I'm serious," Wayne said, although there was a slight smirk on his face, like he thought Me'Shell was just playing games when she said she wasn't certain of how she felt anymore. "What will it take for you to say yes to me again?"

"And I'm serious, too, Wayne. I don't know what it'll take, that is, if I ever say yes to you again," Me'Shell said, pushing Wayne's arm down, and walking toward her father's house.

21

Things were hard right now for Pete. The situation seemed to be right back where it was when Carla would walk in the house, not say a single word to him, retreat straight to her room.

The last couple of nights, Pete stayed in the guest bedroom, lying awake, wondering if his wife was waiting to hear if he would allow her to go out and sleep with some man, or if she had already taken it upon herself and started looking.

They hadn't spoken a single word about it since the first time Carla brought it to him.

Pete needed help in making his decision. He had called Wayne late last night. "You want to go for a run in the morning?" Pete asked him.

"You all right?" Wayne asked.

"Yeah, just a little tired is all," Pete lied. "You want to go for a run, lakefront. We can start in Grant Park, head north?"

"Yeah, that sounds cool. I'll see you tomorrow."

When Pete hung up the phone, he started to feel the slightest bit better. Wayne would help him sort through all this mess, because Wayne had always helped him.

After their run the next morning, while both men walked along the lakefront path, Pete turned to Wayne and said, "She wants to sleep with another man."

Wayne halted. "What?"

"In order for things to be even between us, Carla said she needs to be able to do what I did, go out and sleep with someone."

"And you said what?"

"Fuck no!"

"All right," Wayne said, starting to walk slowly again. Pete continued beside him.

"But I think she's serious."

"Yeah, of course she is. Does that mean you're going to let her do it?"

"She said it's not up to me. She's going to do it whether I approve or not."

Wayne stopped again, turned to Pete, dropped a hand on his shoulder. "So please tell me you're not actually entertaining this idea."

"I don't want to lose her."

"And what do you think her getting fucked by some other man will be doing, guaranteeing that you get her back?"

"I don't know!" Pete said, frustrated. "That's why I'm coming to you. You're always the one with the answers. How do I do this?"

"Tell her she can kiss your ass. She won't go through with it. She says she wants to sleep with another man, but she won't. Trust me, I know she won't," Wayne said.

"How do you know?"

"I just do," Wayne said, sounding confident.

"Then if that's the case, why don't I just tell her that she can?"

"Because she has to realize the reason you stepped out in the first place was because of her. It's her fault. You let her do what she's asking, you're accepting the blame, you're justifying what she's thinking, making her right. And if she believes that, that might just give her reason enough to go out there and sleep with someone else."

"Are you certain about this?" Pete asked, worriedly.

"Just tell her the answer is no. Whatever she says, the answer is no."

22

That night, as Pete lay on the guest bed, his shoes kicked off, trying to read a medical journal by the bed lamp, a soft knock came at the door.

He put the magazine aside, quickly sat up on the edge of the bed. "Come in."

Carla pushed the door open.

"What's up?" Pete said, nervously anticipating what Carla was about to ask him.

She remained in the doorway. "I'm still not asking for your permission on this, but I would like to know where you stand."

"What if I'm against it?" Pete asked.

"Then I'll see that as you not taking responsibility for what you did."

"You were neglecting *me*. It wasn't just my fault that I did what I did," Pete said, mimicking Wayne.

"If you wanted to get back at me for that, then you could've just neglected me, too. You did worse. So don't even pretend it's the same," Carla said. "But like I was saying, if you're against it, then you're not taking responsibility, and if that's the case, then you're telling me you don't want to give me what I need for us to get through this. You don't do that, I leave. I'll hurt for a while, I'll miss you, but eventually I'll get over you, find someone else, and forget what you've done. So it's up to you, Pete. I sleep with a man one time, and we work things out. Or you fight this, I leave, find a man that I'll not only sleep with indefinitely, but that I'll also probably fall in love with, and eventually marry. What do you say?"

Pete thought about Wayne's warnings, heard the man's voice echoing in his head, but Pete quieted that voice and said, "If that's what you want, then go ahead and do it."

23

The next morning as Carla walked past the desks of her coworkers toward her office, she caught sight of Laci, speaking to one of the writers. She waved her toward her office where they could talk.

Laci walked in behind Carla.

"So can you tell me what happened now? I've been worried to death about you."

Carla had called Laci the morning after Pete had told her everything. She was still crying when she told Laci that she would not be coming in to work that morning.

"What's wrong?" Laci had asked.

"I'll tell you next time I see you."

"When will that be?"

"I don't know. Good-bye, Laci," and Carla hung up the phone, even though her friend was still talking.

So now, after Laci sat down in one of the chairs in front of Carla's desk, Laci said, "This has something to do with you finally telling Pete that you were meeting with Wayne, doesn't it?"

"No," Carla said. "I tried, but he beat me to the punch. I never told him, because what he said to me that night made my little indiscretion seem as harmless as I actually thought it was."

"What did he say?"

"That he had cheated on me. He slept with another woman."

"Oh, my god," Laci said, shocked. "You leaving him?"

"No. I spoke with my mother and Camille, and I decided that since Pete was with another woman, then it'd be only right if I were with another man."

Laci relaxed back into her chair, waving Carla off. "Yeah, right."

"No. I'm serious, and I told Pete that's what I'm going to do."

"And he said, hell no, right?" Laci said, springing back up in her chair. "There's no way he'd let you do that."

"He has no choice. I told him that, too. And last night, even though I made him aware I didn't need it, he gave me his permission."

Laci just stared at Carla, her mouth hanging open. "I know you are trippin'. You did not just say that he gave you the Go-out-and-fuck-free card?"

"Yeah, that's what he gave me," Carla said, less than enthused.

"You don't seem too happy about it."

Carla raked her fingers through her hair, looked up at Laci. "I forced it out of him, told him I would leave him, marry someone else if he didn't agree, but I didn't think he actually would. What does this mean now? That he doesn't care if I sleep with some other man? Does it mean he doesn't love me anymore?" Carla asked, standing up, turning her back to Laci, looking out her windows.

"No, Carla," Laci said, standing up, too. "It means just the opposite. Because he doesn't want to lose you, he'll do anything he has to do."

"He should've fought me harder on this," Carla said, turning around.

"And you just would've fought harder. You knew what you wanted, and you weren't going to accept anything less. Isn't that right?"

"Yes," Carla admitted, sounding defeated, lowering herself back into her chair.

"So have you told Wayne yet?" Laci said.

"Told him what?"

"You set this up so you can sleep with him, right? Finally get that out of the way."

"Wayne is Pete's best friend."

"That didn't stop you from meeting him every day, having your little talks."

"Talking and having sex are two different things," Carla said.

"It all falls under the same umbrella of deception and infidelity. Same thing," Laci said.

"Really," Carla said. "If you had a husband, which way would you rather have him deceive you, by talking to another woman, or sleeping with one? Or would it matter, because they're both the same thing?"

"No," Laci said. "Okay. Talking."

"I thought so."

"But why not sleep with him anyway? You've got permission, and it'd be easier than going out there and sleeping with some guy you don't know, or sleeping with Marty from accounting."

"I never said I was going to sleep with Marty from accounting, smart-ass," Carla said, smiling a little. "Just too much history with Wayne. Too complicated. It would tear Pete apart, and now that I've finally gotten over Wayne, I don't need old feelings being brought to the surface."

"So who are you going to sleep with?"

"Fuck, Laci," Carla said, slapping her palm to the desk. "I'm so tired of this happening to me. When Pete told me what he did, I didn't yell, didn't scream, nothing. It was almost as if I knew one day it could happen, so it came as no surprise to me, and there's something really wrong with that. Right now, I just want to grab the first man who says boo to me, take him home, and fuck him on the living room sofa, right when Pete's walking in from work. Let him see how it feels. But what kind of woman would that make me?"

"One who refuses to take shit anymore, right?"

"Or one who has a license from her husband, and plans on using it to be a ho."

"And if you don't go through with it?" Laci asked.

"Then I'll hate myself, because I'll feel as though I've let Pete do whatever he wanted, and I wasn't strong enough to do anything about it."

"Okay, then don't plan to be a ho. Don't focus on going out just to lay some man down. We'll go out to get a couple of drinks, hang out, and you know guys will come on to us like they always do. Only this time, instead of having to beat them off, turn them away because you're married, you can hear them out, listen to their corny-ass jokes, accept the drinks they send us. And if, and only if, you're interested in one of them, you can investigate a little further. Who knows, you might actually find yourself wanting to get in his pants."

Carla shook her head. "Something doesn't seem right about that."

"And how right was Pete doing it to you?"

"You got a point."

"So, tomorrow night. Happy hour at any bar on Rush Street. Take your pick."

"And I don't absolutely have to sleep with anyone? We're just going out to have drinks?"

"That's right."

"And if nothing happens, if I don't go home with some man, you won't think I'm a punk?"

"Just a little bit of a punk," Laci said. "Naw, girl. We'll just have fun, okay?"

"Okay," Carla said, and for the first time she felt a little better about the situation.

Carla's cell phone rang as she was sitting in her car, about to head home at the end of the day.

It was Wayne. She let it ring three more times, pondering whether she wanted to answer.

"Hello," she said, finally picking up.

"We need to meet. I need to talk to you," Wayne said.

"I have nothing to say to you. Considering what you did."

"What did I do?"

"What you withheld from me."

"I'm not having this conversation over the phone," Wayne said. "At Calypso's. I can be there in fifteen minutes. How about you?"

"I didn't say I was coming."

"I'll be there in fifteen minute," Wayne said again. "I need to be seeing you there."

She started her car and headed to the restaurant where she'd met Wayne so often in the past.

When Carla walked in, Wayne was already perched on a stool at the bar.

She took the stool beside him.

He was about to order himself a drink, but he stopped, turned to Carla, and said, "I guess you aren't drinking today?"

Carla ignored Wayne and said to the bartender, "Gin martini. Hold the olive."

They got their drinks and both took a long sip.

"You're a hypocrite," Wayne said.

"And you're a liar. You knew that Pete had slept with someone, didn't you?"

"A day or two before you knew. So what?"

"Why didn't you tell me?" Carla said.

"Why, so you could go through this nonsense you're going through now? So you can be in the pain you're in now? Why should I have told you that?"

"Because he told on you."

"I'm not him. It wasn't his place to tell you about the mistake I made back then, and it sure wasn't mine to tell you about his. But you, demanding that you be allowed to sleep around, because he did it, when you were practically doing it yourself."

"I wasn't doing it."

"Not a week ago, you were hugging me in this very restaurant. If someone were to have walked in, if your husband were to have walked in, you couldn't have told him any different."

"Why are you so concerned about me sleeping around on Pete anyway? If you had it your way, I would've been doing it with you."

Wayne said nothing. He brought his scotch to his lips and took a swallow.

Carla took a sip from her own drink.

Wayne looked back at Carla, then said, "You may be right. But since you told me there was no chance for us, I let all that go. I'm concerned about Pete, now. You aren't really going to go through with this, are you?"

"I don't know."

"You don't?"

"Okay, yes. I'm going to do it," Carla said, seriously.

Wayne shook his head. "Look at what happened to you. This is not who you are."

"This is the third time in a row I've been cheated on by the man I loved, Wayne. I've changed. I've had to. I won't continue to take this shit from you all, cry myself to sleep each night, and hope there's someone out there who won't ever do this to me again."

"I would've never done it to you again."

Carla paused, held the hard stare he was directing at her.

She looked away, picked up her drink, took another sip. "It's too late for that."

"I'm not saying it so you'll take me back. I'm telling you because it's fact," Wayne said. "Don't do this to Pete. If you can't get over it, then just leave him. Don't do it just to get back at him."

"And if I leave, where will I go, Wayne?" Carla said. She knew what he would say. How she could come back to him, that things would be better than they were before, because he truly realized how much she meant to him. It wouldn't be anything that she'd do, but right now, she yearned to hear it. "Who would want me if I wasn't with Pete?"

Wayne stared directly at her, but turned away, and said, "I don't know. But I'm sure someone would come along."

Carla grabbed her purse, stood up to leave, but first she brought her martini glass to her lips and finished the last of the drink in one swallow.

"Wayne, do me a favor. Don't call my phone again."

24

It was the fourth night in a row that Carla and Laci had gone out.

They were at a restaurant on Rush Street, one that doubled as a club on weekends. Popular music blared out of hidden speakers. The place was packed, crammed with men wearing suits and dress shirts, and women wearing backless dresses or low-cut tops with thigh-high skirts and extra-high heels.

Carla felt right at home, feeling no pressure to actually sleep with any of these men. She had taken the last four days to just enjoy all the attention she had been getting. She allowed the men to flirt with her, and she flirted right back.

Tonight Carla wore a low-cut lavender dress, with a split that ran from her knee all the way up her left thigh.

Heads turned as she walked back to the table she shared with Laci. She had just bought them yet another drink. It was Carla's fourth martini, and only Laci's second.

She set the drinks down on the table, not spilling a drop. Carla was even surprised by her own dexterity, considering how tipsy she was. "Girl, you're going to have to catch up. You're three drinks behind," she said.

"Two drinks," Laci corrected.

"Yeah, that's what I said." Carla laughed.

"Besides, somebody's gonna have to drive you home tonight," Laci said. "And somebody's gonna have to hold your hair up, while you puke up your guts in the parking lot."

"Cute," Carla said, holding up her glass and taking a sip. "Ain't nobody puking their guts up. These men wouldn't find that very attractive."

A handsome, broad-shouldered, dark-skinned man wearing a gray suit walked by. He glanced at Carla, then continued on his way, but halted when she called out to him.

"Hey," Carla said, catching the man's attention, then waving him over, spilling a little of her drink as she did.

"What are you doing?" Laci whispered loudly, looking embarrassed by all the other men who turned to see who Carla was calling for.

"What's it look like? I'm trying to get that man to come over here."

When he approached their table, she saw that he was even more attractive than Carla had first thought. He smiled brightly, making the cleft in his chin more prominent. "Can I help you with something?"

Carla giggled a little, then said, "Do you find me attractive?"

The man glanced over at Laci with a questioning look.

Laci looked away, covering her face with a hand, as though she was trying not to be seen.

"Yes," the man said. "I find you very attractive."

"If I said you could make love to me, would you want to?"

The man looked both ways, as if to make sure no one was listening to their conversation, even though the room was so crowded that people were pressed up against his back and were brushing the table as they walked by.

"Of course. Of course I'd want to, but you're wearing a wedding ring. I don't think your husband would like that very much."

Carla waved a hand, dismissing the thought. "No, he wouldn't.

But there's nothing he can do about it. I have permission." She laughed again and took another sip from her drink.

"Really," the man said, smiling, and inching a little closer to Carla. He curled his arm around the back of her chair.

Laci turned her head, not looking very happy about witnessing this.

"So what do I do next?" the man whispered in Carla's ear.

"You got a business card?"

"Yeah," the man said, patting his breast, then reaching into his jacket pocket and pulling one out.

"Drop it right there," Carla said, pointing to the short stack of a little over half a dozen business cards sitting on the table before her. "I'm taking applications. I'll call you if you're the one."

The man looked oddly at her. "Are you serious?"

"Yeah," Carla said, smiling and sipping again from her drink. "But you don't have to if you don't want to. You'll just be the one that's missing out."

"Missing out on what?"

Laci watched as Carla touched the man's chin, brought him closer, whispered something in his ear. The man smiled, chuckled, then Carla kissed him softly on the cheek.

He dropped his card on the table, and said, "Naw, I don't want to miss that."

"I didn't think you would."

That's what she had been doing the better part of the night, getting men's attention, teasing them, leading them on, taking their cards, and sending them on their way.

Laci stood, looked about the room, could see a number of the men that Carla had flirted with. They were all looking at her as they spoke to their friends, their hands cupped over their mouths, as if they were plotting something.

Laci walked around the table, grabbed Carla by the arm, and pulled her up from her chair.

"What are you doing?" Carla said, stumbling slightly.

"Just come with me."

Laci walked behind Carla, half pushing her in the direction of the lady's room, half holding her up, as she wobbled drunkenly on her high heels. While Laci forced Carla along, she had to beat off the advances of laughing men, grabbing at Carla, pulling on her arms, her hands, her dress.

"Don't forget about my card, girl!" one of the men yelled in their direction.

"Go to hell!" Laci yelled out over the booming music.

Once in the restroom, Laci propped Carla up against the sink, stood in front of her, and said, "What the fuck has gotten into you?"

A woman in a dark dress stood looking in the mirror next to them, pulling a hair from her chin with tweezers.

Carla smiled wide, her eyes rolling and then slowly focusing on her friend.

"What do you mean?"

"You're acting like someone who wants to get raped out there."

"Hey," Carla said, waving a finger wildly at Laci. "I'm just a woman who had just a little too much to drink, who's trying to have a good time. I told you nothing's going to happen."

"Not if you ask those men out there. You've really gotten a bit too comfortable with this. You're playing with these men, but you might find out some of them don't play."

"Hey," the woman in the mirror said to Laci. "Give her a break, we all just want to have fun."

"Cyndi Lauper, nobody asked you," Laci snapped. "And before you come out next time, either let the beard grow completely in, or shave, because the five o'clock shadow ain't working."

The woman turned up her nose and stormed out the door.

Laci took Carla by the arm again and led her out of the restroom. "Come on, I'm taking your drunk ass home."

On the way out of the restaurant, they were harassed some more by different men. They were bothered again while Laci led Carla's drunk, stumbling butt down the street. Harassed while Laci helped Carla into the car, and while Laci walked around to the driver's side.

Then two men got out of a car that was parked behind Laci's. "Hey beautiful lady, you need an escort home, or maybe just an escort? Your girl looks kinda drunk."

"She's fine," Laci said, pulling the car door open, jumping in, and quickly pressing the lock.

"See the nonsense you got me going through?" Laci said to Carla, while she was backing out of the parking space.

"Hold it," Carla said, fumbling with the power window buttons. "Let me get their business cards."

"Stop!" Laci screamed at Carla. "Can you just stop for a second till I get you home?"

They were halfway to Carla's house, when Carla's alcohol buzz started to turn from delightful to bordering on painful.

She was resting her head on the side window, trying to stop herself from even thinking about throwing up, when she felt Laci poking at her.

"Carla! Carla!"

"What!" Carla said, raising her heavy head.

"Look back there out the window. That car's been following us since we left the restaurant."

Carla made a lazy attempt to look out the back window. She saw lights, but there were a number of cars behind them.

"Maybe they're just going the same way we are. Ever thought of that?"

"I've driven around this last block twice just to see, and they haven't moved an inch from behind us."

"Are you serious?" Carla said, sitting up a little higher in her seat. She looked over at Laci. With the bright light reflecting out of the rearview mirror, hitting her in the face as she clutched the steering wheel with both hands, she looked more than serious. She looked frightened.

"Okay," Carla said, quickly starting to sober up. As they pulled up at a red light she said, "Just sit here. When the light turns green, don't move. Just sit."

They waited the few moments. The light turned green, Laci did not drive off, and neither did the car behind them.

A car behind that car honked its horn, and then drove around both cars.

"He's not moving," Laci said.

"I know," Carla said, feeling her heart pounding in her chest.

Laci waited till the light turned yellow, then sped off.

The car behind her did the exact same thing.

"What the hell do they want!" Laci yelled, banging a fist against her steering wheel.

Carla dug into her purse, pulled out her phone, dialed a number.

"What are you doing?"

"Calling nine-one-one," Carla said. "Yes, there's a car following us," she said when the operator answered. "It's been for almost twenty minutes. Yes. Yes. Yes. Turn here," Carla told Laci. "Then make a left on Grand. Thank you," Carla said, then hung up the phone.

"What are we doing?"

"Make a left at the next light."

"What are we doing?" Laci said.

"Just make the left."

Laci did. A police station appeared on the right side of the street. She pulled up and parked in front. The black car continued past them. Laci got a look at the guys, and they were the same two who had been parked behind her at the restaurant.

Once they were sure the men had gone, Carla and Laci went

into the station. They were able to get a police escort back to Carla's place. With the police car behind them, Laci looked over at Carla as she was trying to get out of the car. "I hope you know I'm not going out with you anymore," Laci said. "Not until you're done with this nonsense."

"Yeah, okay," Carla said.

"One more thing. I thought you said you wouldn't, but if you really are gonna go through with this, why don't you just fuck somebody you know? See you on Monday."

Laci drove off, the police cruiser following her home, leaving Carla on her front lawn at one in the morning.

25

Pete sat up in bed when he heard the front door open. He saw the sliver of light seep into the guest bedroom from under his door. The glowing green numbers on the alarm clock read 1:02 A.M.

Carla had been coming in past ten every night since Tuesday. The next morning Pete always asked her where she had been.

"Out," was all she'd said each time.

But that could've meant anything. She could've been out having dinner with Laci, or drinks, or maybe doing the same thing, just with some anonymous man, and then afterward off to some hotel, or to his place.

In the mornings, Pete would eat by himself.

Carla had taken time off from work. She didn't tell Pete for how long, just said she needed a break. She slept late, wouldn't come out until after he had left for work, as if she'd rather not see him at all.

At night, Pete would hear her climbing the stairs, going straight to their room, not even stopping to knock on his door, to say she had gotten in all right.

On two of those nights, Pete had stepped out of the guest room, stood just outside of Carla's door, pressed his ear to it and heard her on the phone, laughing and talking in a soft, sexy voice that had once been reserved for only him.

By the tone of the few words he could make out, when she wasn't whispering, he could tell she was talking to a man.

He wondered if it was a guy that she was considering having sex with, or maybe she had already slept with him and it had been so good that she was making plans to do it again.

Those were his thoughts each night before falling off to sleep, and he knew something had to change. He could no longer take imagining her out there, among men she did not know, doing things he dared not even think about.

Pete thought of knocking, telling her that this had to stop. But he knew she would not listen. So he just had to trust what she had told him. That once she had done what she said she was going to do, they would act as though none of it had happened. None of it—not her indiscretion, not his.

But maybe she would allow him to make an alteration to their agreement, Pete thought last night before sleep took him. It was something that he had been entertaining since the day after she had told him that she wanted to sleep with another man, but he hadn't mentioned it, because he thought she'd never actually go along with it. But now he felt he had no other recourse. She had to accept it, whether she liked it or not.

The next day, Carla did not come downstairs till after noon.

It was Saturday, and Pete was in the living room, pushing the noisy vacuum cleaner.

Carla appeared on the stairs, wearing a robe, her hair messy, dark half circles under her eyes.

Pete shut off the machine, looked up at his wife.

"Do you even care that I was trying to sleep?" she said angrily.

"I didn't know you were home. I never know when you're home now."

Carla gave him an evil glance, then was about to turn and head back upstairs when Pete said, "Has it happened yet?"

"Why are you asking?"

"Because I have a right to know," Pete said. "When I did it, I told you. You said you would do the same. Were you lying?"

"No. It hasn't happened yet."

"Then what are you waiting for? It's almost been a week."

"How dare you ask me that question?" Carla said, stepping off the last step toward him. "You have no right."

"I have every right," Pete said, releasing the handle of the vacuum. "I'm your husband. Stretching this thing out is putting us through more stress than we need to go through. I hear you talking on the phone at night. Who are you talking to?"

"That's none of your business," Carla said.

"Is it someone you're considering sleeping with?"

"Like I said, it's none of your—"

"Carla, give this up. It's a meaningless act. We don't—"

"We've already discussed this, Pete," Carla interrupted. "I'm going to do it."

"Then do it!" Pete raised his voice. "Just get it over with so it can be done, and we can start putting our life back together again." He paused. "Or maybe the fact that you haven't done it yet means you don't really want to."

"No, I want to. There's nothing more that I want than that."

"But obviously there's a problem. Maybe nobody out there wants to sleep with you," Pete said, wanting to get a rise out of her, wanting Carla to feel as upset as he did about this situation.

Carla's mouth fell open. It was a verbal slap across the face, exactly what Pete had intended.

"Oh, really," Carla said. "If you only knew all the men who wanted to have me."

"If you're all that, and so many men want you, then there should be no hold-up. Make it happen."

"Fine. When you want it to go down?" Carla said, challenged.

"Tomorrow's never promised," Pete said. "How about tonight?"

"You got it. Tonight it is," Carla said, storming back up the stairs, leaving Pete to realize that he had just given his wife still more incentive to go out there and have sex with some other man.

26

She could've called it off early this morning, Carla thought later that day, sitting at yet another restaurant with a new man beside her, doing his best to interest her in what he was saying.

When Pete had dared her to go out tonight, find some man to sleep with, she could've told him about last night, that some men had been following them, that she had been scared half to death, and that she really didn't want to go through with it, that she had never really wanted to.

But Pete acted as though she couldn't even find a man, and that insult was enough for Carla to forget about how frightened she'd been, enough to ignore the fact that she still believed something wasn't right about going out and sleeping around on her spouse, even though he had done it to her.

And as she sat at the bar, feeling very much like a bloody body floating in shark-infested waters, Carla told herself that maybe it was better if she went ahead and just got it over with. It would teach Pete a lesson, and even if she didn't enjoy the act with a stranger, her husband would always know there would be consequences to foolish actions.

So she sat and spoke to a man, the third who had approached her this evening.

Carla glanced down at her watch, saw that it was five minutes to nine.

She wore a simple black dress, had her hair pinned back, her face fully made up.

She had been at this place, Bijon's on State Street, since seven thirty.

It was nice, dimly lit, had a sophisticated clientele.

When she had arrived, she perched herself at the corner of the bar, ordered a martini, and waited to see what would happen.

Not five minutes later, a man approached her. He was kind looking, with a pleasant smile. He asked if he could join her; Carla said yes. He had her laughing after only a couple of minutes. He was very direct, said that he thought she was beautiful, and wanted to know if they could go somewhere a little more private.

"Where would that be?"

"I'm in Chicago on business," the man said. "I have a suite over at the Omni. We could go there."

Carla was really considering it, till she noticed the wedding band on his finger. She didn't know why she hadn't noticed it earlier.

"You're married," Carla said.

"Yes. And so are you."

"Does your wife know you're out here cheating on her?" Carla said.

The man smiled, laughed a little. "No."

"Well, my husband does. If you'd please excuse me," Carla said, swiveling her back to the man.

What she was out to do, sleep with a man she didn't even know, was one step above the actions of a prostitute, but she would not do it with another woman's husband. A woman who didn't feel the same way Carla did now was the reason she was in the situation in the first place.

The second man who approached Carla was just a waste of time. He had bad teeth, bad skin, and a bad hairpiece.

After trying to be polite, Carla had to tell him in so many words that he revolted her, and would he please just go somewhere else.

But this third man, the one who was talking to her now, wasn't bad on the eyes, a light-skinned fellow with wavy brown hair. He seemed polite enough, asking if the seat next to Carla was taken before sitting down and introducing himself as Keith.

He wasn't married. That was the first thing Carla asked him.

He, too, was in town on business. They had been talking easily for half an hour. Carla didn't feel pushed or pressured. She didn't feel as though the man was even coming on to her, even though she knew he was.

"Would you like another drink?" Keith asked.

Carla looked at the alcohol in the bottom of her glass. She had had only one drink, but she remembered what happened last night.

"It's okay if you don't," Keith said. "I'm not trying to get you drunk or anything."

"I know that," Carla said, relaxing a little more. "I just . . . what the hell—yeah. I'll take another." She smiled.

The bartender brought their drinks, set them down.

Carla picked up her martini. Keith picked up the brown liquor he was drinking.

He raised his glass a little, and said, "To . . . uh . . . two people in a bar."

"To two people in a bar," Carla said, smiling more.

They spoke and laughed while they drank, Carla becoming more comfortable, not knowing if it was Keith's conversation, the second drink, or a little bit of both.

After their drinks, Keith said, "I hope you don't take this as too forward, but I was wondering if you would like to go somewhere with a few less people."

"And where would that be?" Carla smiled, sensing what he'd say.

Keith smiled, too. "Uh, my room. I'm staying over at the Omni."

Carla laughed.

"What's so funny?"

"Only guys who stay at the Omni must be allowed in here."

Keith gave her a look that said he didn't understand.

"You're the second guy tonight staying there that asked me back to his room."

"Look, I'm sorry about that," Keith said, standing up and digging for his wallet.

Carla put a hand on his arm, settled him some. "No, it's okay. I was just laughing at the coincidence."

"Yeah, I guess that was kinda funny."

"Do you still want me to go?" Carla said, deciding that very moment that Keith was the man she would sleep with.

He looked a little surprised by her aggressiveness, then said, "Yeah."

Keith paid for their drinks, then said, "I want you to feel perfectly comfortable about going back with me. I'm the sweetest, safest guy in the world. In the future, you'll find that out."

Carla stopped just before the door, turned to him.

"You okay?" Keith asked.

"I don't want to mislead you, Keith. This isn't going to be the start of something. I'm a married woman," Carla said, showing him her wedding ring.

"I saw that. I just thought you wore it so you wouldn't get hit on."

"But you hit on me anyway."

"Well," Keith said, scratching his head. "What do we do now?"

"I still want to go to your hotel, if you still want me to."

"But you said you're married. I don't want to mess up anything."

"It's a long story. I'll explain it on the way."

27

Carla and Keith walked out of the restaurant, Keith's hand resting gently on the small of Carla's back. Keith raised an arm to hail a cab.

Carla's husband looked on furiously from his car just down the street.

When Carla had left this evening, all dressed up, a trail of perfume in her wake, Pete was sitting in the living room, watching TV.

At first he hadn't intended to follow her. But as he heard her car drive off, he knew that tonight would be the night. He had practically forced her into making sure that it was, and for some reason, Pete felt he had to be there for the occasion. Or at least as close as he could possibly come. He grabbed his car keys, his jacket, and hurried out of the house.

He followed Carla, keeping at least a couple of car lengths between them, in order not to get spotted. He watched as she parked her car, then walked the block over to the restaurant.

Then Pete drove until he found the perfect spot to park, where Carla couldn't see his car when she left, but Pete would be able to see everything himself. He sat there, his car stereo turned down to a hum, his windows down, watching intently for a little longer than an hour and a half.

Pete wanted so badly for his wife to come out of that bar alone.

He would've made sure Carla got back to her car safely, sped home in order to get there before she did, and then begged, pleaded, and done everything he could to convince her not to go through with this.

But that didn't happen.

She came out with a man, smiling, allowing him to touch her in that way that let all three of them know that more was going to happen tonight.

Pete watched as a cab pulled to the curb, as the man Carla was with opened the door and then climbed in beside her. The cab drove off, took a right turn, and Pete started his car and drove after them, telling himself the last thing he would do was lose sight of that cab.

The downtown traffic was much thicker than usual, forcing Pete to cut in and out of lanes and blow through some yellow lights. He would not lose them. As the cab headed east, more cabs merged onto the street.

Pete tightened his grip on the wheel, speeding up toward the oncoming intersection, telling himself he just had to risk it to stay with Carla's cab.

Carla's cab just made the yellow light, and two other cabs blatantly sped through the light after it had just turned red. Pete was about to do the same thing, when he noticed the car adjacent to him, waiting for the green light, was a police cruiser.

"Damn it!" Pete said, striking the seat beside him with his fist. He sat at what felt like the longest light ever; then, when it turned green, he sped off in the direction of Carla's cab.

There was a line of cabs parked on the left side of the street, in front of a restaurant, some criss-crossing the intersection before him, and one driving down the opposite side of the street. He narrowed his eyes to look into each one of them, but Pete knew it was hopeless. "Shit!" he shouted, braking hard in the middle of the street, looking in every direction, realizing there was nothing more he could do.

He had lost her.

28

When they had gotten out of the cab and walked into the hotel lobby, Keith ushered Carla toward the elevator.

"Hold it," Carla said. "What room are you in?"

"Twenty-two fifteen."

"And your last name again?"

"Erikson. Why?"

"Just taking a little precaution," Carla said, walking over to the clerk, around the same age as Carla, behind the reservation desk.

"May I help you?" the attractive woman asked.

"Yes, my name is Carla Barnes, and that man over there," Carla pointed Keith out, "his name is Keith Erikson. I'm going to be his guest for a couple of hours."

Carla leaned a little closer to the woman.

"And to be honest with you, sista, I just met him tonight. He's in room twenty-two fifteen. Can you phone up there in one hour just to make sure that everything is all right? If you know what I mean."

The woman jotted down the pertinent information, smiled, and said, "I know where you're coming from. I got you covered."

On the cab ride over, Carla had explained her situation to Keith, told him everything.

"So, I'm looking for someone to help me out with this," Carla said. "Do you think you can be that person?"

"Yeah," Keith said, not seeming as enthused about her as he had while they were talking at the bar. "I think so."

After they walked into his suite, Keith asked Carla to have a seat on the sofa.

"Do you mind if we go straight to the bedroom? It's already after ten, and I don't want to get in too late," Carla said.

"Sure."

Inside the bedroom, Carla stood nervously looking down at the bed.

Keith stood by the door, watching her.

"You really don't want to do this, do you?" he said.

She turned around, startled, as though she wasn't aware someone was in the room with her.

"I have to do it."

"Will it really make things better between you two?"

"I told you, Keith, it's not about better. I'm so hurt right now, recently I've been wondering if I even want things to get better between us. I need you to do this for me."

Carla reached behind herself, undid her zipper, and let her dress fall to her feet.

Keith walked over to her, took her in his arms, held her tight, and started kissing her on the mouth.

Carla turned her face, allowed him to kiss her on her neck.

This was supposed to turn her on, she thought, but it wasn't working. It was probably his routine, what he did with every woman he made love to. If it was what he needed to get himself ready, then she would allow it.

Carla pulled his jacket off his shoulders, let it drop to the carpet. She undid the buttons of his shirt, pulled it out of the waist of his pants, peeled it off, and let it fall as well. She started unfastening his belt, but he scooped her up off the floor, laid her down on the bed, stood over her, undid the pants himself.

The room was mostly dark except for the street lights that broke through the parted window curtains.

Carla looked up at Keith, saw that he was well built, his shoulders chiseled, his chest wide and muscular.

He slid down his pants. Immediately she saw the bulge in his boxer shorts.

He quickly pulled those down, and Carla felt herself gasp at how large he was. But it wasn't just the size of his penis that had Carla unsettled. The fact that he was another man, and not her husband, threw her.

It had been almost two years since she had been with someone else, and now she lay here, staring in between this man's legs, knowing that he would be inside her.

His manhood jutted out, hard and long before him.

He bent closer.

Carla turned her face away.

Keith reached over her, undid the front clasp of Carla's bra, let it fall open.

He kissed her neck again, worked his way down to her nipples, suckled them, played with them with the tip of his tongue.

They started to harden, but it wasn't because Carla was excited, or at least she told herself that. She didn't know what she was feeling, didn't know how she was supposed to react.

He started working his way down, kissing her belly, her hips, then he grabbed her panties, slid them down her thighs, threw them to the floor.

She was exposed now. Nothing between her and him.

Keith grabbed her thighs in his hands and squeezed.

"You have a beautiful body," he said, his voice throaty.

Carla tried her best to smile.

He moved his palms down to her knees, parted her legs.

He climbed onto the bed, on his knees, between hers, placed his face over her.

He started to kiss her again, just below her belly, on the inside of her thighs, working his way in.

Carla actually heard him licking his lips, felt his warm breath practically blow inside her, and right before she thought she would feel his tongue on her, she reached down, grabbed his face.

"You don't have to do that," Carla said.

"Oh, okay," Keith said, startled, and brought himself up from between her legs.

He climbed out of bed, walked across the room to the dresser.

"I just have to get some protection."

Carla watched him, then turned her head away from him again when he started back toward her.

She told herself she could do this. It wouldn't be long. In her mind, she would go somewhere else, with someone else, and before she knew it, it would be over.

But why go through with it if she felt so reluctant, she asked herself.

She could lie to Pete, tell him that it actually happened. He wouldn't know the difference. The pain she wanted him to feel, he would experience.

But she would know she hadn't gone through with it. And whenever the thought of Pete being with that other woman crept into her head, like it had done so often in the past with Wayne and with Steve, as opposed to just hurting, just feeling like a victim, she'd finally know that she had gotten some sort of revenge, and that he would have to suffer those thoughts as well.

She had to do it.

Keith was back, kneeling between Carla's parted knees again, but this time with a little gold packet in his hand.

"You ready?" he asked.

Carla nodded without speaking.

Keith tore the tiny packet open, rolled the condom down over him, and lay on Carla's bare body.

She started to feel herself panic.

He wasn't as heavy as Pete, his weight was different, but heavy enough where she could not move if he didn't want her to, couldn't escape him if she tried her hardest.

She felt the kisses again on her neck.

Carla tried to turn away from them.

He raised up some on his knees, his arms holding him up, on either side of her head.

"Guide me in," Keith whispered.

"Huh?" Carla panted.

"Grab me, and guide me in," he said again.

"No," Carla heard herself saying, her eyes closed. "Just push in. It's wet enough." She even opened her legs a little wider to accommodate him, and then she waited to feel his foreign body inside her.

After a few moments, she heard Keith say, "Carla, open your eyes."

When she did, he was looking down at her, and he said, "Get up. I can't do this."

29

When Pete heard his wife enter the house, their alarm clock read 11:36 P.M.

He walked out of the guest bedroom, down the stairs, then stopped on the last one when he saw her setting her things down on one of the dining room chairs.

Carla looked up. "Hello," she said, walking toward the kitchen.

"So that's how you operate, huh?"

"What are you talking about?" Carla said, not breaking her stride.

"You pick up strange men from restaurants, and let them take you lord knows where."

Carla froze just inside the kitchen doorway. She turned to face her husband. "You followed me?"

"I wanted to make sure that you didn't do anything stupid, but you did anyway," Pete said, walking farther into the living room. "Where did he take you?"

"You have all the answers, you tell me."

"I lost you in traffic. Where did he take you, Carla?"

"Where do you think? A hotel," Carla snapped.

"So you slept with him?"

"I can't believe you. You push me, dare me to go out there and find some man tonight—"

"I asked did you sleep with him?" Pete said, walking over to Carla, standing right in front of her.

"That's what you wanted, right? You said I couldn't find anyone who'd want to."

"No, that's what you wanted. You started all of this."

"No." Carla raised her voice. "You started it by sleeping with that woman."

"Carla!" Pete said, taking his wife by the arm, shaking her. "Did you fucking sleep with that man or not!"

"No!" she screamed. "And take your fucking hands off of me!"

Pete released her, stepped back.

"I couldn't do it," Carla said, lowering her head.

"Because you shouldn't. Because you know you shouldn't." Pete stepped close to her again, tried to wrap his arms around her. Carla pushed him away.

"Carla, just forget this. I swear I'll never cheat on you again, but please, just drop it."

"No. And stop asking me that. I just need more time."

"To do what? Hang out in bars, solicit men like some high-priced prostitute?"

Carla glared at Pete.

"I'm sorry, but you have no idea what you're doing. Every time you go out there, you're putting yourself at risk. And do you know how I feel, sitting up, watching the clock, wondering what you're doing, if you're having sex with some man. Or worse, if some man has knocked you over the head, stuffed you in his trunk."

"Don't say that," Carla said.

"Why not? It could happen. It has happened to other women. You're my wife," Pete said. "I love you, and I just can't allow you to go out and continue this."

Carla walked over to the dining room table, had a seat, dropped her face in her hands, strands of her hair falling over her forearms.

"You still have no choice," she said, her voice low.

"Then just stop going out like you do."

"And how am I supposed to find the man that I'm—"

"Use somebody at work," Pete said.

"And have everyone at the place I go to every day knowing my business. I don't think so," Carla said, looking up.

"Then let me choose him," Pete said. It had been the other option he had been thinking of, the one thing that would give him the slightest bit of peace, knowing that at least she wouldn't be with someone that would do her harm, someone he knew would not take advantage of the situation.

"What?"

"You heard me. Let me choose the man you sleep with," Pete said.

Carla threw her head back, laughed out loud. "Sure, Pete, head on down to the nursing home and grab me a ninety-year-old with no teeth, and a fresh prescription of Viagra."

"No. I don't mean like that. Someone you'd be attracted to."

"Like who?"

"I don't know," Pete lied. "But if you aren't, then you can turn him down, continue to look yourself."

Carla looked at her husband with skepticism. "I don't know. Something doesn't seem right about this."

"I told you. You have final approval. If you don't like who I choose, don't do it. But if you do," Pete said, pulling a chair next to his wife, sitting down, and looking directly into her face, "I want you to fuck him, and get this shit over with. Think you can do that?"

"Yeah," Carla said. "I can do that."

30

When Wayne and Me'Shell went to visit him the other day, her father came to the door, stepped forward, wrapped his frail arms around his daughter and hugged her tight.

Wayne smiled as he watched the old man rock his child from side to side, kissing her on the cheek. Carla had asked Wayne in the past about meeting her father, but he had always put her off. He wasn't certain if there would be any need, considering he was still pursuing her. But now that he knew the direction of his future with Me'Shell, meeting her old man was something that Wayne wanted to do.

Me'Shell's father let go of her, turned to Wayne, and said, "And who is this fine-looking gentleman?"

Me'Shell didn't answer, so after a moment Wayne said, "I'm Wayne Mason, sir."

To Wayne, Me'Shell's father looked to be at least seventy-five years old if he was a day. His skin was bronze and shiny, wrinkled and worn. His hair was long and white, brushed back like a lion's mane.

"Pleased to meet you, Wayne. Come in, come in," Mr. Jacobs said.

Inside the old, sparsely furnished house, Wayne and Me'Shell sat on a plastic-covered sofa, while her father sat facing them on a chair he had dragged in from the kitchen. He leaned forward on the edge of it, wearing a yellowed wife beater T-shirt and baggy slacks. He had brought the three of them a pitcher of iced tea.

"When Me'Shell called me, said that she was coming over, I got so excited. I haven't seen her in so long."

"It was two weeks ago, Daddy," Me'Shell said.

"You're my only daughter, Shelly. That's a long time."

"Yes, Daddy."

"How has my baby been?"

"Fine, Daddy, but we can't stay. Wayne has something to ask you, and then we really must be going."

"Are you sure?"

"Yeah, Daddy. But I'll call you later tonight, and we can talk for as long as you like."

"Okay," her father said, smiling. "Then what do you have to ask me, young man?"

Wayne didn't like how this all felt, like Me'Shell couldn't care less whether they were to get married or not. And judging by what she had said before they came in, there seemed to be a very good chance that he was going through this particular motion for nothing. But Wayne wasn't a quitter. He had lost Carla, and now that his sights were set on Me'Shell, he would not lose her.

Wayne stood up from the sofa, walked over to Mr. Jacobs, stood before him, and respectfully said, "Sir, I don't know if Me'Shell has informed you of this, but we've been seeing each other for six months now, and we are very much in love. I've grown very accustomed to having her in my life, and I don't believe that life would ever be the same without her. So for that reason, I am humbly asking for your permission to—"

"Marry her?" the old man said, quickly.

"Daddy!" Me'Shell said.

"Is that what you're asking? For Shelly's hand?"

"Yes, sir."

"What do you do for a living, son?"

"I'm a doctor, an orthopedic surgeon."

Me'Shell's father smiled, winked at his daughter.

"Do you have any children? Any baby-mamma-drama, as the kids say?"

"No, sir. I do not."

"You love her? Do you treat her right?"

Wayne glanced over at Me'Shell. "Every day I try a little harder."

"Is that true, Shelly?" her father asked Me'Shell.

"He brought me breakfast in bed this morning, if that counts?"

"That does. I used to do that for your mother on her birthday. So yes, you can have her," Mr. Jacobs said to Wayne, sticking a bony hand out between them. "I mean, you can marry my daughter."

Before Wayne took Mr. Jacobs's hand, Me'Shell rose from her seat.

"Daddy, don't you think you could've given it a bit more thought? You only just met Wayne."

"Sweetheart," her father said, walking over to her in his house shoes, wrapping an arm around her. "You're thirty-six years old."

Me'Shell pushed away from him. "I know how old I am."

"Since your mother passed on ten years ago, and I stopped teaching at the university, I really have no one. It'd be wonderful to have a grandchild before I die."

"Stop talking like that. You said you'd never die," she said, taking his hand.

"That's right, sweetheart. I never will. But I would still like a grandbaby, while I'm still young enough to play with her. This man, Wayne," her father said, turning to look at him, "seems nice. He appears to love you very much. Do you feel the same?"

It took Me'Shell a moment to answer, but she said, "Yes, I do. I love him very much."

"And he wants to marry you, is respectful enough to ask your father first. And because he seems like such a nice man, I said yes, but I guess I should've asked you first. Should I have said yes? Do you want to marry him?"

Me'Shell looked over at Wayne, then to her father, and said, "Daddy, honestly, I don't know."

The drive home was a silent one.

She wanted him to drop her off at home. Wayne wasn't having it. "Why should I take you home? So there can be even more distance put between us?" he said, taking the highway exit that led back to his place.

The next three days, when Wayne came in from work, Me'Shell had very little to say to him.

He accepted that as her taking time to think, even asked if that was what she was doing.

"Yes," she said, one evening when they sat across from each other eating a meal that Wayne had made.

"And when do you think you'll be done? When do you think you'll decide?"

Me'Shell put down her fork. "Is there a time limit? If there is, then I can just leave now."

Wayne sensed her anger, knew he had hurt her. "No, there is no limit. But you know how I feel, and think I know how you feel about me, too. All you have to do is say the word, and we can move on with our life together."

Me'Shell didn't respond, just picked up her fork, lowered her head, and resumed eating.

That night, for the first time since they had gone to Me'Shell's father's house, they made love. Wayne noticed it was especially passionate, seemed so emotional. After Wayne had spent himself inside Me'Shell, all the while feeling that she was holding him exceptionally tight, he glanced down into her eyes. There were tears.

She turned away.

"What's wrong?" he asked.

"I love you, Wayne. I really do. But I can't be hurt. I just can't be, not again. Do you hear me?"

"Yes."

"No," Me'Shell said, holding him tighter. "I mean this. I've been there before, and last week when I walked into that kitchen, it felt like my heart was being ripped out, and you were the one who was doing it. I can't ever go through that again."

"Baby, you won't have to," Wayne said sincerely. "I promise."

31

While they were having lunch at the office, Pete asked Wayne if he would have a couple of drinks with him after work.

"Something happen with Carla?"

"Uh, there's just something that I need to talk to you about, ask of you."

"Ask me now," Wayne said, taking a bite of his sandwich.

"No," Pete said. "It really should wait. Tonight, okay?"

"Whatever you say, man."

While at the bar, Wayne had not brought up what Pete had expressed earlier, and Pete did not mention a word of it, because the place was too crowded and noisy. But after they left and were sitting in Wayne's car, about to drive home, Pete said, "Hold it a minute, Wayne."

"What's up?" Wayne said, turning to Pete.

"Remember when I told you that Carla wanted to sleep with another man."

"Yeah," Wayne said. "And I told you that she never would. That regardless of what she said, tell her no."

Pete was quiet, looked away from Wayne a moment.

"You told her yes. You didn't tell her yes, did you?"

"I had no choice. She would've left."

"Dammit, Pete! She wouldn't have."

"It doesn't matter now. That's what I told her, and she's been going out, coming in at all hours of the night."

"She won't go through with it, Pete. I told you that."

"I don't know that for sure."

"Has she slept with anybody?"

"No. Not yet," Pete said. "At least she says she hasn't."

"Do you believe her?"

"Yes."

"Then what's the problem?"

"I can't take it. The idea that my wife is out there with these men, that anything could happen to her. The thought of her with one of them, some man I don't know, entering my wife—" Pete said, closing his eyes, trying to shake the thought from his mind. "—fucking my wife! I can't take it."

"Why are you telling me this, Pete? I tried to help you. What do you expect me to do now?"

Pete looked directly at Wayne. "She's going to sleep with somebody. She has her mind fixed on it, like that's the only way she'll be able to forgive me. She's gonna sleep with somebody, and I was thinking—"

"Hold it," Wayne said. "You are not about to ask me what I think you are, Pete."

"If you could just—"

"Pete," Wayne said, pointing a finger across the car at him. "Don't even fucking think it."

"But—"

"But nothing, Pete! If you need an answer, it's no. This is the last time I'll say this. Don't you ever again fucking ask me to do that. Do you hear me?"

Pete looked at him, silent.

"I'm serious, Pete. Do you hear me?"

"Yeah. I hear you."

32

After Wayne dropped Pete off, he drove home so angry, grabbing the wheel so tightly he thought he might tear it from the dashboard, flip the car, and tumble down the street in a fiery ball.

Didn't Pete know what he was asking? Didn't he realize what this meant to Wayne?

Later that night, around 12:30 A.M., Wayne sat out on the stairs of his town home, watching the occasional car drive by, sipping from a bottle of beer. The weather was warm, the sky was clear, and Me'Shell had not stayed over that night.

That morning at breakfast, she said she would be staying at her own place that night, that she had to get up early in the morning to do something.

"Do what?" Wayne asked.

She seemed caught off guard, did not answer.

Wayne left it alone, realizing that she might want time away from him still to decide whether she truly wanted to marry him.

It was a good thing, too, because since Pete asked Wayne what he had, the thought of Carla would not leave his head. He needed time, too, at least this night, to force Carla from his mind again.

Wayne lifted his bottle of beer from the step and took a sip. As he lowered it, he saw Pete's car pulling up in front.

Pete got out, started toward Wayne. Wayne stood up, not believing Pete was there, knowing that he could not have come to present his offer again.

"Did you think about what I asked you?" Pete said, stopping at the bottom of the steps.

"Pete, I told you, there's nothing to think about. I'll never do it."

Pete walked up the steps, took Wayne's arm, and urged him to sit down beside him. "Let me explain this to you. I followed her the other night. She left some bar with some man. They took a cab, and then I lost her."

Wayne's heart started to beat hard and fast in his chest.

"Is she all right?"

"Yes."

"Did she—"

"No. But she went to his room, went there to do it. I don't know why it didn't happen. But she's going to. Wayne, for whatever reason, she's fucking bent on it."

"But why me?"

"Because unlike every other man out there, who would want nothing but to fuck my wife, treat her like some piece of ass, I'm having to convince you to even listen to me. I know you don't want this, and if you actually do agree, it'll be against your own will. You'll be doing it for me, not for yourself. And believe it or not, that'll help me deal with this, help me get over it. Then there's the fact that you have something to lose. You're still getting married to Me'Shell, right?"

"Right," Wayne said, not knowing whether it was true.

"Because of Me'Shell, I know you won't go falling back in love with Carla."

"And what if she goes falling back in love with me?"

"You two have been together, before she and I even got together. You did her wrong. She left you. I'm not worried about her going back on her decision. For all those reasons, there is nobody more suited for this than you."

"Fuck, Pete!" Wayne said. "I'm getting married. Doesn't that mean anything to you? You're asking me to cheat on my future wife."

"Yes, I know that. But I need you on this one," Pete said, grabbing Wayne by the shoulder. "We're brothers, right? We've always had each other's back. I need you to have mine now. Just one more time. There's nowhere else I can turn."

"This isn't Susie Taylor," Wayne said. "And we aren't sixteen. There are so many ways this can go. Ways you probably aren't expecting. You think this is no big deal now, but afterward—"

"I'll deal with that," Pete said.

"And if you can't?"

"I will," Pete said, seeming certain. "What's it going to be, Wayne? I would forever owe you for this one."

And Wayne could not help thinking about Me'Shell again, the promise he made. What would he tell her, he thought, unconsciously turning his head back toward the front door, as if she was there in the house.

"Don't tell her anything," Pete said, reading Wayne's mind.

And what about Carla? Would he really be able to be with her, and have nothing more come of it? He wasn't sure. He didn't think so. He'd only just been able to finally put aside his feelings for her. But he knew they still lingered below the surface. But this opportunity had presented itself for a reason, and if something more was meant to happen between him and Carla, then he guessed it would happen. And if it wasn't meant to happen, at least he would be sure, beyond any doubt, that it was meant to be that he and Me'Shell should marry.

Something told him that he would regret this decision, but with his head down and his voice very low, Wayne whispered, "Okay."

"What was that?" Pete said, tightening his grip on Wayne's shoulder.

Wayne raised his head, looked Pete in the eyes, and spoke up. "I said I'll do it."

Pete paused a minute, looking intently back into Wayne's eyes. He swallowed hard, as if he hadn't really expected Wayne to submit to his request. He released his grip, then patted Wayne on the shoulder. Without any expression, Pete said, "Thanks. I truly appreciate this. I'll let Carla know, and then I'll get back to you."

"Okay," Wayne said.

He watched Pete stand, turn and head to his car, jump in, and drive off.

Wayne watched him go, then took another sip from his beer.

33

At work, Carla sat at her desk, her head in her hands, staring at a pencil. There was nothing special about this pencil, she had no particular interest in it. She was just desperate to think about anything other than what had been going on with her.

"I think you need a break," a voice said.

When Carla looked up, Laci was standing in the doorway.

Carla dropped her face back into her hands without responding.

"You haven't been yourself the last couple of days. What's going on?" Laci said, now standing in front of Carla's desk, her arms wrapped around a manila folder pressed to her chest.

"After that Friday night, I didn't think you cared."

"I don't want you to do anything else foolish, and I definitely don't want to be included in it, but I care. I'll always care," Laci said, sitting down. "I'm your best friend. Now tell me what's been going on."

Carla lifted her face, told her best friend everything that had transpired since the last time they had spoken about the matter, and at the end of her announcement, Carla sank back in her chair and admitted, "I'm starting to think this is more trouble than it's worth."

"You're thinking about calling the whole thing off?" Laci asked.

"I don't know. What do you think?"

"Will you be able to live with yourself afterward? And more important, will you be able to live with Pete?"

"I don't know."

"But you said he's supposed to be choosing the guy that he wants you to sleep with."

"I'm almost at the point where I don't care who it is. I just want to get this nonsense over with."

Now, after she had been home for a couple of hours, Carla heard Pete's car door slam closed. She sat up in bed, glanced at the alarm clock, saw that it was 6:35 P.M. She had been trying to take a quick nap, but could not clear her mind enough to find sleep.

A moment later, she heard the front door close, heard Pete walking through the house beneath her on the first floor. She swung her legs over the side of the bed and stared at the bedroom door, listening intently as her husband climbed the stairs, and then there came a knock.

"Come in," she said.

The door opened, and Pete stood behind it. He appeared as haggard, as undone by all that he was going through as Carla felt she looked.

"Am I bothering you? Is this not a good time?" Pete asked.

"No. It's fine. I was just sitting here, is all."

"I would like to talk about what we discussed the other night."

"That's fine."

Pete walked in, sat on the bed beside his wife.

"I found the man. But first I want to tell you that you know him."

"Who is it, Pete?"

"There is no better candidate than him. He's a friend, so it won't be like you're going out and sleeping with a stranger, but because of past circumstances, I won't fear anything building from the one event."

"Pete, who have you chosen?" Carla said, knowing it wasn't who she thought, but fearing that it might be.

"I chose Wayne."

Carla stared at her husband for a moment, as if waiting for the punch line. After she realized there wasn't one, she said, "No, Pete. No way." She stood up and walked toward the middle of the room.

"Why not?" he said, rising.

Carla turned to him. "Hello. I used to date him. We were almost married. Remember that?"

"Yes. But you didn't marry him. You married me."

"Because he cheated on me," Carla said.

"And because you loved me, right?"

"Of course."

"And you still love me, don't you?"

"Yes, I still love you."

"Then what's the problem?" Pete said.

The problem is, Carla thought of saying, that I still have feelings for Wayne. That if I were to be given the permission to sleep with that man, to make love to him the way I used to, to allow him to do the things to me that he used to do, I don't know if you'd ever see me again. That's what she thought of saying, but instead she just said, "It just wouldn't work."

Pete walked over to her. "Carla, it's for one night. It's one time."

And since Carla hadn't been able to tell Pete about all that she had been through with Wayne over the last two months the way she had planned, she thought maybe she could tell him now. She could tell him how Wayne had been pressing her to leave him, that there were times when she had actually considered it. There were times, when over dinner with Wayne, she would look at his smile, those eyes, and tell herself that maybe it was Wayne who she wanted to be with again, forever.

But what good would that do her, would that do Pete?

"I just don't want to," Carla said.

"Then who?" Pete said, obviously irritated. "Who will it be, and how will you find him? Tell me now. I want all this over. I love you and I want you back, so if you still insist on going through with this, tell me who it'll be with if it's not Wayne."

She searched her brain for a moment, looking for eligible men that she could sleep with. Not quite half a dozen sped across her mind, but none as nice looking as Wayne, none that she cared for like she cared for Wayne. And honestly, the more she thought about it, the more she realized she had no real desire to sleep with another man at all. All she wanted to do was get back at Pete somehow, give him a dose of what he had put her through.

But how could she do that, if she didn't commit the sin he had?

"Fine," Carla said.

Pete took her by the shoulders, looked directly into her face. "Then you'll do it?"

"Yes."

"Are you sure?"

"I said I would."

"Okay," Pete said, pulling his wife close to him, wrapping his arms around her. "Everything will be just fine. This will all work out."

Carla's arms remained at her sides; she didn't hug him back. I hope you're right, she thought.

34

The next morning at work, Wayne slipped into his office, closed the door, picked up his phone, and made a call.

When the call was answered, he sat for a moment, not saying a word.

"Hello?" Carla said for the second time.

"It's me, Wayne. We should talk."

"I know. When?"

"My schedule is free for the rest of the day. I can take you to lunch. Grande Luxe Café?"

Carla didn't answer right away; then she said, "Okay. I'll wait outside for you."

When he pulled up in front of Carla's building, he saw her standing there, wearing a skirt suit, her hair pinned back, looking as beautiful as she always had.

She opened the door and climbed in. Turning to Wayne, she smiled a little and said, "Hey."

"Hey," he said back, then drove in the direction of downtown.

The drive took all of ten minutes, but they both looked directly out the windshield, not speaking.

Seated in the restaurant, both Wayne and Carla reached for

their glasses at the same time. Wayne waited to take a drink until Carla had taken a sip. After he set his glass down, he finally said, "Well, we've found ourselves in a peculiar situation, huh?"

"I'm not going through with it, Wayne," Carla said.

"What do you mean?"

"My husband chose you to sleep with me, and he told me you agreed to it—"

"I mean, it's not like I jumped at the chance or anything. I said no at first. He had to convince me."

"None of that matters, Wayne. I'm not going through with it."

"And that's fine," Wayne said, still honestly, though not feeling quite fine with it. "But I just want to know why not. Pete told me you seemed so bent on sleeping with any other man. Is it me?"

"Yes, and no. I decided that I don't want to sleep with some strange man I don't know. But Pete still deserves some punishment."

"I'm not some strange man. You know me."

"And that's exactly why it can't happen. I do know you, and I . . . I . . . might still have feelings for you, to be perfectly honest. But they're dormant now. I felt them start to come to the surface when we were meeting for those two months. That's one of the reasons I had to stop seeing you. But I've gotten them under control again. I've managed to bury them so far down that they aren't a threat to me or to my marriage anymore. It's been over two years since I've been with you, so I can sit here and not be so attracted to you, but if we were to sleep together again, I don't think I'd be able to see you on the street without feeling as though you should be with me." Carla took another drink from her glass. "Besides, you're getting married."

"Yeah, that's right. I'm getting married," Wayne said. "And what Pete did to you, that is just forgotten, water under the bridge? You've forgiven him."

"No," Carla said. "Never. There is no forgiveness for that."

"I see. I cheat on you, and you go marry some other man, my best friend. Pete cheats, and you do nothing to him. What makes you think he won't do it again, since he won't be taught a lesson?"

"He will be taught a lesson."

"I thought you said you weren't going to sleep with anyone," Wayne said.

"I'm not. But he won't know that."

"I don't understand," Wayne said.

"Pete has planned some meeting for the three of us tonight to discuss this arrangement."

"I know," Wayne said. "He told me about it this morning."

"You'll come, we'll sit there, listen to what he has to say as though we're still planning on going through with the whole thing, but really knowing that we won't."

"We won't?" Wayne said.

"No. Because I know that all I need is for him to *feel* what it's like for another man to have his wife. I don't need to know what it feels like to give myself to another man. Do you understand? He'll feel the pain, the regret, for stepping out on me, and he'll believe that if he ever does that again, then I won't hesitate doing it again myself."

"You're going to lie to him is what you're saying," Wayne said, shaking his head.

"You're looking at me like I'm some filthy person."

"You are lying to him."

"Okay," Carla said, sitting up straighter in her chair. "Which is worse? Lying to your husband and not sleeping around on him, or telling him the truth and fucking someone else?"

"Believe it or not, the lying," Wayne said. "Fucking someone else, at least you're being open about it and he'll know what's going on."

"Well, I didn't know what was going on when he slept with that other woman," Carla said. "So this is what's going to happen.

I know you don't have to do this for me, so I'm asking you. Will you do it?"

Wayne looked away for a moment. "And tell me, just why should I not sleep with the woman I once loved, when her husband is giving me the goddamn go ahead. You know how I felt about you, how I feel."

"Because of what you just said. Because you do care for me, and I'm married to Pete now, and I know you care what happens with him."

"I do."

"Then we have a deal?"

Wayne felt as though he had no choice but to accept what she asked.

"Yes, we have a deal."

35

Pete sat at his dining room table, wearing a white shirt, black tie, and a brown suit. He was flipping through the pages of a yellow legal pad, checking his notes from the last day or so.

There were lines and lines, some words scratched out, some traced over to signify importance, others underlined.

These were his thoughts about what was supposed to happen between his best friend and his wife. The events that would be allowed to take place, and things that would be off limits, out of the fucking question during their short time together.

Carla was in the kitchen. He had not spoken to her much since arriving home, and she hadn't pushed him to speak to her. Pete was sure that she sensed the conflict he was going through. He glanced at his watch, saw that it was five minutes to eight, just about time for Wayne to be there.

Pete pulled out the three copies of the contract that he had drawn up. He checked it for the fourth time against all his notes, making sure that he had not left anything out.

The words *oral sex* caught his eye. He fixated on them a moment, blocked the image that was beating at his mind, then dropped his head into his hand, and asked himself what in the hell they were doing. Did Carla really think he'd be able to go through with this?

Just then, he heard his wife say, "Are you all right?"

Pete looked up and saw Carla standing in the kitchen doorway. How he loved her. Pete realized that was the reason he was actually going through with this, because she had said it was the only way they could set things right, which was all he wanted.

"I'm fine," he said.

"Do you want anything? Something to drink?"

"No. Wayne should be here any moment, so—"

And then the doorbell rang.

"That should be him," Pete said.

Carla walked to the door. Pete looked down at the contract.

Pete heard Wayne greeting his wife, Carla welcoming him. He lifted his head to see the two hug. He paid close attention to them as he stood up from his chair and walked across the living room to greet Wayne.

They shook hands. "I didn't know I was attending a funeral," Wayne said, grabbing the bottom of the tie that Pete was wearing. "I feel underdressed. What's the deal?"

"No deal," Pete said. "This just feels appropriate, that's all. Now if you don't mind, I would really like to get right to this," he said, walking back toward the dining room table. He pulled out the chair at the head, and waited for Wayne and Carla to sit down on either side of him.

Pete picked up the papers. "There is a list and a contract," he said. "It covers everything that's going to happen, and what's not going to happen. I made a copy of the contract for each of us, and at the bottom is where each of us will sign to acknowledge that we accept what is written here."

Pete pulled a pen from his inside breast pocket and held it out to his wife. "Carla, you can sign first."

"I think I want to see what's on that list before I sign anything. I believe I'm entitled to that," Carla said.

Pete looked over at Wayne.

"Whatever you want to do, man," Wayne said.

Pete set the pen down, picked up the papers.

He cleared his throat and began to read: "The agreed meeting between Wayne Mason and Carla Barnes will take place on Saturday, three days from now."

"Why then?" Carla asked.

"Because I want this over as soon as possible. Is there another day that you would prefer?"

"No. I guess not." Carla said. "Saturday's okay."

"Said meeting will take place at the Hyatt Regency downtown."

"Why the Hyatt?" Carla interrupted again.

"No particular reason," Pete said. "You can go wherever you want. I just chose that hotel. Is there a problem?"

"No."

"Can I continue?" Pete asked.

"Yes. Please. I'm sorry," Carla said.

Pete continued to read from his list on the contract, stating that the meeting was to start at 8 P.M. and end at 8 A.M. the following day.

"Intercourse will be had one time, and one time only."

Pete did not look up at Carla, but as he continued looking at his list, he paused as if waiting for her to interrupt. When she did not, he said, "A condom will be used." Pete paused again. "There will be no oral sex. There will be no kissing. There will be no—"

"I'm not saying I have a problem with that," Carla said. "But tell me, why won't there be any kissing?"

Pete put the papers down on the table, interlaced his fingers and addressed Carla as if she were a legal client and not his wife.

"Because kissing is a show of emotion. Considering this is an act of revenge, and not a consummation of love or feelings for one another, there should be no need for kissing."

"Did you love or feel emotion for the woman you slept with?" Carla asked.

"No."

"Did you kiss her?"

Pete did not answer. He looked to Wayne. Wayne looked down at his hands.

"Strike that then," Carla said. "I don't think it'll happen, but if I feel the need or the desire, I'll do it because you did it."

Just then an image of Carla naked and sweaty, riding Wayne, moaning, strands of her hair stuck to her face, entered Pete's mind. She opened her full lips, leaned over Wayne, covered his mouth with her own as she continued to gyrate above him.

Pete shut his eyes, forced the thought out of his mind, grabbed the pen, and drew a line through his written demand.

"Are you happy?" he asked, looking up at Carla.

"Satisfied."

Pete picked up his papers and continued: "There will be no showering together, no spooning while sleeping, no discussion of your past relationship. You will leave the hotel no later than eight the following morning, and you will never sleep together again, or speak of it."

Pete looked up at Wayne and Carla. "That's all. If you agree with what I've written, then you can sign here."

He gave the pen to Carla, slid her the three copies of the contract.

She signed on the line designated on each page.

She then passed the papers and pen over to Wayne.

Wayne grabbed the pen, was about to sign, but looked up at Pete. "You sure about this, buddy?"

"Just sign, Wayne."

Wayne did as he was told.

"Good," Pete said, taking his copy and the pen. "Now if you'll excuse me for a moment, I have to go to the washroom."

Pete stepped away from the table, feeling light-headed and slightly nauseated.

He walked down the hall, closed himself in the bathroom, and immediately ran the cold water. He held a washcloth under the stream, wetting it, wringing it out, then holding it to his face, as he kept himself from crumpling to the floor with the other hand firmly on the corner of the sink.

Just then he felt a rumbling in his stomach, felt his insides threatening to spill out of him, but he swallowed hard, controlling the urge.

He had to hold himself together. They hadn't even slept together yet.

Later that night, Pete knocked softly on their bedroom door.

"Come in," Carla said.

Pete stopped just two steps into the room. "What will happen when this is over?"

Carla closed her magazine and said, "Just like you said, it'll be over, like it never happened. We'll go back to the way we were. You'll sleep in here again. Everything will be fine."

"How do you know that?"

"I just do."

"Can't we get back there without going through this? Isn't there another way? Any other way?" Pete sat down on the bed beside her. "I know there is. We can do it if we really want to. I know we can."

"No, Pete," Carla said. "We can't."

He sat there, just staring at his wife, wishing he could somehow impress on her how much this was hurting him. Pete knew she could see it on his face, in his eyes. He knew the pain was visible, knew he was on the verge of tears. But she obviously chose to ignore that. She had made her decision. He needed to accept that, regardless of how much it hurt.

Pete stood up from the bed, looked down at his wife, and simply said, "Okay."

36

When Wayne returned home from the meeting, he stood just outside his door before sliding in the key. He took three huge breaths, and while exhaling told himself to forget about everything that just happened.

No, he would not be sleeping with Carla, but just the fact that he was planning this elaborate plot made him feel as though he was once again deceiving Me'Shell, especially since he told her he would never again. She had chosen to trust him once more, after the promise he had made to her.

Last night when Wayne walked in, Me'Shell was sitting on his living room sofa, her hands folded on her knees, waiting in silence.

He hadn't spoken to her since the night she said she had some things to think about, and now she was in his front room, sitting quiet, blank-faced.

"Me'Shell," Wayne said, walking over and standing in front of her. "You okay?"

She looked up at him, but didn't speak.

Wayne lowered himself to his knees, took her hands in his. "What's going on?"

"Promise me again that you won't ever hurt me."

"I promise," Wayne said.

"I want you to mean it."

"I do."

Me'Shell looked deep into Wayne's eyes, seeming to try to determine if he was being honest. "I want to marry you, but I don't want to be made a fool of."

"I won't make a fool of you."

"I don't want to be cheated on."

"I won't cheat on you."

"And don't ever lie to me," Me'Shell said.

"I won't. I swear it."

Me'Shell stared at Wayne for a moment, still no expression on her face. "You promise?"

"I do."

"Promise, promise?"

"I promise, promise," Wayne said.

That smile that Wayne loved so much suddenly spread across Me'Shell's lips.

He stood, pulled her from the sofa, and took her in his arms, lifting her off the floor. "Then that means we're gonna get married?"

"Yes," she said, kissing him. "But first you got to give me my ring back."

They had made love that night, sat up in bed, fed each other ice cream and talked about their future together. Me'Shell loved to imagine the home they would share, the children they would have, the years they would spend growing old together. And Wayne loved to see how that talk would light her face.

But now, as Wayne walked in the door, saw Me'Shell eagerly walking over to greet him, smiling as she had been doing non-stop since their talk, he knew he could not hide this from her.

Later that night, while they lay in the dark, Wayne was so troubled that he could not find sleep. "There's something I have to tell you, Me'Shell," he said suddenly.

"What?" There was caution in her tone.

"Tomorrow night, I've agreed to go to a hotel room with Carla and sleep with her."

Me'Shell lay silent in Wayne's arms. After a moment, she said, "You're joking, right?"

"No. I'm not."

She quickly rolled out of Wayne's arms, and Wayne threw his arm over his face, squinting against the bright bed lamp as Me'Shell clicked it on.

Sitting up on her knees in bed and facing Wayne, she asked sharply, "What are you talking about?"

He told her everything. How Pete had cheated, how Carla wanted revenge and this was how she had planned it. And he told her she no longer wanted to go through with it.

"So she just wants us to pretend," Wayne said, thankful that Me'Shell didn't seem as angry as he thought she would be.

"Do you want to do this with her?"

"Not really."

"Then why are you?"

"Because Pete's my best friend, and I guess Carla is kind of, too, now, I guess. This is what she thinks will allow her to get over the pain of Pete's cheating on her. She thinks it will keep them together, as strange as that sounds."

"Can't she just go to the hotel by herself? Can't she just lie and say you were there, if she's lying about sleeping with you?"

"I thought about that already," Wayne said. "But she doesn't know whether Pete will follow her, doesn't know whether he can check the hotel register somehow. She just wants to make sure that he believes this actually happened, so he'll never cheat again."

Me'Shell wrapped her arms around herself, lowered her head.

Wayne moved over to her, pulled her close to him. "You don't trust me?"

"It's not that. It's just—"

"Because if you don't, I'll tell her that I won't do it."

Me'Shell looked up. "You'd do that?"

"If you want me to."

She looked away. "I don't. I just don't want to lose you. I can't forget that kiss between you two."

Wayne moved behind Me'Shell, wrapped himself completely around her, held her tight. "There isn't a woman that can take me from you. Not even her. You hear me?"

"Yeah," Me'Shell said. "You still going to marry me?"

"If you'll still have me," Wayne said.

"Yeah, I guess."

"Even after Saturday night?"

"Yeah. Do what you have to do to help your best friends, but you better not touch that girl."

"I wouldn't dream of it."

Two hours later, Wayne opened his eyes to what he thought was the sound of the doorbell.

He turned to Me'Shell, whispered her name, but she was still asleep.

He was about to go back to sleep himself, when he heard the sound again.

He carefully climbed out of bed, and in the dark he threw on a T-shirt and some sweat pants over his boxers.

He hurried downstairs, peeked out the window beside the door, and saw Pete standing there. Wayne opened the door and asked, "Is everything okay?"

"Yeah. Everything's fine." Pete looked exhausted. His clothes were wrinkled, stubble dirtied his cheeks and chin, and Wayne detected the faint smell of alcohol. "I was out this way and thought I'd see if you wanted to go for a walk."

Wayne looked over his shoulder at the clock in the living room to confirm the time. "It's almost midnight."

"So?"

"All right. Let me put some shoes on."

The two men walked in silence down the peaceful, tree-lined residential street, no one stirring but them. They strolled for a while before a word was spoken, and then Wayne ventured to say, "You having second thoughts about this thing?"

"What, about you having sex with my wife?" Pete said, waving it off with a hand, as though it was nothing.

"We can still call it off," Wayne said. "It's not too late."

"I'm not worrying about that, Wayne. I trust you. We've been friends since we were ten."

"Practically brothers."

"Yeah, practically brothers. But how often does a man's brother sleep with that man's wife? This could change us, and that's what I'm worried about."

"What do you mean, change us?" Wayne asked.

"I don't know," Pete said. "I try to think about it, try to work out what will happen afterward, how it might affect us, might affect me and Carla, but I can't. I just don't want us to stop being who we are, because I love you, man."

Pete reached out, hugged Wayne.

"Same here," Wayne said.

They hugged for a long moment, then Wayne stepped away and said, "I'm not doing it. I've decided. Let's just call it off."

"No," Pete said. "You have to. Just do it and get it over with. We'll be fine."

"You sure?"

"There's no other way."

"That's not what I asked you," Wayne said.

"Yeah . . . I'm sure."

37

Today was the day. It was finally Saturday, and Carla stood in her bedroom, over the weekend bag that she was packing to take to the hotel.

She folded the short black nightgown she had just bought yesterday, and placed it on top of her other things.

Why had she bought it when she already had night clothes? She had a couple of pairs of perfectly good flannel and cotton pajamas, but those were still tucked away in her dresser drawer.

Was she trying to impress Wayne? She told herself no.

She took the nightgown out of the bag, looked toward her dresser, thought of swapping it for a pair of the cotton jammies, but caught herself. If she couldn't remain faithful to her husband, even in that black nightgown, then she had no business being married to him.

Carla put the nightgown back in the bag.

"Everything will be fine," she said, pulling the zipper closed.

She heard Pete come in and climb the stairs. She listened as he walked down the hall, past her room, and closed himself in the guest bedroom.

She had not seen him since late last night, when he had knocked on her door and told her he was going out for some fresh air. He looked troubled then, worn, not himself.

Concerned, she had sat up in bed and asked, "Are you okay?"

Pete hadn't answered, just stood there with a hand on the doorknob, staring at her. "What do you think?"

Carla didn't respond.

"I thought so," he said. "I'm going out."

She didn't know what time he came in but she heard him stirring about in the guest bedroom.

He was going through it, Carla knew. But what could she do?

She had to do this and there was no turning back.

She went into the bathroom, got her toothbrush and toothpaste, and packed them. She shouldered her bag, walked to the closed bedroom door, and stopped just before it.

She wondered if she should even walk down the hall and say good-bye to him?

Would he try to stop her? Knowing her husband, of course he would. He would try to reason with her at first, and when that didn't work, he would get emotional, beg her. Carla didn't want to see him like that, did not want to have to deal with it.

She wasn't really going to sleep with Wayne, she told herself. Carla put her hand on the doorknob, turned it gently, and pulled the door open, telling herself that if Pete wasn't damn near standing at the front door, arms and legs spread, blocking her exit, she would just leave. They would sort through everything when she returned.

When Carla stuck her head out and looked down the hall, she was thankful that the guest bedroom door was still closed. She moved silently down the hall toward the stairs, so if her husband did come out, he wouldn't think she was trying to sneak out. As she walked down the steps, she looked back over her shoulder, still watching out for him.

When Carla finally made it to the front door without seeing Pete, she felt a twinge of guilt, knowing he would've wanted to see her before she left. It was for the best that he hadn't she told herself as she left.

38

Pete watched her go. He was in their bedroom now, looking down from the window.

A moment ago, from the guest bedroom, Pete had heard Carla open their bedroom door, knew that she was leaving.

He wondered if she would say good-bye, if she even cared enough to do that. But as he watched her car pull out of the driveway, it was clear that she didn't.

Pete hurried to the closet, grabbed a jacket, punched his fists through the sleeves as he sped down the hallway and flew down the stairs.

Inside his car, speeding down a congested street, he dialed Wayne's number on his cell phone. When he didn't pick up, Pete shouted into the phone. "Wayne, don't leave yet. I'm coming by your house. Wait for me, okay." Pete was about to hang up, then yelled into the phone again. "Call me back if you get this."

He couldn't get through to his wife, and he knew it was because she was so hurt by what he had done. That was what gave her the motivation to go through with this.

But Pete knew Wayne didn't really want to go through with it either. He hoped Wayne would listen to him, would recognize the damage this act would do to every single relationship involved in it. And as Pete whipped his car around the corner onto Wayne's block, he was hopeful, too, because just last night, Wayne had told him he was willing to bow out.

Pete prayed that he had not missed him, prayed that it was not too late, because Pete knew that if this thing did go down, he didn't think he'd really be able to forgive anyone involved, Carla, Wayne, not even himself.

Pete started to slow down, and what was close to a smile appeared on his face, as he saw Wayne lowering himself into his car in front of his house.

He hadn't left yet.

Pete pulled up next to him, their cars facing opposite directions. He rolled down his window and motioned for Wayne to do the same.

"Pete, what's going on?" Wayne said, after his window powered down.

"I need to talk to you. I'm going to park right there. Don't leave, okay."

"Okay."

"I'm serious," Pete said. "Don't leave."

"Okay, Pete. I said I won't go anywhere."

Pete parked his car down the street, a couple of cars away, and started running toward his friend, who had gotten out and was leaning against his own car.

"What's up?" Wayne said.

"Where were you going?"

Wayne looked at him oddly, smiled uncomfortably. "You know. I was going to . . . to the hotel."

"You can't," Pete said.

Wayne said nothing for a moment, just looked at Pete. "What do you mean, I can't?"

"I changed my mind, Wayne. I can't let you go through with this."

"But just last night when I offered to—"

"I know. But like I said, I don't want you to go now."

Wayne looked in the other direction, down the street, then back at Pete. "And what's Carla going to say about this? You even said that this is the only thing that's going to allow you two to start over again. You don't let this happen, either she's going to resent you, which could end in the two of you getting divorced, or she's going to sleep with another man, but do it behind your back."

"I'll take that chance."

"Really. Carla sneaking off at lunchtime, after work, saying that she's meeting with clients or friends when she's out getting fucked by some coworker. You'd chance that?"

Pete clamped his hands to his skull, squeezed, and yelled, "No! I don't want to fucking chance that, but I don't want this either. I won't be able to take it."

"It's one night. It won't be that bad."

"How can you say that?" Pete said, grabbing Wayne by the shoulders. "You're not in my position."

"Pete, it's nothing to worry about."

"What!" Pete said, starting to look angry. "This is my wife. The woman I love, and you're going to fuck her, but it's nothing for me to worry about?"

Wayne leveled a heavy stare at Pete, and said again, this time much slower, "There's nothing to worry about."

The anger in Pete's face started to dissolve a little, his grip weakening a tad.

"Why are you saying that?"

"I'm just saying," Wayne said.

"What are you trying to say?"

"I'm not trying to say anything, Pete. But that you don't have anything to worry about," Wayne said, turning to his car and opening the door. "Now I should be going."

"No!" Pete said, slamming Wayne's car door shut. "There's something that you aren't telling me, isn't there? I want to know."

"No," Wayne said. "Just do this the way we all planned and things will work out for the best."

"Fuck you!" Pete said, quickly grabbing Wayne around the collar.

Pete slammed him against his car, but Wayne countered, quickly hit him with a hard shot to the belly, knocking the wind out of him. Pete dropped to his knees, wrapping both arms around his stomach, breathing erratically, trying to catch his breath.

Wayne stood over him. "Sorry, buddy. But I said, just fucking trust me, okay. All of this will work out for the best. You'll see."

Wayne opened his car door, Pete rolling out of the way, into the middle of the residential street.

"Wayne!" Pete called.

Wayne started his car, rolled down the window. "Go home, Pete. Everything will be fine in the morning."

"Wayne! This is my wife!" Pete said, spit flying from his mouth, tears threatening to fall from his eyes.

Wayne continued to ignore him. He maneuvered the car out of the parking spot as Pete rose to his feet. And as Wayne pulled out, started slowly down the street, Pete staggered toward him, his arm stretched out, yelling as loud as he could.

Finally, after several steps, Pete stopped, too winded, too emotionally distraught to continue. He bent over, dropped his hands to his knees, huffing and puffing, saliva spilling from his mouth.

It's over, Pete thought. It's actually going to happen.

But then Pete heard a car door slam, and when he looked up, Wayne was walking back toward him.

When Wayne approached him, Pete stood, wiped his mouth. "I'm sorry for acting this way, but you have to understand—"

"She's not going to do it, Pete," Wayne said.

"What are you talking about? She's not going to do what?"

"When you said it was me you wanted her to sleep with, she said she wouldn't do it. She wants you to think that she did, because she wants you to know how it feels to go through what she's going through. But she loves you too much, man. She can't do it."

Pete couldn't believe what he was hearing. A huge smile stretched across his face, and then all of a sudden, he threw himself into Wayne, wrapping his arms around his brother's neck.

"You're bullshittin'!" Pete yelled into Wayne's ear. "You are, aren't you?"

"Pete," Wayne said, pulling Pete's arms from around him, pushing his friend away. "I'm not. But you aren't supposed to know this," Wayne said, very seriously. "Do you hear me?"

"Yeah."

"So this means, tomorrow morning when Carla walks in, you have to act like you would've if I hadn't told you a thing. And just to get used to it, you should start acting like that now."

"All right."

"That means wiping that big-ass grin off your face."

Pete smoothed a hand down his face, as though he could literally smear the expression away. He looked at Wayne with a more serious expression. "I'm sorry. I'm just happy. I could almost cry, man, I'm so happy. Thank you."

"Don't thank me," Wayne said. "I didn't do anything. You just got a good woman who loves you."

"I know," Pete said. "I know."

39

Carla sat on the sofa in the hotel suite, watching TV.

She wasn't really watching it, but staring in that general direction. She was too nervous to care what was happening on the screen. Her mind was on what she would do once Wayne arrived, what she would say to him, if anything, and what he would say back.

"Calm the hell down, Carla," she scolded herself.

She had been there an hour already, and had half gone crazy.

She unpacked all her clothes, placed the few items in the dresser drawers, and hung the others on hangers in the closet as though she was staying longer than just twelve hours. Then she sat herself down in front of the television, placed her cell phone on the coffee table, and stared at it.

After walking out on Pete without saying a word, she had started to feel guilty. She thought of calling him, telling him that everything was fine with her. But he was supposed to be suffering, wondering whether or not she was in the throes of passion right now, if she was on her back, or on her stomach, feeling a pleasure that he could never give her. Carla dialed his number anyway.

The phone rang only once, then her husband picked up. "Hello," he said.

"I'm sorry for walking out without letting you know, but—"

"You don't have to explain, sweetheart. I understand. You gotta do what you gotta do. I brought this on us, and like you said, it's time for me to accept the consequences of my actions. Do what you have to do, Carla. I know we'll be able to move past this."

"Oh," Carla said, somewhat shocked by Pete's newfound acceptance. She had called half thinking that he would beg her once again not to go through with this, that maybe, just maybe, she would've taken that one last step back, and canceled the entire charade. It would've only been partly because she didn't want her husband suffering anymore, but it also had to do with the fear of being alone in this room with Wayne.

"So, you're okay then?"

"Don't get me wrong. It's killing me, but if this is what it takes for us to start over, then I'll accept it."

"Well, good, Pete. I just wanted to make sure that things were okay. I guess I'll see you tomorrow morning."

Carla said good-bye, then disconnected the call.

Just then the hotel room door opened.

Carla swung her head in that direction to see Wayne walk in, a duffel bag slung over his shoulder, a key card in his hand. He closed the door behind him. "You okay?"

"Yeah," Carla said, not sounding certain.

"You sure?" Wayne said, walking over to her.

"Yeah."

"I'm going to put my bag in the bedroom. That okay?"

"Sure."

When Wayne came back, he sat down on the sofa with Carla and looked around, as if searching for something to say. Then he said, "Not a bad room, huh."

"Did you talk to Pete today?" Carla asked.

"No. Why?"

"No reason," Carla said, turning a little on the sofa to face Wayne. "It's no big deal."

"Good. So do I get a hello hug, or what?"

Carla smiled a little, shaking her head. "I thought I told you—"

"I ain't trying nothing." Wayne smiled back. "We got this hotel room for twelve hours, if we're going to waste your husband's money and not use it for what it's meant to be used for, we might as well be comfortable around each other."

Carla admitted to herself that he had a point. She was feeling a little standoffish toward Wayne, so she stood up and opened her arms.

Wayne stood up too, stepped closer to her.

They hugged, Wayne holding her soft and close, and Carla didn't want to accept the fact that the man felt good against her body.

"I'm not going to deny that it's good to see you," Wayne said softly.

"Get off of me," Carla said, pushing her palms into Wayne's chest, squirming away from him. "You ain't slick. I told you that."

"Not trying to be," Wayne said, holding both his hands up. "What should we do now? Play checkers, write poetry?"

Carla grabbed the remote and sat back down on the sofa. "Have a seat. We can order a movie, or see what's on cable."

"If your husband knew what we were doing," Wayne said, plopping down next to Carla, "oh boy, he'd kill us."

"Very funny."

Halfway through the movie, Wayne stood up and said, "I'm gonna see what's in the mini-bar. Want anything?"

"Whatever is nonalcoholic."

"Okay."

When he came back, he spilled two handfuls of tiny alcohol-filled bottles across the table.

"There wasn't anything without alcohol?"

"Yeah, but we have to save those as chasers, for when we drink the stuff with alcohol."

Carla looked at Wayne a moment, then laughed. "Just make me a vodka and cranberry. And hurry up, you're missing a good part."

After Wayne and Carla's third drink, or was it their fourth, Carla couldn't really remember, Wayne had reached down and grabbed Carla's ankles. "What are you doing?" she said, a little shocked and just a little drunk.

"Oh, stop it. I'm going to give you a massage. You remember how we used to sit and watch TV, and you'd always ask me to massage your feet. You always said how good I was."

"That was then, Wayne."

"Really. So you're saying you couldn't go for one now?"

Carla remembered back to how wonderful those massages had been.

"I think I've even gotten better," Wayne said.

"Okay," Carla said, letting him lift her feet into his lap. "But no funny stuff."

"Just relax and watch the movie. Don't you worry about what I do down here."

It only took a moment of his hands rubbing her feet, before Carla felt her body starting to melt. He had gotten better, and she didn't know if it was the massage, the alcohol, or a combination, but Carla was beginning to feel more relaxed than she had in a very long time.

She continued watching the movie, taking an occasional sip from her drink, every so often raising her head from the pillow to look down at Wayne, dutifully massaging her feet, ankles, and calves. He took his time, was dedicated to the task, and it made Carla remember how he approached everything that way, including lovemaking.

A flash image of the two of them in the act appeared in her head. She did not fight it, but allowed it in for just a moment. He was on top of her, she was on her back, pillow pushed under her hips to raise her up. He held her ankles spread apart as wide as his arms could stretch, and Carla could remember him, before her, sweaty and moaning, on his knees, sliding ever so slowly in and out of her.

The way he moved his body had always entranced her, and now, on the couch, getting her massage, her eyes fell closed, and she was transported somewhere else. She unconsciously licked her lips, as she felt Wayne's soft hands smooth all the tension and stress from her feet. And then as he laid one foot down on his lap to grasp the other, Carla felt something else, something that she hoped she didn't. But as her foot rested there, she knew it was his erect penis pressing against her ankle.

Carla quickly raised her head, looking at Wayne, conveying to him her concern.

"It's okay," Wayne said. "Just because I'm excited, doesn't mean something's going to happen."

"No," Carla said, pulling her feet away from him. "I'm not thinking that. It's just that . . ." she looked at the TV and was thankful that the end credits were rolling. "The movie is over. And I think I need a shower."

She stood and grabbed her empty glass from the table. "Do you think you can make me one more of these. I could use it."

"Sure," Wayne said, standing up.

And Carla didn't want to look, but she couldn't stop her eyes from staring at the bulge in his pants.

A moment later, Carla heard Wayne say, "I said, are you okay?"

"What?" Carla said, snapping out of her momentary trance.

"I asked if you were okay, but it seemed like you were busy looking at something else. So I'm asking you again." Wayne smiled.

"I'm sorry," Carla said, embarrassed. "Yeah, I'm fine."

When Wayne took her glass and stepped over to the mini-bar to make her another drink, Carla slapped both her hands to her face, covering it, realizing she was making a fool of herself.

Wayne returned with the drink. "Here you go. Need anything else?"

"No. The drink is enough. And once I take this shower, I'll be fine."

"Leave it running when you're done, okay. I want to take one after you," Wayne said.

Wayne watched her turn, wobble just a little, then disappear into the bedroom. He flopped onto the sofa, grabbed his glass, and downed what was left in it. What the hell was he doing, he asked himself. He gave himself no reply. He had done nothing that he wasn't supposed to be doing, nothing that Me'Shell or Pete would be angry at him for.

But if they had scrutinized what he was thinking, maybe they would've been just the slightest bit pissed.

Wayne continued to sit there, listening as Carla ran the shower water.

Nothing was going to happen tonight. He had made that promise to Pete, to his fiancée, and Carla had made that promise to him, so why would he even want to go back on that?

He didn't.

But as he sat there, as he listened to that water running, he could not help but let his imagination follow Carla into that bathroom, and into that shower. In his mind, he saw her, the water crashing against her beautiful body, spilling over her curves. He saw her lathering up, her hands smoothing the soap over her thighs, her ass and—

"Cool it!" Wayne said, jumping up from the sofa, covering his ears with his hands, as though that was the route used by his thoughts to gain entry into his head.

"Just cool it. I can do this," Wayne said, but found himself taking slow steps toward the bathroom door. There would be no crime in just taking a listen.

Wayne pressed his ear to the door, heard the water splashing, and he wondered what would happen if he were to just walk in. He wasn't really going to do it, he thought, placing a hand on the doorknob. He was just wondering, kind of entertaining the possibilities.

But just then, the door opened.

Wayne stumbled back, surprised.

Carla, a bath towel around her, shrieked with shock, the towel falling to the floor, leaving her standing naked.

Wayne's eyes bulged.

Carla shrieked again, slamming the door.

"Damn!" Wayne said to himself. He picked up the towel up from the carpet and tried to figure out what he could say so that he wouldn't seem like so much of a pervert. He leaned up against the door and said, "I wasn't going to come in."

"Then why were you at the door?"

"I was going to ask did you need your drink freshened," he said, thinking quickly.

"Bullshit, Wayne. You just made the drink. Now give me back my towel."

"You gotta open the door."

"No. Just leave it on the knob and go."

"You sure."

"Yeah!"

Carla stood inside the steam-filled bathroom, naked behind the door. She counted to ten, cracked the door open, and saw Wayne still there, smiling and holding the towel.

"You aren't mad at me, are you," Wayne said, peeking in. "I've already seen your stuff before anyway."

"No," Carla said, snatching the towel from Wayne's hand. "I'm not mad. You're just a pervert."

"I'm really not, but you still look great."

"Pervert!" Carla said, slamming the door. She rested her back against it, smiling and shaking her head.

40

An hour later, both Carla and Wayne had finished their showers. They were sitting on the sofa again, and Carla was wearing the nightgown she had packed. Wayne wore a pair of silk boxers and a tank T-shirt.

They had said nothing to one another, outside of making the occasional comment on the movie they were watching.

Carla felt a tension between them, probably due to how late it was getting, the fact that they had this room, and that they could do anything they wanted with it, even had permission from her husband.

They continued sitting there until Carla sat up, grabbed the remote, and muted the television.

Wayne turned to her. "What's wrong?"

"I never apologized to you," Carla said.

"For what?"

"For going behind your back and marrying Pete. It was spiteful, it was evil, and just plain wrong, and I'm sorry."

"Wow. That happened a year ago. Why the apology now?"

"I don't know," Carla said. "I guess I finally realize that you do regret what you did, and that maybe you didn't deserve the pain I caused you by marrying Pete."

Wayne sighed. "Did you really love him when you two got married?"

"Yeah."

"Then it wasn't wrong."

"But I did know it would hurt you."

"Well, then, that was wrong," Wayne said, looking down at his hands.

There was a long silence before Carla said, "I've been thinking. Everything, all of this, is happening for a reason. Pete cheating on me, him telling me that he did, all of that putting you and me in this room together. I love Pete, and we're happy together, but I've never really gotten over you. I believe I made the right decision in letting you go, in marrying the man that I have, but seeing you when I do, talking to you, I sometimes hate myself for what I did. I think that maybe if I could've just gotten over what you did, accepted your apology, that we could've been so happy together."

Wayne scooted over to her, took her hands. "Don't do that to yourself. You did what you thought was right, and nothing good will come from second guessing yourself."

"But I do, Wayne," Carla said. "And no matter how many times you tell me I shouldn't, no matter how much I know what you say is true, it won't stop me from doing it. And what's so bad about it, is that I want to stop. I want to for once wake up in the morning and not have you on my mind. I want to go a full day without wanting to call you, wanting to hear your voice. But I can't, and it's killing me. Every time I see my husband, talk with him, sleep with him, and you are in my head, it makes me feel filthy," Carla said, a tear coming to her eye. She quickly wiped it away. "It makes me feel like a liar, a fake. Although I know that I love Pete, I don't know if he's the only man that I love. And that is not only unfair to him—it's also unfair to me."

Carla gently pulled her hands from Wayne's and wrapped her arms around herself.

"I can't take not knowing anymore, Wayne."

"Not knowing what?"

"If Pete is the only man I love. I want to know that if I had the opportunity to choose, it would be him, without a second thought, that I would pick."

"I wish there was something I could do to ease what you're going through," Wayne said.

"There is."

"What is it? Name it."

"My husband has given me that opportunity. I know that I said that I wouldn't, but—"

"Carla," Wayne said, standing from the sofa. "You aren't about to say—"

"You're getting married. You love Me'Shell, or you wouldn't have asked her. But don't you want to know, for sure, that she is the one, the only woman that you would want to be with."

"But when I was trying to get back with you—"

"I wasn't hearing it. I know. But that was before this happened with Pete. And I don't know if it opened my eyes, don't know if it's just timing, or what. But we're here now, with the blessing of my husband, allowing us to be with each other again, for one night, like we used to be, to know if we should continue our separate ways, or think about getting back together. Wayne," Carla said, standing, walking over and stopping before him. "I want to know. I need to know." She grabbed his hand, held it for a moment. "Help me find out," she said, then turned around and walked into the bedroom, leaving Wayne there to think about it.

Fuck! Wayne thought to himself. Fuck! Fuck! Fuck!

He paced the living room, knowing that he should not do what Carla asked of him, what he promised he wouldn't.

This was his best friend's wife. He could not do that.

But Wayne remembered, she had been his fiancée first. Wayne was going to marry her, and yes, they would've been together now, so happy, if it hadn't been for Pete. He had taken Carla away from him, had married her, and had been with her ever since. Would it be that wrong if Wayne were to be with her one last time?

He thought about her argument, and he thought she had a point. This could make everything clear for the both of them.

If things weren't what they used to be for them, the two of them could walk out of this room tomorrow morning and be so much better for it. They could truly be with their respective partners, and never think twice about each other. But if they still had feelings for one another, if Wayne still loved Carla like he always thought he could've, and she still loved him, then it would only be right that they confirmed that, and then reexamined the choices they were about to make.

He stopped just before he got to the door, asked himself one last time. Was he sure of this? Was this the right thing to do? His answer came quick, and was certain. It was no.

But as Wayne walked into the darkened room, smelling Carla's scent, he knew he would do it anyway.

41

When Wayne walked into that hotel bedroom, he was already stripping off his T-shirt and sliding down his boxers.

When he slid underneath the sheet, he could feel that Carla was naked as well, lying on her back. Her arms reached out to pull him on top of her. She opened her legs, let him fall in between them.

He could feel the heat right away, the moisture that wetted the inside of her thighs, that grazed the hard tip of him.

She wrapped her arms around him, raised her head, feeling for his lips.

He pressed his mouth to hers, sank his tongue in, kissed her heavily, their heads turning about.

She held him tight, opened her legs more, clamped them around his ass, was trying to pull him in.

"Hold it," Wayne said. "Are you sure about this?"

"Yes." Her voice was throaty, but it was sure. She had answered right away. There was no doubt present.

She was pressing him again to enter her. He could feel the softness of her clit, his dick sliding across it.

"Do you have any protection? I didn't bring anything," Wayne said.

"No. We're fine. Just don't come in me."

He knew that wasn't right, but he agreed. He raised himself on his hands, then carefully slid inside. It had been so long, but the memory of how she felt came back to him immediately. She was a little tight, her pussy gripping him, but she was wet, and he moved, just the head, teasing her.

She moaned. Her body tightened, her legs clamping against his hips like a vise.

"Oh, baby," she said.

"Do you like it?"

"Oh."

"Do you remember me?"

"Yes."

Wayne pulled himself out, then pushed back in again, half of himself. He rose up a little on his knees, on his elbows, elevated himself slightly, his dick firm and long, extending down into her. He grabbed her legs, looped his arms around them, let the back of her knees rest in the bend of his elbows, and then he started to pump his hips, sliding in and out, long strokes and short.

Carla panted, tilted her head back, but he found her mouth, kissed her, would not let her move.

She whipped her head about.

"Baby, baby, baby!" she cried, and he knew what got to her, had known for the past year and a half he had been deprived of her, because he had been doing it for the two years they were together.

He continued working, stroking her long now, letting her feel the very tip of him, his entire shaft, then the very base at the end of each stroke, until he felt her entire body tighten, heard the high-pitched whine seep from behind her clenched teeth, and he knew she was coming for him.

He made her come four times more during that session.

They made love twice more. Once before going to bed, again when Wayne woke up, found Carla on top of him, riding him.

He slept soundly after that, not regretting what they had done, nor worrying what the morning would bring.

But when he woke, Wayne found himself in bed alone.

He rose up, looked around, then called out, "Carla?"

He looked over toward the bathroom. The door was open, and it was empty.

"Carla," Wayne called again, jumping out of bed, sliding on his pants, and hurrying out into the living room.

She wasn't there either, and neither were any of her things.

Wayne rushed back into the living room, checked the closet, and saw that her bag was gone.

He ran for the door of the suite, swung it open, looked down the hall, and saw Carla standing in front of the elevator. He walked quickly, barefoot and bare chested to her side. "What are you doing?"

"I have to go," Carla said, not turning to look him in the face.

"Why? It's only six A.M.."

"I just do."

"It's not wrong what we did."

"I didn't say it was."

"Then why are you leaving? Just come back," Wayne said, grabbing her hand.

Carla yanked away from him.

Wayne backed away, his feelings hurt. "Okay," he said. "Okay." He turned and walked back to the suite.

Wayne sat outside in his car, staring up at his home.

Me'Shell was there.

Wayne wasn't sure whether or not she was awake, but he knew that the moment she saw him, she would be able to tell that something heavy was on his mind. Would she know just what that was? Would she know that last night, when he was faced with the decision of whether or not to cheat on her, he decided he would?

He had no idea of what last night meant. Had Carla found out what she was searching for, or had she been overcome with guilt for doing exactly what she said she wasn't going to do?

More important, Wayne needed to ask himself the exact same question. After spending the night and making love to Carla for the specific reason of determining who he should be with, Wayne still wasn't sure.

But he knew, as he stepped out of his car, grabbed his duffel, and started toward the house, none of that would help him decide what to tell Me'Shell.

42

What happened last night was supposed to happen, Carla told herself, as she stood just outside the front door of her house, her weekend bag slung over her shoulder.

She knew Pete would probably be waiting right inside, would probably stare into her eyes, asking himself, if not asking her as well, whether she had enjoyed having sex with Wayne.

She would try to mask her emotions, act indifferent, as though she had felt nothing when Wayne was on top of her, inside of her, kissing her, whispering things in her ear, while she held tight to him.

She hadn't experienced that in so long, and now she could not stop thinking about him. "Stop it, Carla. Just stop it!" she whispered harshly to herself.

She exhaled, turned the key in the lock, and pushed open the door.

Pete was sitting on the living room sofa, no TV running, no music, just sitting, waiting. It looked as though he had been there for some time.

He got up quickly to meet her, pulled the bag from her shoulder, set it down, then wrapped his arms around her and held her tight.

"How are you?" he asked, his voice soft, sincere.

Carla held on to him. She wanted to cry, she felt so much guilt after going back on the promise she had made to herself.

"I don't know," she admitted.

Pete leaned away from her, looked into her eyes. "It doesn't matter, because it's over. We did it, what we needed to do, and it's over with. And now we can go back to our lives."

Pete actually managed a smile, which shocked Carla a little.

When she thought that he wouldn't have a single word for her, thought that he would look at her with disgust in his eyes, he was actually smiling, being very understanding, and accepting everything that had happened.

He was a far better man than she had even thought, which made it so much harder to deal with the feelings that were emerging after last night.

"Why don't you go up to bed. I put fresh linen on it. Sleep for a while. You look tired."

"I think you're right," Carla said.

43

Me'Shell was asleep when Wayne walked quietly into his bedroom, stood beside the bed, and looked down at her.

She slept peacefully, a smile on her face that told Wayne one thing, that she wasn't worrying at all about what had happened last night, wasn't worried that he had slipped up and made love to Carla.

It was a good thing she trusted him like that. And bad that he did not respect that trust.

Wayne disrobed silently. He considered sliding in under the covers with her, for he was glad that all this was over, wanting nothing more than just to be beside her, hold her. But he felt unclean, even though he had showered this morning before leaving the hotel.

So he decided to wash once more.

He stepped into his own shower, lathered up, and rinsed off three times, making sure there was no sign or scent of Carla left on him.

Wayne was about to give himself one more wash, when he was startled by the shower curtain being pulled back. He spun around to find Me'Shell, naked and smiling behind him.

"Hey baby," she said, giving him a kiss and a hug.

Wayne hugged her back, fearing that she sensed everything that had happened but was just waiting till he was man enough to tell her himself.

"So how did it go?" Me'Shell asked, releasing him, taking the bar of soap from his hand and smoothing it across his chest.

"Watched a few movies, and talked."

"I hope about how much you loved me."

"That's exactly what we talked about," Wayne said, feeling as low as he ever had in his life for deceiving this woman.

When Wayne woke up four hours later, he opened his eyes and found himself alone once again.

After the shower, they had climbed in bed together. Me'Shell snuggled close to him, kissed him on his neck, lowered her hand below the sheet, reached for Wayne, began to massage him.

"I was jealous last night."

"You didn't think that I was doing anything, did you?" Wayne said, afraid he sounded too defensive.

"No. I just never want another woman to spend another night with you. That's my place. And once we're married, it will be for the rest of my life."

"I know," Wayne said.

Me'Shell continued to try to arouse him.

It wasn't happening.

She was about to lower her head beneath the sheet. Wayne stopped her.

"No," he said. "I think I'm just tired."

"I understand," Me'Shell said, but she sounded disappointed. She moved closer to him, hugged him, placing his head against her breasts. "Just go to sleep."

Now, seeing that Me'Shell was gone, he thought something must be wrong. He got out of bed quickly, slipped on a pair of track pants and a T-shirt and went downstairs.

He imagined Me'Shell on the phone, receiving from Carla or Pete the news that he had done exactly what he told her he would not do. He looked around, and when he didn't see Me'Shell anywhere, he thought again that maybe Carla hadn't been able to hold their secret any longer. Maybe she had told Pete, and Pete had called Me'Shell, and she had driven over there to get the gory details.

Wayne anxiously stepped to the patio doors and frantically slid them open. To his relief, Me'Shell was sitting there on a deck chair, sipping from a glass of lemonade.

"Hey, sleepy head," she said, looking up.

"Hey," Wayne said back.

"You okay? You look like something's on your mind."

"No. I'm fine," Wayne said, taking the chair next to hers.

"Are you hungry? I can fix you something."

"No, everything is perfect," Wayne said, taking Me'Shell's hand in his. But he was lying to her, and to himself.

He had tried to put his night with Carla out of his mind, but while he slept that was all he dreamed of. The events that had taken place, things that Wayne had never thought would happen, but did. And now he was more confused than ever.

He loved Me'Shell, but he still thought he might love Carla, too, and if there was any question as to whether that was true, their night together definitely confirmed it.

But what difference did that make now, Wayne asked himself, staring across at Me'Shell. He was to marry her. They were to be husband and wife, as Pete and Carla were. So there was nothing more to think about.

But as Carla had said, what if they realized that they still loved one another; wouldn't it be wrong to further deny themselves being together?

The problem was that Wayne did not know now how Carla felt. She might have left so early this morning because she just did not want to face her real feelings.

Wayne asked himself if it even mattered how Carla felt about him. His answer was no. There were more important things that he had to think about, like what he would do with the woman who was sitting beside him. Wayne had to decide whether to keep last night a secret, or be honest with her.

He looked over at her, Me'Shell smiling contently, apparently thinking she had nothing to be concerned about. He had deceived her before, promised her he would never do that again. He was serious about that. So Wayne knew there could only be one way to handle this.

Me'Shell turned to Wayne, the smile still on her face. She looked lovingly at him, brought his hand to her lips and kissed it.

"I was thinking," she said. "Why are we waiting, planning a huge wedding, when we don't need all of that. I love you, you love me. Everyone knows that. We don't have to prove it to them with a production, a reception, and all that other stuff."

"What do you mean?" Wayne asked.

"We can just do it, baby. Just get married."

"When?"

"Now. Today. Tomorrow. Sometime this week," Me'Shell said, her excitement mounting with each word she spoke. "I don't want to wait any longer to be Mrs. Me'Shell Mason, and there's no reason why I should have to. Right?"

Wayne shifted nervously in his chair, sweat accumulating in his palm. He pulled his hand from hers and said, "Maybe there is."

"Really, Dr. Mason, would you like to tell me what that is?" Me'Shell said, as if Wayne was joking.

"Because I lied to you. Something did happen last night. I slept with Carla."

Me'Shell smiled, as if thinking that what he'd said was a joke. After Wayne did not make an attempt to correct himself, the smile disappeared from Me'Shell's face. Wayne saw shock replace that smile, then disappointment, followed by what he knew was deep pain.

Me'Shell quickly got up from her chair, walked slowly to the edge of the deck, placed her hands on the rail, her back to Wayne.

She turned around, tears on her face. "Did it mean anything?" she asked.

"What do you mean?"

"Did it mean something!" Me'Shell said, raising her voice, quickly wiping tears from her face. "Was it more than just sex?"

"Yes. No," Wayne corrected, then settled on, "I don't know."

Another tear spilled from Me'Shell's eye, rolled down her cheek. "You don't love me?"

"I do," Wayne said.

"You don't want to marry me?"

"I still want to marry you, Me'Shell," Wayne said, with as much sincerity as he could muster.

"Then why are you telling me this? Last night, I lay in bed, crying, knowing that you could've slept with her, that it could've happened. I'm not a fool. But I told myself I wouldn't think about it, and if it did happen, I knew it would be for the last time, something you just needed to get out of your system. I told myself that she could have you for one night, if it meant I would have you for the rest of my life. But you're sitting there telling me about it. Why? Why couldn't you have just kept it to yourself?"

"Because I lied to you once, and I promised I'd never do it again."

"It wouldn't have been a lie," Me'Shell said, waving her hands about. "I wasn't going to ask!"

Wayne rose from his chair, took a step toward her, his head lowered. "I had to tell you, because I slept around before on someone I loved, and that was what ended my relationship with her. I don't want that to happen again. Not with you," Wayne said. "And . . ."

"And what?" Me'Shell said.

"And you needed to know so you'll understand why, even though I still want us to get married, I'm going to have to spend some time with Carla."

Me'Shell looked puzzled, as the tears began to dry on her cheeks. "What are you saying to me?"

"Me'Shell," Wayne said, walking up to her and putting his arms around her waist. "I love you, and I want you to be my wife. But I had feelings for Carla, and the way we ended . . . I just need to know that I don't still have those same feelings."

Me'Shell shoved Wayne away with both hands. "Are you fucking crazy!" she said. "Because I was foolish enough to see you after you told me about some woman you would've left me for the first time, you think you can just pull that shit whenever you want? You think just because I love you, because I've given my heart to you, and trusted that you'd never . . . that you'd never . . ." Me'Shell couldn't hold in her emotion any longer. She dropped her face into her hands and wept.

Wayne touched her arm.

She swatted his hand away. "Don't you ever, ever, touch me again!"

Wayne stood there, feeling horrible, knowing that after all he had put her through, he had no right to ask her what he had.

When Me'Shell lifted her face, it was wet with tears. "Goodbye, Wayne," she said, turning to leave.

"I do love you," he said.

Me'Shell stopped, turned, walked back to him, slapped him across the face.

He reeled from her assault, and when he turned back, Me'Shell was on her way into the house.

He did not follow her, knew he had no right asking her to stay any longer.

44

Four nights later, Pete raised himself up on his elbows, sweat on his brow, and stared down at his wife.

Her eyes were closed, her head turned away.

Pete was inside her, had been for the past fifteen minutes, had been pumping away, trying to coax her into enjoying what he was doing, but she just lay there, her eyes averted, her mind someplace else.

"Carla," Pete said.

She opened her eyes, turned her head to him. "What, sweetheart?"

"What's wrong with you?"

"Nothing."

"Are you sure? You're acting as though you'd rather be any place but here."

"I'm sorry, Pete," Carla said, sincerely. "I'm tired. It's been a long day. I promise tomorrow it'll be better."

"No," Pete said, shaking his head. "No." He pulled himself out of his wife.

Carla reached for her husband, trying to stop him. "Pete. Please, just finish."

He got up and stood before her, naked. "I don't want to just finish. I've been doing that for the last four days. What is going on with you? Ever since you came back from that hotel, you've acted as though you don't want to be here with me. You barely talk to me."

Carla sat up in bed, pulled the sheet up to her breasts. "Like I said, I'm sorry, but work has been—"

"Don't give me that excuse about work again. That's what you said before, and even if it is true," Pete said, "I don't want to hear it now. There's something else bothering you. What is it?"

Carla lowered her head, wrapped her arms around herself, as though wishing she could just disappear.

Pete knew what was bothering her. She was still feeling guilty, and it was amazing that even though she hadn't actually slept with Wayne, the mere idea that she believed Pete thought she had, was enough to make her feel guilty.

"Is it because of what happened at the hotel?" Pete said, again.

Carla lifted her head, nodded, then looked down again.

Pete sat beside her, curled an arm around her back, pulled her close to his chest. "That's going to happen. But there's no reason to feel that way. We talked about all of this. I gave you permission. I knew that it was going to happen, it has, and if I can be okay with it, then you can, too."

Carla did not respond to a word Pete said. He placed a hand under her chin, raised her head to look at him.

"Carla, the most important thing here is that we love each other. I slept with another woman. It was the biggest mistake of my life, but I don't love her. She meant nothing to me. You slept with Wayne in order for things to be right with us, but I know I'm the one you love, not him. We're past all of that. Really, everything is fine."

"Okay," Carla said, softly, but her expression had not changed. None of the guilt Pete knew she was feeling seemed to have dissipated, and Pete thought that was strange. He had told her that he was cool, that he had forgiven her, and if that was all that was truly bothering her, why wasn't she all of a sudden guilt free, as Pete felt she should've been?

Then next afternoon, while sitting in Wayne's office at work, Pete asked Wayne that exact question. Wayne sat behind his desk, his lab coat and tie still on, a pencil between his teeth, seeming to really give it some thought.

"I don't know. Just give it time. Everything will be fine, I promise you," Wayne said. "She'll decide what is most important to her, her guilt or the man she's supposed to be with, and everything will be the way it's supposed to be."

"Thanks, Wayne," Pete said, slapping his brother on the knee, and standing up from his chair. "I can always count on you to make things better."

45

Toward the end of her workday, Carla sat behind her desk and watched as her cell phone rang beside her.

It was set on vibrate.

She did not pick it up, because she knew who it was. After it had stopped ringing, she reached out, grabbed it, and checked to confirm that she was right.

It was Wayne again, as she had suspected. He had been calling five or ten times a day for the last four days, but Carla never once picked up or even took the time to listen to his messages.

She knew why he was calling, and she knew he had reason.

It was wrong the way she had run out of the hotel that morning with no explanation.

When he stopped her in the hallway, just before she got on the elevator, she had been so close to throwing herself at him, confessing that she still loved him, had never stopped, that all she wanted was to be with him again. But she knew all the hell that would cause, knew it while she lay in bed with him sleeping beside her that morning. She even knew it the moment after he had slid into her for the first time that night. It had all come rushing back to her, the love she felt for him, and the pain, the regret she felt after dumping him two years before.

And now Wayne was calling, obviously wanting to know just what the hell was up, where everything lay.

It had been her idea that they sleep together. She was the one who'd said that if they still had feelings for each other they should not deny them. But now she was doing exactly the opposite of what she had recommended.

This morning, there were no calls from Wayne. This afternoon, and most of the evening, nothing as well. She thought he had finally given up, but then her cell phone rang, and now she had to accept the fact that it was wrong to just try to disappear after she had opened up this can of worms again.

Carla's desk phone rang.

"Yeah, Laci," Carla said, snapping up the phone.

"Call for you on line four."

"Who is it?"

"Dr. Mason."

"Tell him I'm unavailable."

"He said he knew you'd say that, and to tell you that he's not going to accept it."

"Then tell him that I'm gone for the day," Carla said.

After a moment of no response, Carla said, "Laci?"

"Yeah. I'm here."

"Did you hear what I said?"

"Yeah, I heard you."

"Then tell him that," Carla demanded. "Please."

"Yes, ma'am," Laci said, clicking off.

Carla watched as the little clear square above the label, LINE 4 blinked, then lit without interruption, and a moment later went out. She slumped in her chair, relieved that situation had been resolved, at least for the moment.

A knock came at her door.

"Go away," Carla yelled to the door.

Another knock came.

"I said, go away."

The door opened anyway, and Laci walked in, closed the door behind her, and approached Carla's desk.

Carla sat up in her chair.

"Can you tell me what happened to my best friend?" Laci said.

"What are you talking about?" Carla said.

"The woman who used to run this magazine. The woman who used to be nice to people, would speak to folks when she walked through the office, instead of roll her eyes, or grunt, if she said anything at all. I just thought I'd ask you, because I haven't seen her in a while, and I was starting to get a little worried," Laci said, turning and heading back toward the door.

"Laci," Carla said, standing up from her desk. "Stop."

"Yes, miss. Can I help you?"

"I slept with him."

"You slept with who?"

"I slept with Wayne."

"Oh, my God," Laci said, walking back and sitting down in front of Carla's desk. "Don't tell me, and now you think you're falling back in love with him."

"No." Carla said. "Now I know I love him. I think I truly never stopped."

"Sweetheart," Laci said, looking sadly at Carla. She stood up and walked around the desk.

Carla stood up, too, accepting the hug that Laci gave her. "Everything is going to work out," Laci said, rubbing Carla's back.

When they sat down again, Carla said, "I don't know that they are."

"You still love your husband, don't you?"

"Of course I do, but I haven't been able to show him that, because all I can do is think of Wayne. I'm so confused."

"Forget Wayne," Laci said.

"I can't."

"Pete is your husband. You're married to him. You want to stay that way, don't you?"

"I don't know," Carla said.

"Let me rephrase that. Can you stay married to him? Would life be hell, would you look across the bed every morning when you wake up and want to tell him that you can't stand the sight of him? Would you want to tell him that you resent his very existence because you chose him over Wayne?"

"No," Carla said. "It wouldn't be anything like that. My marriage is good, and if I do stay married to Pete, it will continue to be good."

"Then what's the problem?"

"I think it would be better with Wayne," Carla said, hanging her head, ashamed of her feelings.

"No," Laci said, standing up from her chair and waving her arms about. "Hell no! You need to end things now."

Carla said, "I've come this far, and I feel all this has happened for a reason. I need to know for sure, one way or the other, with whom I'm supposed to be. I need to pursue this."

"Nothing can come from this but pain," Laci said.

Carla turned to her, and said, "I imagine nothing can be more painful than being with the wrong person for the rest of your life."

46

That evening, Wayne paced back and forth across his living room, wondering just what the hell was going on with Carla.

Wayne hit the redial button on his phone, waiting the four times the phone rang, and then he hung up angrily, feeling like a fool, when he heard Carla's recording.

He stopped in the middle of the living room and stared at the sofa. He could imagine Me'Shell there, saw himself beside her. He remembered how they would sit, wrapped up in each other, watching TV, laughing or just talking.

But now all that was gone, and Wayne wondered if he'd been a fool to have done what he had, been as honest as he was. He had to have been.

He wondered if Carla was at home with Pete, eating dinner, everything fine between the two of them now, since she had finally gotten Wayne out of her system.

But Wayne knew that wasn't the case, that was, if he went by what Pete had told him earlier. Carla was bothered by something, and Wayne believed it was that night she had spent time with him. It couldn't have been anything else.

But why the hell wasn't she answering his calls? If it was that night, he could've talked to her about it. They could've shared their feelings, come to some conclusion, and at least decided upon the next step.

He could grab his jacket and keys, just go over there. He didn't know what he would tell Pete, but he was sure he would come up with something on the drive. And if nothing hit him, he would just say that he was there to see how Pete was doing. He never needed an excuse to drop by before now.

Wayne went to the closet, snatched his jacket from the hanger, walked to the dining room table, grabbed his car keys, all the while feeling his anger building. He told himself that this mess would be resolved tonight. He didn't know how, but it would be.

When he flung open the door, he was startled to see Carla standing in front of him, poised to ring his doorbell.

Wayne stood speechless.

Carla did the same, her face flushed, her chest heaving.

"Why haven't you taken my calls?" Wayne said. "Why haven't you gotten in touch with me?"

Carla didn't respond, just continued to stare at Wayne with wide eyes.

"I needed to talk to you," Wayne said, desperation and anger in his voice. "I needed to know what was going on. How you felt. What we would—"

Before Wayne could finish his sentence, Carla took hold of his face, pressed her lips onto his, kissed him deeply.

Wayne locked his arms around her, pulled her tight, kissed her back.

When the kiss ended, Carla said, "You want to know how I feel. I love you."

Wayne stared into Carla's eyes, almost not believing what he had just heard, for she had not said those words in so long. "I love you, too," Wayne said.

Some six hours later, Wayne still held Carla in his arms. They lay on the living room sofa, Carla on top of Wayne, the lights out, darkness around them.

The sound of Wayne's ringing phone cut through the silence, and Wayne tensed, about to slide out from under her.

"Don't," she said.

"If it's him, I have to get it. He's been calling all night."

"Don't."

"I have to at least check," Wayne said, gently sliding his way out from under Carla's body. He picked up the phone from the dining room table, turned it over to view the caller ID.

Carla had followed him, was now standing just in front of him.

"It's Pete," Wayne said.

"Don't answer it," Carla said, the cordless phone now ringing in Wayne's hand.

"I have to. What will he think if he can't get a hold of you at twelve thirty in the morning, and can't reach me either. He'll put it together sooner or later."

"Just don't." And right after Carla said that, the phone stopped ringing. She looked at Wayne. "Now turn the ringer off."

"I can't do that."

The phone rang again, and again it was Pete. This time Wayne answered before Carla could stop him.

"Hello," Wayne said, something near fear on his face.

Carla stood in front of him, silent, wide eyed. She could hear Pete's voice:

"Wayne, have you seen Carla? She hasn't come home from work, and I can't find her."

"What do you mean, you can't find her? Have you tried calling her?" Wayne said.

"Of course, I tried calling her cell phone. I've been calling her like crazy, and she just doesn't answer. I left her messages, called her at work, even drove to her job, but it's locked up now. I don't know what's going on."

"Calm down, Pete," Wayne said, looking directly at Carla. "Maybe she just went out with some of her friends."

"I called her friend Laci, and she's not with her."

"I'm sure Carla has other friends, Pete. Don't worry. She's out, eating dinner, or having a drink with some coworkers. I'm telling you, she should be walking through your door any minute," Wayne said, grabbing Carla by the arm, and trying to turn her toward his front door.

Carla shook her head, stood right there.

"I'm worried, Wayne," Pete said. "What if something happened to her."

"Nothing has happened to her."

"You haven't seen her, have you?" Pete said.

"Seen her? Your wife?" Wayne said, more for Carla's benefit than his own. "No. But if I do, I'll call you right away. But till she comes back home, don't worry, Pete. Everything will be fine."

Wayne hung up, grabbed Carla by the arm again, and tried to lead her toward the door. "You gotta go."

"No," Carla said, standing her ground. "I'm staying here tonight."

"What!"

"I haven't seen you in five days, and I haven't been able to get you out of my head. Now that I'm here, I don't want to go. Not yet."

"Carla," Wayne said. "You can't stay."

"You don't want me to?"

"I'm not saying that, but—"

"Then I'm staying with you," Carla said, grabbing Wayne's hand, and leading him toward the stairs.

"And Pete? What are you going to tell him?"

"I'll worry about that."

Upstairs, sometime later, Carla and Wayne lay in his bed, in his dark bedroom, a window partially open, a cool, night breeze occasionally blowing in through a dancing curtain.

They had not made love and were not naked.

Wayne wore a pair of boxers, Carla wore one of his medical school T-shirts.

They lay diagonally across the king-size bed, holding hands and staring up at the ceiling.

"What does this remind you of?" Carla said.

"Every single night we spent when we were still together."

"Feels weird, doesn't it?"

"What?" Wayne said. "Like if you think hard enough, it's like the last two years never happened? Feels like we've always been together? Weird like that?"

"Yeah," Carla said. "But I don't have to think that hard to feel that. Remember just before we'd fall asleep, you'd ask me if I had only one wish, what would it be?"

"Yeah."

"And do you remember what I'd always answer?"

"Yeah, that you wanted to be with me forever."

"Ask me now," Carla said.

"No."

"Why not?"

"Because I'm scared of the answer," Wayne said. "Because I think you might be caught up in something. We slept together, it's been a while, and now you tell me you love me. But what if it's just infatuation, or something?"

"What time is it, Wayne?"

"What does that have to do with anything?"

"I want you to look over at the clock and tell me what time it is."

Wayne read the red numerals on his digital alarm. "It's three twenty-three in the morning."

"And at three twenty-three in the morning, if I didn't really feel that I loved you, do you think I'd be here with you and not my husband?"

"Carla," Wayne said, rising from the bed, turning, and sitting on the edge of it with his back to her.

"What is it, Wayne? If it was because of what I did to you, how I left you two years ago, then I apologize." She hugged him from behind. "I was wrong to do it. I was just so angry—you had hurt me so bad—that I wanted to do the same thing to you. But now, looking back, I know how wrong it was, how cowardly and hateful it was. Is that why you don't want me back?"

"Carla," Wayne said, turning quickly on her. "I want you back. I've always wanted you back. But it's just not that easy. Your husband is at home right now, sitting up, worried sick that something has happened to you. Does that mean anything to you? Do you even care about him anymore?"

"Of course I care," Carla said, standing up from the bed in front of him. "But in this exchange, regardless of who we all end up with, someone is going to get hurt. If you want that to be you, and you honestly don't care about me anymore, then just tell me, and I'll leave."

"No," Wayne said, reaching out and grabbing Carla's hand, pulling her to him. She stepped into the space between his knees.

"Then how do we do this?" Wayne asked. "You just can't up and leave Pete."

"You and I have spent just one night," Carla said. "I'm not foolish enough to think that means we should spend the rest of our lives together yet, but I want to start seeing you again. That way we'll know for sure if we want to be together."

"What do you mean, 'seeing' me?"

"See you. Like every couple of days, go out to dinner, see a movie, spend time together."

"Like date?" Wayne said.

"Yeah."

Wayne looked up at her, feeling an uncertainty like none other he had felt before. "If we do this, it won't be easy, and feelings are going to be hurt. Really hurt. Are you sure you want to go through with this?"

"Yeah," Carla said, leaning down and kissing him. "I'm sure."

47

That morning, the sun rose at 6:42, and Pete knew that first-hand, because he was sitting outside on his front steps, witnessing it.

He had not slept a moment of the night, thinking of his wife, for he was worried out of his mind. But an hour later, that worry was quickly replaced by extreme anger, as he watched Carla pull into the driveway, step out of her car, and walk toward him, as though it was the previous evening and she was just coming home from work.

Pete stood up and looked at his wife incredulously, as she turned onto the walkway that led to the steps.

"I called the police," Pete said. "I called them and they said they could do nothing because you have to be gone for thirty-six hours. But I told them I didn't give a fuck about the time requirements. They said not to worry, that you were just probably out somewhere and hadn't made it back yet. But I told them, that's not my wife. That she would've called, or at least picked up her phone. I was wrong."

By the time Pete had finished speaking, Carla was standing on the step just below him, as if waiting for him to move so she could pass.

"I'm sorry," was all that Carla offered.

"'I'm sorry?'" Pete echoed. "I'm sorry. I was worried sick about you. I thought you were dead," he said, raising his voice.

"Can we talk about this inside," Carla said. "You'll wake the neighbors."

"I don't care about the neighbors. Where were you?"

"Can we please go inside, Pete. I'll tell you everything then."

"No! I want to know now. Tell me where you were," Pete insisted.

"Fine," Carla said. "I was at Wayne's."

Pete's face went blank. He froze there for a moment, as Carla walked around him and let herself into the house.

Pete turned, followed her inside, closed the door, and stood in the center of the living room. "Why were you at Wayne's?" he said, his voice much lower now.

"I'm sorry. I should've called and at least told you that I was okay," Carla apologized.

"Why were you at Wayne's?" Pete asked again, in the exact same tone.

Carla looked at her husband for a long moment, then walked to the dining room table and said, "Maybe you should sit down first."

Pete quietly obeyed his wife's request, took a seat, and rested his palms on his knees like a grade-school student.

Carla sat down just in front of him. "I'm tired of all the secrets, the deception. There are some things you should know, Pete."

"Like what?" Pete said, trying to keep calm, conceal the fact that he was raging inside.

"That Wayne and I are going to start seeing each other."

Pete looked at his wife as though she must've bumped her head while she was out last night. "What are you talking about?" he asked. "Seeing each other?"

"Because of Saturday night. Because of what happened, and I know this is exactly what wasn't supposed to occur, but it hurts me to tell you that I've developed feelings for him again. He has not stopped caring for me, and last night, while I was over there, we've agreed to start seeing each other to see if it's something that we should pursue."

Pete started laughing. When he finished, he said, "That's bullshit. Now I don't know what you're trying to hide, what you were doing last night, if you were out with one of those men you met while you were trying to choose, but you need to stop telling me lies, and be honest with me."

Carla shook her head, looked as though this was truly hurting her, but she continued. "Pete, I am being honest with you."

"Bullshit!" Pete yelled, hammering his fist on the table, as he sprang up from his chair, finally letting his anger have its way with him. He seized the top of his chair and slung it hard to the floor, startling Carla, her eyes closing tight, her body tensing.

"You're lying to me, and I don't know why you're trying to use my best friend as an excuse, but you need to tell me what's really going on."

"Pete," Carla said. "You called Wayne's house last night like five or six times. You called him again, he didn't pick up, and then when you called him back, he picked up on the first ring. It was exactly twelve thirty."

Pete looked at his wife strangely, asking himself just how she knew that. After thinking about it and not being able to come up with an alternate answer, he told himself it didn't matter, because he still didn't believe she was over there.

Carla must've read that on his face, because she continued by saying, "You asked him if he had seen me, and he told you no. He told you not to worry, that I was probably out drinking with a friend, or having dinner, and that everything would be fine."

She was right. There was no denying that. He couldn't believe what he was hearing. "So, you were over there. But you're still lying about sleeping with him Saturday."

"Pete, I'm not."

"You are. Because, he wasn't supposed to, but Wayne told me that you weren't going to go through with it. He told me you were going just so I would know what it felt like to think that you had actually slept with him, but he told me that you couldn't go through with it. So I know you didn't do it."

"I didn't think that I could. But I did, Pete," Carla said. "I wouldn't be telling you this if it didn't happen. But it did. We slept together, and we both realize that we still have feelings for each other, and that's why we feel the need to start seeing one another again."

"No," Pete said, shaking his head, feeling like it was about to explode. "I don't believe you!"

"It's true, Pete."

Pete locked his angry gaze on his wife, took a step toward her that placed him right in her face, his fists closed at his sides. His entire body was trembling with rage, but he would not hurt her.

"You slept with him?" Pete asked, from behind clenched teeth. "And you better not lie to me."

"I'm sorry. But the answer is yes."

"And you were there last night? Spent the night with him?"

Again, Carla answered, "Yes."

That was all that Pete needed to hear, he told himself as he spun and headed toward the door.

"Pete! Where are you going?" he heard his wife call from behind him.

But he no longer cared to speak to her. It was Wayne he needed to see.

Half an hour later, when Pete burst through the glass double doors of the orthopedic practice, the waiting room was half filled with patients.

That didn't matter to Pete, because when he saw Wayne, standing there and talking to a middle-aged man in a cast, everyone else became invisible to him.

Pete saw that Wayne turned, saw Pete coming toward him.

He smiled, actually smiled, like everything was fine between them, like he hadn't lied to him, hadn't fucked his wife, hadn't spent the night with her just last night, and probably fucked her then, too.

Wayne extended a hand, started to greet him, like it was any other morning. But before he could get a single word out, Pete was on him, had thrown himself across the room at Wayne, tackled him to the floor, straddled him.

Pete rained blows down upon Wayne's face, striking him with some, missing with others, his fists banging into the thin carpet that covered the waiting room floor.

While he was pummeling Wayne, tears spilled from Pete's eyes as he yelled out, "I trusted you. You said you wouldn't do it. And I fucking trusted you!"

Wayne fought, squirmed to get out from under Pete, but he could not.

Pete threw one more punch at Wayne, slamming into his jaw, before Pete was pulled away, kicking and punching, by arms and hands he could not see.

"How could you do this to me?" Pete cried, as he was held by every limb, and dragged farther away from Wayne. "I loved you, trusted you. You were my fucking brother!"

48

When Carla got the phone call from Wayne, she could hardly understand him. At first the only word she could make out was *hospital*, and that's when she started to panic.

"What did you say!"

He mumbled something else, said something about Pete coming to the job and beating him up.

"Where are you?"

Wayne told her not to worry, that he would be all right, that he would call her later. At least that's what it sounded like.

"I said, where are you!" Carla demanded, the phone pressed hard against the side of her face, her eyes starting to tear up.

Half an hour later, when Carla rushed through the doors of the Northwestern Hospital emergency room, she saw Wayne sitting in a wheelchair, pushed up against a wall.

She hurried toward him and as she approached, it became clear why Wayne was having trouble speaking. Carla kneeled beside his chair, saw the stitches in his lower lip, the dark purple bruising around his left eye, the swelling of his right cheek, and the blood-stained gauze in his nostrils.

She shook her head, trying to stop new tears from coming to her eyes. She took Wayne's hand. "Are you all right?"

Wayne managed a smile, wincing a little. "Nothing broken, just a few stitches, bruising, and some swelling. My mouth was packed with gauze when I spoke to you earlier, but I'm better now. Doc said he thinks I'll live."

"What the hell did he do to you?"

"What he had every right to do," Wayne said, getting up from the wheelchair and walking toward the exit. "Where did you park?"

"Wayne," Carla called from behind him. "What did he do?"

"Can we talk in the car? I had enough of my personal business put out in the street when your husband attacked me in front of my patients this morning. Now can we go?"

Carla drove home, constantly turning to Wayne. He was angry, wouldn't speak to her.

"Tell me what's going on. What happened, Wayne?"

He sat with his arms crossed, watching the road, as Carla drove him home.

When she parked in front of his house, she turned to Wayne and said, "I'm not leaving till you tell me what happened." She was shocked by how bad he looked.

"You told him," Wayne said. "Why? Why in the hell did you do that?"

"Because I'm tired of sneaking around behind his back."

"Dammit!" Wayne said, slamming a fist against the dashboard. "Did you have to tell him now?"

"Then when, Wayne? Is there a perfect time for this kind of news?"

"I'm going to have to apologize to him," Wayne said, ignoring her last statement.

"Apologize. For what? He's the one who beat you up."

"He trusted me, Carla. I told him nothing was going to happen that night, and it did. And not only that, you tell him that we're going to start seeing each other."

"Do you want to call this all off?" Carla said, frustrated. "Because if this is too much for you—"

"No," Wayne said. "I'm not saying that. But I'm still going to apologize to him. And I'm sure he's going to want to talk more about you and me *seeing* each other."

"Then I'll just have to talk to him."

"Are you sure?"

"If it's going to happen, he might as well know about it."

49

When Carla got home, she went up to Pete's office and pressed her ear to the closed door, listening for movement.

She heard nothing, but knocked anyway. There was no answer.

"Pete, I know you're in there. I need to talk to you."

"I don't have anything to say."

Carla turned the doorknob. The door was locked.

"Pete, we really need to talk about all this. Staying locked in your office won't help anything."

"I have nothing to say to you!" Pete yelled.

"But I have something to say to you. What I told you this morning, about seeing Wayne, I still plan on doing that. Don't you want to know what I mean? Don't you want to know why? Just open the door and we can discuss it. Please."

Carla waited a few long moments and heard nothing. Just as she was about to walk away, she heard the lock turning and saw the door open just a crack. She pushed the door open the rest of the way and walked in. The blinds were drawn and Pete's lamp burned on his desk at its lowest setting.

Pete slumped back into his leather desk chair, while Carla stood beside one of the two office chairs.

"Sit down," Pete said, glancing at her.

"Can you sit in this chair next to mine, instead of behind your desk when we discuss this. I feel like an employee this way."

"You've lost the right to be treated as my wife," Pete said, sitting up in his chair. "You're the one who wanted to talk. So sit down or leave."

Carla took the seat, despite Pete's harsh tone.

"He deserved what he got," Pete said.

"I'm not here to talk about that. I'm here to tell you what's going to happen with me and Wayne, and why I'm going to do it."

"Fine. Speak."

"Wayne and I are going to spend time together," Carla said.

"You want to sleep with him again?" Pete asked, a look of disgust on his face.

"No. This is not about that."

"You want to leave me?"

"No, Pete. I'm not saying that I want to leave you."

"Then what the hell are you talking about? I don't know what you're saying to me. You say you don't want to leave me, but you want to see Wayne. What is it you want! You can't have us both!"

"To know, Pete," Carla said. "To know who I really belong with. To be certain. I would've had that opportunity a year and a half ago, but you took that from me when you told me that Wayne cheated."

"I did you a favor."

"No!" Carla said, standing up from the chair. "You did yourself a favor. I didn't have to know that, Pete. Afterward, Wayne realized it was a mistake, told you he thought that, but you told me anyway. And you did that because you were looking out for me? He was your best friend, Pete."

"I know that, but I had my reasons," Pete said.

"It doesn't matter. Best friends don't do that to each other. But because you knew what happened in my last relationship, because you knew how I would take it, you had to run and tell me what he'd done. And you got the desired result, didn't you? I left him," Carla said. "And you were right there, playing the shoulder to cry on. You didn't even give me a minute to decide if I was really making the right decision. Didn't give me a chance to allow Wayne to come back in the picture, let him talk me into giving him another chance, because you knew it could happen. Instead, you got as close to me as you could, and when you thought the time was right, while I was still weak, you proposed to me."

"Are you saying you married me because you were weak, and not because you loved me?" Pete asked.

"No. I loved you. But in every breakup, there is that period when you have the right and the time to wonder if you made the right decision. People go back and forth, get back together again just to break up, sometimes two and three times, before they know for sure. But because of you, I did not have that opportunity. I've resented you for that till this day," Carla said, sitting down again. "But now I'm taking it back. I'm going to see Wayne until I know for sure that it isn't him I should be with."

"And I'm supposed to sit here and continue to let you fuck—"

"I won't sleep with him. I told you that. This is not about sex."

"And what about me? You don't love me at all, anymore?"

"I do. You're still my husband, but I have to do this."

Pete sat behind his desk, dropped his forehead in his palm, looked as though he was giving it serious thought.

Carla sat before him, waiting, her breath tight in her chest.

Pete looked up at Carla, the pain he felt evident on his face. "I don't know why you even came in here to tell me this, because there's no way I'll ever allow it. You're my wife. We are married, and despite how much you feel you need to do this, it is not an option. The answer is hell no."

Carla swallowed hard. "I'm not asking for your permission. I don't want to be dishonest with you again. I'm just informing you, so you'll know," Carla said, standing up and heading for the door.

She was about to leave when Pete said, “And what if I say you have to make a decision now, between the two of us?”

“I won’t do that. I can’t do that.”

“And if I say I won’t stay around here and allow you to do this to me?”

“Then I’d say you need to do whatever you need to do.”

50

Pete finally emerged from his office hours later. The sun had gone down, the house was dark around him.

He was looking for Carla, and hoping that he could convince her to rethink this thing, because of the irreparable damage it could do to their marriage.

"Carla," he called, hoping she might still be home. But she was gone, had left without even telling him again, even though she knew he was there in his office. Pete wondered if this was what their marriage had become. Him sleeping with strange women, her sneaking around seeing his best friend, each one trying to hurt the other, not even caring enough to let the other know when they left the house or where they were going.

Pete lowered himself onto the living room sofa. The situation was bad now, he thought, but if things continued down this path, if he allowed them to, then they could only get worse.

Carla told him she didn't want to be dishonest with him any longer, and despite how much it truly hurt, Pete appreciated that.

When he asked her if she still loved him, she said she did.

Pete didn't think that she was lying. Regardless of all the foul things she was doing, Pete still believed Carla loved him.

But he knew love was not enough.

She had to continue to respect him, because if she didn't, she would think she could do anything she wanted, hurt him any way she wanted to, and expect him to just endure it. And if he did that, as he was right now, she would surely lose whatever love she did still have for him—she would go with Wayne.

Pete rose from the sofa, knowing full well what he had to do.

Half an hour later, Pete sat on the floor, his back against his bed, staring at the huge suitcase he had just packed.

No matter how much he wanted to stay, he had to leave. But whenever he tried to pick up his bag, he felt weak, dizzy. He settled himself on the floor beside the bed, thought about what his wife had said to him earlier—that she had resented him for telling her that Wayne had cheated on her. Pete wondered if that was why she was putting him through this hell. Did he deserve this? he asked himself, as he dug his fingers into his scalp. He had told her about Wayne's cheating because he felt she deserved better. Because if it hadn't been for Wayne, Pete and Carla would've continued dating, and they probably would have married anyway.

But Pete's brother Wayne, who always had everything, a father, a mother, a home to live in, and every single girl he laid his eyes on, just had to have the one woman who Pete truly felt he could have something with.

Pete accepted the fact that as kids, the girls just liked Wayne. He had gotten over Wayne being smarter than he was, better looking, having people who truly loved him, because they were his natural parents, and not just feeling obligated to him, because they took on the responsibility, like Pete always felt he was for Wayne's parents.

Pete had gotten over all that, because when he moved out of that house, when he finished medical school, passed his boards, became a doctor, he no longer had to live in his brother's shadow. Pete loved Wayne and his adoptive parents, but he was a grown man, and would no longer have to come second, be overlooked by Wayne, who always seemed to get all the attention.

But it had happened again those two years ago, when Wayne stole Carla from him.

Wayne didn't even want her, or he wouldn't have cheated on her.

He had told Wayne not to do it, but Wayne did it anyway, only confirming how little he cared about Carla.

Pete loved the girl, so he told her about Wayne's transgression. He ran to her and told her, despite the fact that Wayne was his best friend, his brother. Pete told Carla partly because he felt Carla deserved a man who would respect her, and partly because he knew Wayne would quickly get over her and find someone to replace her. Which he did.

But now, Carla said that she resented Pete. After all that he had done, trying to save her from the pain he thought she would have to endure with Wayne—she resented him.

He couldn't take that from her anymore. He had to go.

Pete stood up, bent down, and clutched the luggage by its handle, but again he felt weak, light-headed. He fought through it, lifted the heavy bag, and started for the door. He stopped to look around the bedroom; memories of the times he shared with his wife, both good and bad, flooded his brain.

Pete forced himself to drag his bag out of the bedroom and into the hall. At the top of the stairs, he looked down and cursed himself, hung his head and released the bag, letting it fall to its side.

He couldn't.

No matter how badly Carla was treating him, he loved her too much. And even though he knew it was foolish to hold on, Pete could not deny that Carla told him there still was a chance that she could choose him over Wayne.

At that moment, Pete decided that he would do whatever it took to swing things in his favor, and then just hope for the best.

51

At the same time, Wayne sat parked outside Pete's house, the motor still running, wondering if he should get out and actually ring the man's doorbell.

Wayne hadn't gone back to work, and he figured that Pete hadn't either.

While sitting at home, the painkillers the ER doctor prescribed for him only marginally relieving his discomfort, Wayne entertained the thought of calling Pete.

Half an hour ago he had actually dialed Pete's number, was about to let the phone ring, but then quickly hung up, knowing that a telephone apology wouldn't be nearly good enough.

So now, Wayne had decided to confront Pete, at least to let him know all that went down.

As Wayne knocked, he could see that there weren't any lights on inside, and he felt almost relieved by the possibility that Pete might not even be there.

There was no answer, so he knocked again, and all of a sudden the door swung open. Pete was standing there, looking tired and depressed.

"I need to talk," Wayne found the courage to say.

"I have nothing to say to you," Pete said.

"You don't have to say anything. I just want you to hear me out. I want to apologize. Can I come in?" Wayne asked.

"No. You can never come in my house again."

"Then come out."

Pete looked as though he was giving the request some thought, then said, "No. I don't need my neighbors peering out their windows at me, because I don't know what I might say or do after I hear what you have to tell me."

"Then I'll drive us to the park down the street. No one was there when I passed it. This won't take long, Pete."

Pete looked back into the darkened house, checked to make sure the lock was turned, then pulled the door closed.

After they reached the park, they got out of the car and walked to a park bench, where Pete sat down heavily.

Wayne stood just off to the side and both of them looked out toward the vacant basketball courts.

"I'm sorry about what happened at the hotel," Wayne said, still not facing Pete.

"You said it wouldn't happen. You said Carla wouldn't go through with it, and I thought that even if she did change her mind, the promise you made me would've meant something."

"It did."

"Bullshit, Wayne," Pete said, finally turning to look at him. "Why did you even lie to me, tell me that, if you knew you were going to sleep with her. At least I would've known it was going to happen. At least I wouldn't have been walking around like some damn fool, believing you, thinking that everything was fine, only to find out from my wife that the two of you had slept together anyway."

"I didn't plan for it to happen, it just did."

"I see, Wayne," Pete said, standing up. "The two of you were talking, then all of a sudden, your dick just slid into my wife. Fuck you," Pete said, starting back toward the car. "Take me back to my house."

"No," Wayne called to Pete. "We still have issues we have to discuss."

"I have nothing else to say to you."

"How about the fact that I still have feelings for Carla, and she feels the same about me."

Pete stopped in his tracks but said nothing.

"That's why she said something to you about us seeing each other."

"Yeah," Pete said, turning around, taking steps back toward Wayne. "She said something about that, and I'm telling you that's not going to happen."

"I think that's her decision to make, not yours."

Pete moved closer to Wayne, his fists balled up at his sides, as though he was about to strike him.

Wayne raised his hands, crouched and moved into a defensive position. "This morning you caught me off guard. It won't be as easy this time."

Pete stared at Wayne for a long, hard moment, at the damage he had done to his face, then turned away, saying, "Leave her alone. She would stop it if you weren't encouraging her."

"No, she wouldn't. She wants to see if there is anything left between us, if we should still be together. And I want to know that, too."

"Stop it!" Pete yelled, turning away from Wayne. "This is my wife you're talking about."

"I know that," Wayne said, "But I love your wife!"

Pete spun around, a look of utter disbelief on his face, for this was the first time Wayne had spoken those words about Carla to Pete since she had left him.

"That's right," Wayne continued. "And I'm not sure if I've ever stopped."

"What are you talking about?" Pete said.

"The two months while you two were having problems. It wasn't because things were hectic at work, it was because she was seeing me. Because she was conflicted by her feelings for me."

"You were sleeping with my wife then?" Pete said, looking like he wanted to charge Wayne again.

"No. We were just meeting, going out for coffee, talking. But it was about us, the possibility of getting back together."

"You worthless son of a bitch," Pete said.

"What did you expect? You tell Carla that I cheated, she marries you, and because of that, I just magically fall out of love with her?"

"You accepted it. You were at my fucking wedding, my best man!"

"I did that because our friendship was that important to me, because I had always promised, whoever you married, I was going to stand up for you," Wayne said. "I did that because I loved you, not because I stopped loving her."

"So what now?" Pete said. "You're just going to see Carla, as though she's single, as though she's not my wife, hadn't taken vows, disrespecting both of us."

"Don't you talk about respect," Wayne said, stepping toward Pete, and for the first time showing anger. "You went behind my back. You knew how much I loved her, that I was excited about getting married, and you knew that telling her would end all of that, but you did it anyway. Where's the respect in that, Pete?"

Pete said nothing, hung his head low.

Wayne circled him, stopping just in front of him. "Why did you do it? You never fucking told me why you did it."

"I had my reasons," Pete said, his voice low.

"And I don't mean to hurt you by doing this, but I have my reasons for doing what I'm about to do."

Pete raised his head. "I'm not accepting that. You need to tell Carla that this isn't going to happen."

"Pete," Wayne said. "Nobody is saying that we're going to end up together. We just want to see if her decision to marry you was a mistake."

Pete let out a pathetic chuckle. "You're laughable, Wayne. Think about what you just said. That my wife could've made a mistake in marrying me, but you aren't trying to hurt me. Wayne, I don't care what your reasons are. I don't care what hers are, either. You just stop seeing my wife," Pete said, turning back toward his house.

"And if I don't?" Wayne said.

Pete turned and walked back to face Wayne. "Then I swear, you will fucking be sorry."

52

When Pete got back, Carla was in the kitchen, drinking a glass of water.

He walked in behind her, and she set down the glass. "I saw a suitcase upstairs. What is that for?"

"I packed it, because I was going to leave you," Pete said, and he thought he saw worry creep into Carla's expression. "But I couldn't do it," he said, and then he noticed that she looked the slightest bit relieved.

"Oh," she said.

"Do you want to know why?"

"If you want to tell me," Carla said.

"Because I love you too much, and I'm not ready to give up on us, regardless of how much you want to."

"I never said that."

"You're just seeing another man because you want to prove to me how strong our marriage is. Is that it?"

"You know what," Carla said, waving a hand in frustration, turning toward the door. "We've been through all this."

"Wait," Pete said, taking Carla's hand. "I'm sorry. I know. We have. Just stay."

Carla listened.

"Can I ask you a question," Pete said.

"Yes."

"Tell me again why you were distant with me for those couple of months."

Carla gave a her husband a strange look. "Why?"

"Because I just want to know."

"We were behind some issues, missed some deadlines at work, and things got really hectic."

Pete lifted the glass Carla had been drinking from, turned it up, finished the last of the water, set it back down on the counter, and said, "I want you to listen to what I say, and appreciate what I do, because this will prove to you how much I want things to get better for us."

"What are you talking about, Pete?"

"I'm talking about you lying to me. There were no late issues, because you were seeing Wayne during those two months. He told me everything, Carla. That he's been after you since you left him. Why didn't you tell me that?"

"I . . ."

"It's not important," Pete said, raising a finger, to hush his wife. "Because although I see now that even though you weren't having sex with him, you were cheating with Wayne long before I stepped out on you. I'm going to forgive that, if you say that you will drop all this nonsense about continuing to see him."

"I can't do that."

"I am not the only one that's wrong here. You were seeing him behind my back, and now you want permission to do it. And you have the nerve to blame it all on me. How dare you! When you married me, you weren't really over him, were you?"

Carla looked away.

"Answer me!" Pete yelled.

"No."

"You were still in love with him, which means this marriage was destined to fail. We had no chance. And you sleeping with another man had nothing to do with my cheating on you—it was just an opportunity for you to get back with Wayne."

"That's not true," Carla said. "You suggested Wayne on your own."

"But you didn't fight me on it. Didn't even question it. Just went right along. But now everything is out," Pete said, walking right up to Carla, who stepped away, pressed her back against the counter.

"So because we are married, and you are my wife, and that takes precedence over everything else, I'm asking you to please not see Wayne again. Will you do that for me?"

"I can't," Carla said. "I'm sorry, and I told you why, but I can't."

"Then now I'm telling you," Pete said, raising his finger again to her face. "Do not let me find out that you have seen him again, or there will be problems."

"Don't threaten me, Pete. I'm not afraid of you."

"I'm not threatening you, and I don't want you to be afraid of me. I'm just giving you valuable information that I think you need to seriously consider."

53

Carla sat in her office at the magazine, Laci pacing in front of her desk.

"You should pack your things and get the hell out of there, and then call the police on his ass."

"Why?" Carla said, seeming relatively calm. "He hasn't done anything."

"It's not about what he's done. It's what he's gonna do. What he's threatened to do."

"He hasn't threatened to do anything. Pete is angry, and he has a right to be, but he's not a violent man."

"And what do you call him beating the hell out of Wayne? Nonviolent?"

"That has never happened before, and nothing like it will ever happen again. Trust me."

"Famous last words," Laci said. "Famous last words. So you're going to stop seeing Wayne?"

Carla stood from her chair. "No," she said, confidently. "I told Pete that I'm not afraid of him, and I meant it. Everything I said that I'm going to do, I'm going to follow through on."

"And what if Pete decides he's going to follow through on his promises?"

"I don't think that's going to happen. But if it does, we'll cross that bridge when we come to it."

That evening, Carla and Wayne lay stripped down to their underwear, facing each other in his bed. They kissed and caressed, Wayne pulling his fingers through Carla's hair, Carla rubbing Wayne's evening beard and kissing the spots on his face that had not been injured in his tussle with her husband.

Candles burned on his dresser and on his nightstands, as one of Carla's favorite CDs played in his bedside stereo.

They had been lying there like that for better than an hour, since Carla had rung his doorbell at 6 P.M., after coming from work.

Pete had given her a warning last night, but she would not be intimidated. She'd told her husband that she was going to see Wayne, and that's exactly what she planned to do.

Carla threw her arms around Wayne's neck, slid closer to him, kissing him on the ear, whispering to him, "I don't know why we're torturing ourselves like this. Who's great idea was this anyway?"

"You mean to lie in bed, practically naked, horny as hell, teasing one another?"

"Yeah," Carla said.

"Uh, that would've been yours."

"You didn't have to go along. You could've just said no."

"Yeah, right," Wayne said. "I was hoping to get lucky."

"Well, since you know that's not going to happen, let's get back to the game." Carla rolled onto her back, and asked, "If we were to get married, what kind of car would we drive?"

"Uh, a Range Rover for me," Wayne said. "And, something sensible . . . uh, how about a 'ninety-two Hyundai for you. Oh yeah, with a baby car seat, and old bumper stickers on the back."

"A Hyundai!" Carla said, rolling over, jumping on Wayne, straddling him. "Don't you know part of the reason why I'm here right now is because you're a doctor and you make ridiculous amounts of money. If you aren't planning on spending way too much of it on me once we're married, then I'm leaving right now."

"Okay. How about a Suzuki?" Wayne said.

"How about a Benz?"

"What's wrong with your Beamer?"

"I need an upgrade. I want a Benz, brand spankin' new. The biggest one they make," Carla said.

"Are you worth all that?"

"You'd only find out after we're married. Now it's your turn. Ask me something."

Wayne grabbed Carla's hand, brought it to his lips, kissed it, and said, "If we were to get married, and had a child, what would we name it?"

"It wouldn't be an it," Carla said. "The baby would be a girl, and we'd name her Morning."

"You mean like the time of day. Have you been thinking about that one for a while, or did it just pop into your head?"

"It's beautiful. Don't you think? Morning," Carla said, reciting the name again. "Like the perpetual rebirth of the world and every living thing in it. A pure start, a fresh beginning—Morning."

"Kind of like us," Wayne said.

"Yeah," Carla said, smiling and giving Wayne a quick kiss on the lips.

"And if we had two more kids, what would we name them? Noon and Night?"

"Your jokes stink."

"You know you love them."

"No, Dr. Mason," Carla said, sliding off Wayne's body, and lying beside him. "What I love is you."

"And I you," Wayne said, rolling on top of Carla. "But can you believe it?"

"What?"

"That we're here, now, like this. I always knew we were meant to be together, that you were the person I would ultimately be with, even when you were married to Pete. But it would get hard some times. Sometimes I would think, when I was trying to get you to hear me out, to tell you how sorry I was, that you would never listen to me."

"I was listening, Wayne."

"I would do everything I could, even things I knew that I shouldn't have been doing, not because I was disrespectful of what you and Pete had, but because I knew it should've been us. All I wanted you to do was know that."

"I knew it."

"And now it feels like it could actually happen."

"How do you feel about that?" Carla said, reaching up to touch to his face.

Wayne looked down at Carla, and what she could see by the candlelight, the half that was not cloaked in shadows, was something very near sadness. "I'm happy, because we're back together, at least in some way," he said. "And I think God made us for one another. Soul mates, you know. But I also think of my brother. I think of Pete, I think of Me'Shell and wonder whether my happiness should come at the expense of their pain."

Carla stared up at Wayne. "You're thinking about them now, aren't you?"

"Yes."

"Do you regret leaving Me'Shell?"

Wayne turned more toward her to make his point. "No. I'm not saying that. And even though I knew they would have to be hurt in order for us to pursue something together, I just wish it didn't have to be that way." He paused. "But no, I want you here."

"I know that. And it's okay for you to think about them. It's why I've always loved you the way I do, because you're so compassionate."

Wayne sighed deeply, pulled away from Carla, and sat on the edge of the bed, facing away from her.

"It's seven thirty. You should probably get going, before he goes crazy again."

Hearing that, she considered telling Wayne about the threat Pete had made last night, but she realized all that would do was have Wayne worrying needlessly about actions she knew Pete had no intentions of carrying out.

Carla stepped out of bed and stood in front of Wayne, draping her arms around his shoulders.

"Will you be all right?"

He managed a smile, took her by the waist and pulled her closer. "Only if I can see you tomorrow. We can go out, window shop or something. Because if I have you in my bed again, I won't be responsible for what I might do."

"You got yourself a deal."

54

When Carla walked in, it was five minutes to eight.

The patio doors were open. She imagined Pete was out there, which would give her the opportunity to go up to their room without him knowing she was even home.

That's exactly what Carla was about to do, heading over toward the stairs, and then she stopped herself, knowing that she was wrong for trying to avoid her own husband.

They were going through some things, but she didn't have to treat him as though he was a stranger, she told herself, as she started toward the patio doors.

Carla stepped out onto the deck, and Pete was there, sitting on the top step, half a bottle of beer beside him, staring up at the star-filled sky.

"How's it going?" Carla said, not knowing what to expect from him, what he would say.

Pete turned, looked back at her, smiled a little. "Hey. Where were you?"

Carla froze, paused, was caught off guard, even though she should've expected that very question.

"Never mind," Pete said. "How was work today? Busy?"

"As always."

"How about for you?" Carla asked.

Pete didn't answer right away, for he was taking a sip from his beer. When he set it down, he said, "I didn't go in today. I'm taking a little time off, I think."

Carla didn't dare ask him why. She was pretty sure she knew the answer.

"You know how long it's been since I had a vacation? Or just had time to sit out on the deck and stare up at the stars?"

"No. How long?"

"I don't know," Pete said. "But if you can't remember, that's probably a little too long. What do you think?"

"I guess you're right," Carla said, feeling herself relax a little, and she realized that it had been so long since she had felt this comfortable with him. "You mind if I sit out here with you?"

"Do you want to?" Pete said, sounding surprised.

"Sure," Carla said, sitting on the step just below him, leaning against the banister posts.

Pete and Carla gazed up at the sparkling stars overhead for a while in silence, until he said, "I don't want to argue about this anymore with you, Carla."

"Okay."

"But I have to ask you one last question."

"Pete," Carla said, placing a hand on his knee. "Maybe we shouldn't discuss—"

"What did he do to you?"

"Pete, why are you doing this to yourself?"

"What did Wayne do to you that night at the hotel to make you want to sleep with him?" Pete said, sadly.

"I'm not going to do this tonight," Carla said, standing up and starting back toward the door.

"Carla, please!" Pete called.

And Carla thought she heard an emotion in her husband's voice that she had never heard before. She spun around, and the man looked like a child, his chin sunk into his chest, seemingly on the verge of tears.

"I love you so much," Pete continued, his voice quivering. "Everything was going fine for us, and then one day it was like you just didn't care anymore. You weren't yourself. But I will not believe it was because you were loving Wayne when you should've been loving me. I won't believe it!" Pete said loudly, as the tears spilled over.

"Pete," Carla said, taking a step back toward her husband. "It wasn't that."

"Then what did he say to you? What did he do?"

"It doesn't matter," Carla said, going to him and wrapping her arms around him, holding him tight, shushing him.

"Did he trick you?" Pete said, holding on to Carla as if he had nothing else. "Because you could've told me. You could've told me and I would've done something."

Carla continued to hold her husband, but he felt weak, his knees giving way, and she lowered herself with him to the steps, never letting go of him.

"He didn't trick me, but it doesn't matter, because that night is over," Carla said, smoothing her hand back and forth across Pete's back, trying not cry herself. "I'm here now, and I'm not going back to that hotel."

"But you're leaving. I can feel it, and it's driving me crazy," Pete said, crying even harder now, which triggered tears from Carla's eyes.

"A man isn't supposed to have to go through this, knowing his wife is loving another man. He can only bear so much pain," Pete said, still holding tight to Carla, rocking her back and forth.

"I'm sorry, baby," Carla said, holding onto him as tightly as she could, all the while trying to ease his pain. "I'm so sorry."

"I just want it to stop," Pete cried. "Make it stop. Please make it stop."

55

This morning was a busy one for Wayne.

Upon walking into the clinic, his secretary said, "Doctor Barnes won't be coming in this morning, or for the rest of the week."

"Did he say when he would be coming back?" Wayne asked.

"No."

"Did you ask him, Mary?"

"Yes, and he didn't say."

"Well, what *did* he say?" Wayne said, feeling himself becoming frustrated.

"Nothing. He just hung up."

Wayne saw all his patients, and all of Pete's, too.

He thought of calling Pete but decided against it. Half of the practice was his, and Wayne knew he wasn't so irresponsible that he would allow all that was going on to affect it for much longer.

Wayne dealt with the extra work as best he could and concentrated on the thought of seeing Carla later.

But when they did get together, went to Water Tower Place mall, Carla was distant.

He noticed that from the moment they met in front of Marshall Fields and he leaned in to kiss her lips.

She turned her head slightly, seeming to prefer a kiss on her cheek.

He made light conversation, as they took the escalator and walked the halls. Wayne made most of the comments on the clothes displayed in the windows, or whatever other items they had gone in a particular store to see.

After nearly forty-five minutes of Carla pretending she was listening to what he was saying, of Carla half holding his hand, and half acting like she even wanted to be there, Wayne suggested they go to in the food court for something to eat.

He wasn't very hungry, and Carla said she had no appetite, so they settled on the coffee shop in the center of the busy, people-filled dining area.

Wayne brought an iced coffee and a muffin back to the table. He sat across from Carla, who seemed to be mentally somewhere else.

"Tell me what's going on," Wayne said.

"Nothing," Carla said, looking down at her hands folded in her lap.

"You aren't even looking at me when you talk to me. You might have only looked me in the eye twice since we met today. Yesterday, everything was fine, but—"

"And everything is fine today," Carla said. "I just feel a little tired."

"Why?"

"I was up late."

"Why?"

Carla looked off in another direction.

"Why?" Wayne urged again.

"Because Pete was having a rough night. He broke down crying and asking all sorts of questions, and—"

"What kind of questions?" Wayne asked.

"I don't know, because most of it was babble. All I could do was hold him and tell him that everything was going to be all right."

"And what did you mean by that?"

Carla looked up at Wayne. "What do you mean, what did I mean by that?"

"You know what I'm asking. Does that mean you're going to be with him? Are you bailing out on this? You reconsidering everything we talked about?"

"No," Carla said, seeming annoyed by Wayne's questions. "I'm not bailing out or reconsidering. You're not the only one concerned about how this is affecting Pete. Yes, I want to see what, if anything, there is for you and me, Wayne. But let's not forget that Pete is still my husband, and I do still love him," Carla said. She closed her eyes for a moment, then said, "I really think I need to be going."

She stood up.

"I'm sorry," Wayne said, standing up, too. "That was selfish of me," he said, taking Carla in an embrace in the middle of the crowded food court, some people looking in their direction, most minding their own business. "I guess I just got a little jealous." Wayne kissed her on the cheek.

Carla hugged him back.

"Are you all right? Do you need anything?" he asked.

"Just for you to be understanding," Carla said.

And Wayne was about to answer her, tell her that he would be from this moment on, but someone had caught his eye, a woman, one he had hoped wasn't who he thought she was, but a moment later, Wayne saw that it was indeed Me'Shell.

She was halfway across the huge food court, at the register of another restaurant, but upon turning around, her eyes immediately locked with Wayne's, and he could see all the hurt on her face.

At that moment, all he wanted to do was disappear and take Carla with him, because although Carla's back was to Me'Shell, it was clear from the expression on Me'Shell's face that she knew it was Carla that Wayne was holding so tightly, out in the middle of everything for everyone to see.

Wayne wanted to look away, but he found it was impossible.

He unwillingly held Me'Shell's gaze for another moment, until Carla pulled away and kissed him lightly on the lips.

"I'll call you when I get the time," Carla said.

"All right," Wayne said, looking away from Me'Shell. "Take care, and let me know if you need anything." When Wayne looked back up, his ex-fiancée was gone.

56

Pete hadn't meant to break down in front of his wife like that.

He had told himself that he was going to be strong, that he was going to behave as though nothing bothered him, that he would allow her to do what she needed to do.

But seeing her, knowing that she had just come from Wayne's house, the emotions just came from nowhere, and no matter how much he tried, he could not hide or control them. They rushed to the surface, faster and more powerful than he anticipated, and that's why he was bawling like a child.

But she was there for him.

Carla held him, cried with him, apologized a million times for what she was putting him through, and would not leave his side.

She held him tight as they both fell off to sleep some time around three.

He was thankful for the attention and love she had given him last night, but what Pete could not deny was the fact that Carla never once said that she would stop seeing Wayne.

She told Pete that she loved him and things would get better, but she didn't say how, when, or if the situation would actually improve for himself or for Wayne.

Before Carla left for work this morning, she had leaned over

Pete and kissed him good-bye, something she hadn't done in months.

Pete stirred, gently took her wrist, and said, "I'll see you after work?"

Carla paused a moment before saying, "Yeah. I have a couple of errands to run, but I'll be back afterward. Do you need anything?"

"Just you," Pete said, sitting up in bed a little to give his wife another kiss.

But this evening, Pete paced about the house, looking at the clock, saw that it was ten minutes to six.

He had called Carla's office, spoken to Laci, and found out that Carla had left a little before five.

She was probably running those errands, Pete told himself, but when he called her phone a total of three times, she did not answer. That made him suspicious, made him think things that he didn't want to think.

He had gotten in his car, trying not to imagine his wife was with Wayne, but he knew that she was, could just feel it. Even though he had warned her, she still persisted. And Wayne, he didn't even want to think about the man who had claimed to be his best friend, his brother for so many years.

Pete had hurt him, beat him in the face like he hated him, and Pete was truly sorry about that. But despite the beating, the warning, Wayne would not listen. He just wouldn't, and that's why when Pete finally stopped his car, he was looking up at a police station.

He got out, stalled for a moment, knowing that if he continued with what he was thinking, things could forever change for him and Wayne.

Pete gave it another moment of thought, thinking about where Carla probably was that minute, and decided that this had to be done.

Pete was greeted by an aging male officer, with graying hair and a thick unkempt mustache. He sat behind a long counter with two other officers.

"May I help you, sir?" the officer asked.

"I'm here to fill out a report."

"What's the complaint?" the officer said, pulling a form from a stack, and setting the point of his pen on the first line.

"My wife is committing adultery, and I want you to arrest the man she's seeing."

The officer slowly looked up from the form to Pete. "Sir, maybe that's something you should discuss with the man, or your wife."

"I've already done that, and they continue as though I've given them no warning."

"Then maybe you should have another talk."

"Adultery is a crime in Illinois. Is that correct?" Pete said, annoyed.

"To tell you the truth sir, I know it used to be, but I don't know if it still is."

The officer swiveled around in his chair toward the officer at the other end of the counter. "Meyers," he called to the other cop. "Screwing around on your spouse, that still a crime?"

"Uh, yeah. Can't remember the last time someone filed a complaint, or the last time we actually picked someone up for it, but yeah, that's still a no-no," the officer replied.

The mustached cop turned back to Pete. "I guess you're right."

"So what happens now?" Pete asked.

"You fill out the report. We put out a warrant for your wife and this guy's arrest."

"Hold it," Pete said. "I just want to press charges against him. Can I do that?"

"Sir, just makes our job easier," the officer said. "So, if you know where he lives, we go and pick him up and take him to jail."

"Can I tell you where he works? Will that do?" Pete said.

"Sure thing," the officer said, his pen raised above the form. "What's his name?"

"Wayne Mason," Pete said.

57

No matter how much he tried, Wayne could not get Me'Shell out of his mind, the look on her face, her evident pain.

All the way home after leaving the mall, Wayne watched his cell phone, checked more than once to make sure the thing wasn't on silent or vibrate, just in case she called.

After getting home, he tried to watch TV, tried to settle himself, stop thinking about what she must've thought when she saw him hugging and kissing Carla. He needed to stop thinking about what she was probably going through at that moment.

But Wayne had to ask himself if he still had feelings for the woman.

He stopped pacing, stood in the middle of his living room, the butts of his palms pushed into his eyes, telling himself that could not be the case. It just couldn't be, because if it was, he wouldn't have dismissed her so quickly, treated her so badly.

Wayne thought about that, how he had mistreated her yet again, when all she did was love him, be sweet, honest, and selfless.

He had told himself he would never do that again, after she had walked in on him kissing Carla. He had gone so far as to take her and ask her father for her hand in marriage, and what had he done after that? Exactly the thing he said he would not do.

Wayne fell back onto his sofa, tried to close his mind to the series of thoughts he was experiencing, but he could not.

There was a question he needed to ask himself. Did he still love her?

"Yes," he said, aloud, anger in his voice.

But he loved Carla more, didn't he?

He had done the right thing, he persuaded himself, letting his head fall back against the sofa, closing his eyes. He had to tell himself that if he had it to do all over again, he would've done the exact same thing. Because even if he did change his mind and wanted Me'Shell back, she would never have him, Wayne told himself. Or would she?

58

Later that night, Pete lay in bed with his wife again. It was past midnight, and they had been lying there and holding each other for the last hour.

"I am really sorry about how all this is happening," Carla said, her voice soft, low.

"It's not your fault," Pete said, snuggling closer to her. "And I think it's best we not even talk about it anymore, because something tells me everything is going to work out the way it's supposed to."

Carla moved closer to him, tilting her head up, kissing him on the corner of his jaw.

"Last night, remember when I said I haven't taken a vacation in forever?" Pete said.

"Yeah."

Pete pulled away from Carla, sat up in bed. "Well, I think we should get away," he said, sounding excited. "In light of everything that's going on, let's get away. It would do us good."

It had only been a matter of hours since Pete had filled out the police report, and going by the reputation of most city services, Pete figured he had a little time, maybe a couple of days, even possibly a week before they showed up at the clinic. But when they did come to put the cuffs on Wayne, Pete knew Carla would be the first person he'd call, and Pete wanted his wife safely outside of cell phone range, or at least so far away that there would be nothing she could do.

"What do you think?" Pete said, the excited grin still on his face.

"Where are you thinking of?" Carla asked, not seeming totally against the idea.

"How about Aruba? We've always wanted to go there."

Carla frowned a little, shook her head. "I don't want to be away from the magazine that long."

Pete knew that meant she didn't want to be away from Wayne that long. But he did not give up. "Okay, then the weekend. Two days. We drive up to Lake Geneva. Relax, do a little boating, toast some marshmallows by a campfire."

Carla sat up, looked as though she was envisioning what Pete was offering, and seeming to like what was playing out in her head.

"Come on. We could sleep under the stars in sleeping bags."

"You know the only thing I'm sleeping in is a bed," Carla said.

"Okay, then we could push the bed outside, and sleep under the stars in a bed. C'mon, it'll be fun. We'll forget about everything that's happening here and just enjoy ourselves."

"Can you let me check what's coming up at work tomorrow, before I give you a definite yes?"

"Just say yes, now," Pete urged.

"I can't, Pete."

Again, he knew what was going on, but he said, "Sure. Find out. But if nothing serious is pending, will you go?"

Pete knew that this could be a major moment in turning things around for them.

Carla had to think about it longer than Pete liked, but she finally said, "Sure. I'll go."

"Great," Pete said, scooting over to Carla and giving her a quick kiss on the lips. After he pulled away and saw that she was still looking him in the face, Pete leaned in again, kissed her mouth once more, slower, more passionately.

He felt himself getting aroused.

It had been so long since he had made love to Carla that he felt close to exploding just from kissing her.

Pete caressed her arm, and laid her down on the bed. He positioned himself on top of her, continuing to kiss her.

He kissed her cheek, her ear, and started down her neck.

"I missed you so much," Pete whispered, rubbing one of her breasts, lifting up her top, kissing her nipple, sucking her.

He remained there for a moment, kissing her left breast, then her right, massaging them in his hands, not hearing his wife responding to what he was doing, but so involved himself, that it did not matter to him.

He smoothed the side of his face across her soft, flat belly, slid a hand under her behind, squeezed it, and then he sunk his fingers inside the waist of his wife's satin shorts and started to pull them down.

"Wait, Pete," Carla said, her hands on top of his.

"What?"

"We shouldn't."

"Why not?" he said, pulling himself up, so he could lie face to face with his wife.

"Because . . . it's just not the right time."

"Is it because you're on your cycle?"

"I'm not on. It's just that—"

"But aren't you normally—"

"Pete, I said I'm not on. It's just not the right time. Can you understand that?"

Once again, Pete knew this probably had something to do with Wayne. Carla said that while she was seeing him, she wouldn't have sex with Wayne, but Pete never thought she meant the same for him.

"I understand," Pete said, doing his best not to become angry, trying to come off as sympathetic as he could, hoping that would make his wife's decision to leave with him on their trip easier.

Pete rolled over, turned his back to his wife.

Carla hugged him from behind, kissed his neck, and said, "Thank you."

An hour later, while Carla was deep in sleep, Pete stood over the toilet, his boxers fallen to his feet, angrily masturbating. After his body tightened, and he had released himself, he experienced something, although fleeting, he had never felt for Wayne. Hate.

59

The next day, Wayne stood beside his desk at work.

He was frozen by indecision, by what Pete had just said to him.

A moment ago, there was a knock on Wayne's door, and when he said "Come in," he was both surprised and pleased to see Pete.

Pete walked in, just stared at Wayne for a long moment, then said, "Do you remember when we were in medical school? That time I got into it with Craig Lipton because he just wouldn't leave me alone, and I beat him so badly he had to go to the hospital. I didn't mean to do that, but it was like something snapped in me. I didn't even know what I was doing."

"Yeah," Wayne said, not knowing what had brought on this subject, if it was supposed to be some sort of threat.

"But when it was over, I saw him at my feet, bleeding. It all came back."

"They were going to expel you."

"But you told them how he wouldn't leave me alone. How he messed with me every chance he got. But they weren't hearing that," Pete said. "One semester till graduation and they were trying to expel me . . . until you told them that if I didn't graduate, then you wouldn't either."

"Yeah, I said that."

"That was telling 'em, Wayne," Pete said. "But I guess you were surprised when they said they didn't give a shit."

"Yeah. But they changed their tune when I convinced my father to tell them that he would pull all the donation money he was giving to the university every year."

"Yeah, they practically said I didn't even have to finish the last semester, and I could still graduate," Pete said, chuckling a little.

Wayne laughed with him until Pete stopped.

"I couldn't believe you did that for me."

"And I would do it till this day. You know I would, Pete."

Pete didn't respond to the comment, but turned to the wall behind him, looked at a framed photo of him and Wayne, an elderly man standing between them, all three of them smiling.

"And how about the first day we opened the clinic." Pete took the frame from the wall and held it out for him to see.

"Yeah, I remember old Mr. Ruben, our first patient, all the attention we gave him," Wayne said. "What did he always say, Pete?"

"That if heaven was like this, he wouldn't mind dying. Those were the days," Pete said, walking back to the wall and rehanging the photo.

"And we will never have times like those again if we continue to stay at odds with each other," Wayne said. "We need to work this out. What do you think? I know we can get through this."

"Wayne—" Pete said, turning around.

"Pete, I know it feels fucked up now, but that's how I felt when you married Carla. But I got over that. I dealt with it for the sake of our friendship."

"You dealt with that so you could stay near her, so you could steal her back when the opportunity presented itself."

"It may seem like that," Wayne said, standing up from his chair. "But after a while I did accept it. When you told me that you were going to tell Carla you cheated, I told you not to, because I knew it would cause you trouble. If all I was thinking about was getting Carla back, I would've said, sure, go right ahead and tell her."

"And how about when we were sixteen. We said we'd never let a woman get in the way of our friendship."

"The pact?" Pete said.

"Yeah. The pact."

"We aren't sixteen anymore. Haven't been in a long time."

"Pete," Wayne said, stepping from around his desk and over to him. He placed a hand behind Pete's neck. "I love you, man. Tell me you won't miss our friendship. Yeah, our offices will still be down the hall from one another's, but what will we have if we aren't even talking?"

Pete gently took Wayne's hand away. "We won't even have the offices. That's what I came to tell you. I know Carla was with you yesterday. I told you not to see her. I warned you that I would do something, and still you didn't listen. You don't respect my wishes, or my marriage. Why would I think you'd still respect my friendship."

Pete walked toward the door, and before he walked out and closed it, he said, "Find yourself a new partner, Wayne. I'm leaving the practice."

Wayne stood there, frozen, not believing what Pete had just said. His childhood friend, the man he had known for almost thirty years was about to exit his life, totally and for good.

If Wayne let him leave the practice, there was a good chance that he'd never see Pete again.

Taking that into consideration, Wayne wondered if the possibility of being with Carla was worth losing Pete? She gave him no guarantees that they would even be together, that this dating thing would even work out.

But if Wayne just stepped out now, told Pete not to worry any longer, that he would no longer fight for Carla, he could save his friendship, his practice, and still remain close to Carla, even if it was just as a friend of her husband's.

If nothing else, it was a thought, Wayne told himself. He didn't know if that was exactly what he would come to Pete with, but he would tell him something. The last thing Wayne wanted to do was see his best friend leave.

Wayne started to walk down the hall to Pete's office, when he was startled by the two uniformed police officers standing in his doorway, a static-filled voice coming from one officer's walkie-talkie.

"Can I help you?" Wayne said.

"Are you Wayne Mason?" the officer with the bushy mustache said.

"Yes, I'm Doctor Mason. What can I do for you?"

"You can turn around so I can put these handcuffs on you. Sir, you're under arrest for adultery."

60

Pete didn't know exactly how to feel, as he watched Wayne being led out in handcuffs like a common criminal, past all of his patients in the waiting room.

He told himself that Wayne deserved it, that if he had only listened to Pete, then this wouldn't have happened.

But Pete couldn't help but feel sorry for the man as well, and he felt some guilt, too.

The short conversation they had in his office had struck a chord with Pete. In the past Wayne had done so much for him. But the line had to be drawn on gratitude.

But as Pete was driving home from work later that day, he was surprised that the police had followed up on the warrant so quickly. He had thought they wouldn't show up until the next day at the earliest, after he and Carla were already on the road, hours away.

But that wasn't the way it had happened, and when Pete got home at a little after one in the afternoon, he just hoped that Carla hadn't heard about what he'd done.

When he saw her suitcase packed and sitting near the door, he took it as a good sign. Pete would go upstairs, do a quick repacking job of some of the clothes he had recently unpacked, and rush them out of the city, hopefully so far out in the woods, that she'd have no phone service, not be able to receive Wayne's call.

He was on his way upstairs when Carla hurried into the living room from down the hall, her car keys in her hand, a worried look on her face.

When she saw her husband, she stopped and gave him a look that made it clear she knew everything.

"Is everything all right?" Pete asked, hoping he was wrong.

"You're a bastard!" Carla said, shoving past him toward the door.

Pete grabbed hold of her. "Where are you going?"

"To bail Wayne out. What was on your mind, having him arrested?"

"I had a right. What he's doing is illegal, and if he doesn't want to listen to me, maybe he'll hear the police."

"And to think, after everything we discussed the last couple of nights, that I was seriously considering stopping all this. To think I was actually looking forward to spending time alone with you."

"We can still go," Pete said, holding her arm tighter. "Nothing has changed. You and me, last night. We can just go."

"Keep on thinking that, Pete. Now let go of my arm."

"Where are you going?"

"I already told you," Carla said, pulling away from Pete, heading toward the door.

"Stop, goddammit!" Pete yelled louder than he had ever before. "What the fuck is wrong with you? You are about to walk out on your husband to save some man from being punished for what he has done to me. Don't you understand what you're doing? Or has he just got you so twisted around his finger that you're willing to do anything for him?"

"I'm not twisted around his finger."

"What did he do to you?" Pete said. "You never answered my question from the other night. What did he do to you to make you act like this?"

"I told you, I'm not going to talk about that."

"Did he pay you, like a prostitute? Or maybe you were cheaper than that. Maybe all he needed to give you was a little game and a chicken dinner like the women on Thirty-fifth Street."

"I'm telling you, Pete," Carla said angrily. "You need to watch your mouth, before you get your feelings hurt."

"My feelings have already been hurt. Over and over and over again, by you. There's nothing more you can do," Pete taunted. "So you might as well tell me. Did he give it to you good? Did he fuck you the way you liked?"

"Stop it."

"Did you give it to him doggy style, let him fuck you from behind?" Pete persisted.

"Stop it!" Carla yelled.

"Did you suck his dick like some stank-ass trick?" Pete said.

Carla didn't answer that. At first she seemed to have shut down, but then she said, "Fine. You want to know, then yeah, I gave it to him doggy style, and yeah, he hit it exactly the way I like it, but you wouldn't know what I was talking about, because your shit is always so weak. And you know what, Pete. We didn't follow your little contract, either. I fucked him more than once. We fucked three times, Pete," Carla said, holding up as many fingers in front of him. "And it was good, it was great! I came like eight times. Came so hard that the mattress was soaked, but we didn't care, just kept on fucking anyway, wanted to soak it all the way through to the floor, it was so damn good. And to answer your last question. I most definitely sucked his dick. I let him come in my mouth, and the rest I let him shoot all over my face. Isn't that how stank-ass tricks do it, Pete?"

Pete did all he could to control himself, to stop himself from doing what his body was so desperately begging him to do. He tried, but failed, and felt his arm slicing the air, his open hand slapping his wife across the face.

Her head whipped around, her body following, spiraling to the floor.

Pete stepped closer to Carla, looked down at her.

But even though he was angrier with her than he had ever been, he was still conflicted. He wanted to reach down, pick her up, hold her and tell her that everything was going to be all right, that they would be fine. It was what he prayed for, what he still wanted for them, but he didn't know if that would ever be possible again after this.

Carla pulled herself quickly from the floor, hair falling in her face, hiding her tear-stained cheeks. She headed again for the door.

"Carla, I'm sorry," Pete said. "Don't go."

"Fuck you, Pete!" Carla said.

"You walk out that door, bail Wayne out, then you've made your choice."

Carla halted for a moment, then said, "If that's how you see it, then it's settled. The choice is made."

61

As Wayne sat behind bars, waiting for Carla to come to his rescue, everything became painfully clear to him.

This morning, when Pete told him he no longer wanted to be his partner, Wayne knew he could not let that happen.

Sitting in that cell, hearing the loud voices, cursing, yelling, echoing around him, he thought about his feelings for Carla, tried to measure just how deeply they ran.

There was no denying that he loved her, but was it the same love that he had felt for her those two years ago when he was going to marry her, or had he been so actively pursuing her because he was trying to recapture what had been stolen from him?

Wayne had never seriously asked himself these questions before, knowing that they would force him to give strong answers, might make him accept things he didn't want to accept.

But with everything that was going on, the very real possibility of not only losing his brother, but also his partner, Wayne decided that even if he would forever feel the pain of letting Carla go, it was what he needed to do. For himself, for Carla, and for Pete.

But his decision wasn't solely selfless. It had something to do with Me'Shell. Maybe it took seeing her once again to jar loose the feelings that he had stored away so deeply in his mind, but he couldn't stop thinking about her.

He remembered the times they had spent together and how much he loved just being around her. Unlike the questions that would pop up when dealing with Carla, who did she really love, who would she ultimately choose, Wayne was always certain that Me'Shell loved no one but him, would damn near give her life for him, and it was sad that it took him till this moment to realize just how much that meant.

So when the officer unlocked Wayne's cell and told him that his bail had been posted, Wayne knew what he would have to do.

While Carla was driving him home, angry as hell, cursing and honking at cars, Wayne was in an entirely different place.

He saw himself telling Pete that he would no longer pursue Carla. Wayne would tell him that their friendship meant too much to him and that their pact would remain unbroken. The smallest smile appeared on Wayne's lips at the thought of him and Pete embracing, how happy Pete would be when he received the news that Wayne was now so eager to give him.

And then there was Me'Shell. He would buy her a dozen of the most beautiful roses. No, two dozen, and he would appear at her house, the ring in his possession, and once again, he would propose. But this time he would mean it. Better yet, this time he would kidnap her. They'd board a plane tonight, fly to Vegas and get married, once and for all.

That's exactly what he'd do, Wayne thought, smiling even wider, until Carla pulled her car to a stop in front of Wayne's house and turned to him.

"I still can't believe he did that to you," Carla said.

And then Wayne was forced to think about the woman beside him, what all this news would mean to her. He would tell her that he changed his mind, simple as that. That he was sorry for pursuing her, for ruining her marriage. He truly was. He would tell her that he hoped everything would turn out all right for her and Pete, and that he would do anything in his power to ensure that it did. But he knew that wouldn't fly with her. She would be angry, she would hate him, and he would probably lose her friendship. But if he had a decision to make regarding which relationship he would keep, Wayne decided that moment it would be Pete's.

"Wayne, did you hear me?" Carla said. "Why did Pete do this to you?"

"He must've been pretty angry," Wayne said, returning from his thoughts.

"It doesn't matter. I thought I knew him, but I guess I didn't. Wayne," Carla said, shifting toward him in her seat, "I think I'm going to leave him."

"No," Wayne said. "You shouldn't make that type of decision in the heat of the moment. He thought he had reason to do what he did, and in his mind it was justified. That doesn't mean he's not the same man he's always been."

"Maybe you're right. Can we go inside and talk about it? There's just so much going through my head right now."

"Uh," Wayne hesitated. "There are some things I really need to do. Can we get together later?"

Carla looked oddly at him. "I just told you that I think I'm going to leave my husband, something that I thought you'd be somewhat happy to hear, at least mildly interested. But now you want me to go?"

"Carla, I know you're going through some things right now, but I'm going through this with you. I just spent most of the day in jail," Wayne said. "There are just some things I need to take care of, and then we can talk about all of this as much as you want. Is that okay with you?"

"You're right. I'm sorry."

Wayne leaned over and gave Carla a hug.

"Call me on my cell phone when you're done, because I think I'm going to be at Laci's. I'm in no hurry to say anything to Pete right now."

62

So that was how they wanted to play things, Pete thought to himself.

Carla had gone to Wayne's rescue, even after Pete told her she would be making her decision if she went. Fine, there was nothing Pete could do about that. His wife chose to hurt him time after time, not caring about the condition that left him in, because she knew he would not leave her, and he could never knowingly hurt her the same way.

But Wayne was a different case.

Pete knew when Carla showed up, Wayne would be happy to see her, allow her to be there for him, as though she was his wife, and not Pete's, even after all Pete had done, all he had threatened the man with, Wayne just didn't care.

But unlike with Carla, where Pete could not stand the thought of hurting her, Pete could do harm to Wayne. It had only taken a moment after Carla had stormed out of the door, for Pete to realize what would hurt Wayne the most.

Pete jumped in his car, drove twenty-five minutes to her apartment, and he was happy to find Me'Shell at home to answer his knock.

She was surprised to see him there, but she was cordial and

when Pete asked whether he could talk with her, Me'Shell stepped aside and said, "Sure, come on in."

Pete looked around her small one bedroom apartment, and after he'd accepted her invitation to take a seat on the sofa, Me'Shell said, "So what brings you here?"

"I'm not going to play stupid and act as though you don't know what's been going on. Wayne has been seeing my wife, had been seeing her for some time, before I even found out about it."

"Pete, I'm so sorry," Me'Shell said. "Wayne had told me, and even though I wanted to go to you, I didn't think it was my place."

"And I appreciate that, Me'Shell. Your concern says enough. You're a truly considerate person, as I feel I am, but unfortunately, neither Wayne nor Carla care about anyone but themselves."

Me'Shell didn't respond, didn't say a word.

"You don't feel the same way?"

"Pete, Wayne has treated me badly, but . . . it doesn't change the fact that I still love him."

"And I love Carla. But that doesn't mean you can't get angry, fed up over the way he's treated you. That he proposed to you, just to leave you for someone that he once had a relationship with, that he had supposedly gotten over, but didn't. That doesn't piss you off, just a little?"

"Pete—"

"Just a little bit. Because you know, they're probably together right now. Like I said, they've been spending time together. Dating."

Me'Shell lowered her head. "I saw them yesterday together at Water Tower. They were hugging, kissing."

A jealous wave passed over Pete, but he controlled himself, knowing there was something here he needed to do. "And how did that make you feel?"

"Like he had never loved me. Like he lied to me, like he used me, just to get back with your wife."

"Me'Shell," Pete said, scooting closer to her on the couch, taking one of her hands, holding it with both of his. "I have to admit, that is why I'm here today."

"What are you talking about?"

"We are the ones who care, the ones who are open and honest with our feelings for them. But it doesn't matter. They know that it hurts us, but they're seeing each other, sleeping together. I know this is going to sound strange, but maybe we ought to do the same thing."

"What? Sleep together?"

"Yes."

Me'Shell looked strangely at Pete, but did not lean across and slap him as he thought she might have.

"Tell me what you're talking about," she said.

As Pete walked away from Me'Shell's apartment an hour later, he was happy, satisfied with what had gone down. The deal was made, the deed was done, and he couldn't wait till the next time he spoke to his so-called brother, because now Wayne would truly experience firsthand what Pete had been going through.

63

Half an hour later, Wayne waited nervously as Pete's cell phone rang.

"C'mon, Pete, pick up the phone," Wayne murmured. "I finally got some good news for you."

The phone rang two more times, and then Wayne heard Pete's voice on the other end.

"Why are you calling me?" he said.

"Because we need to talk. I have something very important to tell you. Can we meet? It won't take long, and I believe this will be something you'll want to hear."

Pete didn't answer for a moment, then said, "Yeah, we can meet. I think there's something I have to say that you'll want to hear yourself."

64

He wasn't going to bargain with Wayne, Pete told himself, as he walked back and forth in front of his car, looking out for Wayne's arrival.

They had agreed to meet in a parking lot, off Sixty-third and Lakeshore Drive. Pete told himself there was nothing that man had to say to him that he wanted to hear.

Wayne would want to strike some deal, try to reason with him about why he should be allowed to continue to see Carla, or maybe he'd try to come off even more bold, and tell Pete why he should just be allowed to marry her. Pete decided he would not hear a word from the man.

As Pete caught sight of Wayne's car pulling into the lot, he told himself he was there for one reason, to drop the bomb on him that he had made with Me'Shell—and he hoped it would do the damage that he had intended.

Wayne parked his car and stepped out. Wayne wore a smile, Pete a scowl. Wayne extended his hand toward Pete. "I'm here," Pete said, looking Wayne in the face. "We don't have to shake."

"Okay," Wayne said. "Then I'll just get to it. Yesterday, when I was in Water Tower mall—"

"With my wife," Pete said.

"What was that?"

"With my wife. You were telling a story, I just figured it might as well be the whole story. So," Pete said, continuing the story for Wayne. "While you were at Water Tower with my wife . . ."

"Okay," Wayne said. "When I was there, I saw—"

"Let me guess," Pete interrupted again. "Me'Shell. You saw Me'Shell there."

"Wow. How did you know that?"

"Because I spoke to her today."

"What do you mean, you spoke to her today?"

"Well," Pete said, leaning casually on a white Ford parked in front of them. "Actually, we did a little more than talk."

A look of concern appeared on Wayne's face, a look that Pete was happily hoping to see.

"I don't understand what you're talking about. What the hell were you doing over there anyway?"

"Wayne, there were some things on my mind that I really needed to talk about. Normally I'd do that with my wife, but since she was out spending time with you, I figured I had to find someone else. So I thought, since you were with Carla, then you definitely wouldn't be with Me'Shell. I called her. She said to come on by, which I did, and you wouldn't believe it," Pete said with a mocking smile. "One thing led to another, and we just landed in bed together."

"You're lying," Wayne said, looking angrier with each passing moment.

"I don't know how it happened, we were just chatting, and I guess, just the same way it happened at the hotel, my dick just slipped inside of her."

"You're a fucking liar!" Wayne said, staring hatefully at Pete, trembling with rage.

"Really, Wayne? Don't believe me? Go over there. Ask her for yourself. That is, if she's woken up yet. Because after the way I pounded that ass, she fell right to sleep," Pete said, smiling.

After that, Wayne rushed at Pete before he could realize what was happening. Wayne swung at him, hitting Pete with a punch that surprised him and dropped him to a knee.

But Pete wasn't dazed, wasn't hurt. He stood up quickly, rubbing a hand across his jaw, smiling and laughing a little, watching as Wayne ran to his car.

He called out to him, "And when you see her, tell her we're still on for tomorrow. There's some other tricks I want to try on her."

65

When Wayne got to Me'Shell's apartment, he threw his car door open, raced up the stairs, and banged wildly on her apartment door.

"Open up, Me'Shell. I know you're in there. Open up!"

The door was flung open and Me'Shell stood behind it.

It was all a lie, Wayne just knew, and she would tell him that. She would erase everything Pete said, all the images that had flooded Wayne's mind as he had sped over there like a madman.

"What is it! What are you doing here?" Me'Shell said. Gone was the smile she always had for him. She stared at him angrily.

Wayne pushed past her, into her apartment.

"I didn't say you could come in," she said. She was wearing a T-shirt with no bra over a pair of boxer shorts, and Wayne took notice. It looked like something she had thrown on after a shower, like she used to do when she was with Wayne, after he had made love to her.

"What were you doing this afternoon?" Wayne asked.

"What does that have to do with anything?"

"What were you doing?"

"That's none of your business."

"Were you with anyone?" Wayne asked.

"If there's something you want to know, why don't you just come out and ask me."

"Fine," Wayne said, swallowing hard, almost afraid to ask the question for fear of what the answer would be. "Was Pete here?"

And without hesitation, Me'Shell said, "Yes."

The answer shook Wayne, surprised him, made him even more fearful to ask his next question, but he had to know.

"What was he doing here?"

"We had sex," Me'Shell said, as though she did not care one bit as to how that remark affected Wayne.

Wayne stood there, his entire body numb, his legs feeling only as strong as twigs. "What?" he said.

"You heard me, Wayne. We had sex," Me'Shell said, anger in her voice. "He came over here, we talked, one thing led to another, and we were in my bed having sex."

"No," Wayne said, shaking his head.

"How does it feel, Wayne?"

"No," Wayne said again, trying to cover his ears with his hands, but Me'Shell wouldn't let him, kept pulling them away. "You wouldn't do that!"

"Why wouldn't I? Do you think you're the only one who can hurt someone, the only one who can just sleep the fuck around, forget that he has made promises to someone and just do what the fuck he wants, no matter how much that hurts someone else, no matter how much that person loves you? Well, I can do the same thing, Wayne. And I've done it," Me'Shell said, spitefully. She walked to the door, opened it. "Welcome to my world, Wayne. Now get the fuck out!"

66

"That'll be seven fifty-five," the Walgreen's cashier said to Carla.

She dug in her purse, gave the woman some crumpled bills. Her cell phone rang as she walked toward the door, trying to drop her change back into her purse.

"Hello," she said.

"It's Wayne. What are you doing?"

"Nothing, just leaving Walgreen's, buying a . . . never mind. I'm just leaving Walgreen's, why?

"Remember what you said earlier, about leaving Pete."

"Yeah."

"I think that may be a good idea now. Why don't you come by so we can talk more about it."

"Okay," Carla said, smiling. "I'll be right over."

67

"He hit me," Carla admitted sadly, after she had been at Wayne's for only a few minutes.

Wayne had sat her down and looked in her eyes. He knew that something was wrong. She tried to tell him it was nothing, but after he had asked for the third time, Carla had told him.

"Why?" Wayne said.

"Some things I said, that I shouldn't have."

Wayne stood, anger on his face. "Something has to be done. I need to go over there."

"No!" Carla said, grabbing him by the wrist, pulling him back down beside her. "Just leave it alone."

"Then what are we supposed to do?" Wayne asked. "I'm not going to just let him put his hands on you like that."

"I don't know, Wayne," Carla said, standing up and grabbing her purse from the end table. "I don't even want to think about it anymore. I have to use the bathroom."

She walked down the hall, closed herself in, and fell against the door, dropping her head into her palms.

"Please, don't let this be happening," she said to herself.

But she knew that it was, even before she dug into her purse and pulled out the Walgreen's bag with the home pregnancy test in it.

Her period came exactly the same time every month, and if it ever deviated, it would only be a day late.

But as Carla thought Pete suspected the other night, she should've been on her cycle that very moment. She was an entire week late, which never, ever happened. She would've dismissed it as effects from stress—Lord knows she had enough of it—but her body was giving her different signals.

She had been pregnant once before, in her twenties. She had it terminated, but she knew almost the day after she conceived that she was pregnant. She could just tell, and now her body was giving her the exact same hints.

She pulled the box out of the bag, tore it open, and peeled the wand out of the plastic. She ran the faucets to disguise what she was doing.

She prayed, "God, please not now. I want children, and I know they are a blessing, but not now." Carla looked down at the two little windows, then turned away before anything could appear.

She never thought it would be this way.

She had had sex with both Wayne and Pete. She had told Wayne not to come in her, and she thought he had withdrawn each time, but it still could've been his. There was always that slim chance.

What would she do?

How the hell would she tell either of them?

Should she get another abortion?

She fell against the bathroom wall again, pressed her palms to it, dropped her forehead against it, and with her eyes closed, prayed again.

She turned and checked the test.

When Carla returned from the bathroom, she set her purse down on the coffee table and sat down beside Wayne. He didn't speak to her, was just staring off into space, his mind somewhere else.

"Wayne," Carla said, placing a hand softly on his. "What's wrong?"

"There's something I have to tell you."

"What?"

"It must've been out of spite, to get back at me for seeing you." Wayne turned to look at Carla. "Pete slept with Me'Shell."

Carla gasped, could not believe what she had just heard. "No. He wouldn't do that."

"He told me he did," Wayne said.

"He was just trying—"

"I confirmed it with her. They did it." Wayne looked away, hurt. "I'm not telling you this to put more distance between you and Pete. I just think you should know what's going on."

Carla placed a hand on Wayne's shoulder, trying to comfort him. "I'm sorry."

"I could say the same thing to you. But this doesn't affect me now. Me'Shell is no longer mine, and she can do what she wants, with whom she wants."

He tried to sound as though none of what he had found out mattered to him, but Carla knew he was affected by it, just as she had been.

Carla slid closer to Wayne, wrapped her arms around him. "If we get nothing more from this information, it tells us that we no longer have to worry about their feelings, because they sure as hell aren't worried about ours."

68

When Carla opened her eyes again, a blurry Wayne was coming into focus.

"Wake up, Carla."

At first she didn't know where she was, didn't remember what had happened the hours before she had lain down, then it all of a sudden came to her. They must've fallen asleep.

She sprang up from the sofa. "What time is it?"

"Eleven forty-five," Wayne said.

Carla was exhausted. She ran a hand through her hair. "I gotta go."

"If Pete hit you, and you've been gone this long, maybe it's not a good idea for you to go back tonight," Wayne said, worry on his face.

"I'm not going to stay. I have a bag already packed in the living room. I'll get that, and come right back."

"Then I'll come with you."

"No. The last thing we need right now is you rolling up in the car with me," Carla said, grabbing her purse. She checked her phone. "Besides, he hasn't called me once. He probably doesn't even care that I'm gone."

69

It was after midnight and Pete sat in the dark, on the edge of the bed, waiting for his wife to come home.

He had been looking out the window, off and on, for the last two hours or so.

He could not believe she would take off like that, and stay gone till after midnight, when Pete knew exactly where she was going.

He thought countless times about calling her, but decided that he would not try to force her to come home. He would wait to see just when common sense told her it was time to come back.

And now, as he saw headlights hit the bedroom window, he got up and looked out to see that it was indeed Carla pulling into the driveway.

He made his way out of the bedroom and stopped at the top of the stairs, asking himself, what Wayne and his wife could have been doing for more than twelve hours.

Pete tried to calm himself, but those images that Carla had left him with came back: images of her and Wayne in that hotel room, the images of Wayne fucking his wife, of Carla taking him in her mouth. The thoughts continued to strike him like a physical pain.

He told himself to be cool, but it would be hard. So very hard.

The entire house was dark, and he could not hear a thing. But when Pete leaned over the banister he could see, in the faint bit of light from the street lamps outside, Carla trying to sneak into the living room.

She disappeared from his sight, and when he tried to lean out a little farther, the banister made a small creaking sound.

He saw Carla's shadowy image freeze, look over her shoulder in his direction.

Pete held his breath.

After a moment, Carla grabbed her suitcase and started to pull it toward the door.

He knew what she was up to now. She was leaving him. Going back to Wayne, to sleep with him again, to let him do whatever he wanted to her.

Pete would not allow that, not again. He threw himself down the stairs, moving so fast that he missed a few steps, almost falling as he stumbled down.

Carla screamed, hurried toward the open door dragging the suitcase, but Pete was on her. He grabbed her around the waist and kicked the door closed with his foot. He whirled her around to the sofa, Carla losing her grip on the suitcase.

"You were with him, weren't you?" Pete said.

Carla had landed face first in the sofa cushions. She was trying to turn around to see Pete, but he grabbed her by her hair, forced her face back into the sofa.

"You were fucking him again, and now you're coming back to get your things so you can go back to him!"

"Stop it, Pete," Carla yelled. But Pete did not release his grip. With his other hand, he reached around in front of her, trying to undo her pants.

"No!" she screamed out, trying to fight him, kick him.

He forced her face deeper into the cushions. She was having trouble breathing.

Pete pressed his body into hers, restricting her movement.

"You can fuck him, but you don't want to fuck me!" he said.

Carla felt her belt buckle come loose, felt her pants and panties being pulled down to her knees.

She fought some more, with everything she had. "No, Pete!" she cried again. "Please!" But her screams were muffled.

He was going to rape her. She could not believe it, but she knew it was going to happen.

She felt him release her hair, felt him grab hold firmly to her behind with both hands. She felt the hard tip of his penis clumsily pushing into her cheeks, trying to find his way inside her.

With everything she had, Carla pushed back from the sofa with her arms. It did not free her, but it allowed her to breathe, and it allowed Pete to hear her when she screamed, "Pete, please don't do this. I'm pregnant!"

Immediately his grip loosened and his hands fell away completely. Carla squirmed away from him, to the far corner of the couch, pulling up her pants.

She fumbled for the light switch, almost knocking the lamp over but finally turning it on.

Light was shed on Pete, standing a few feet from her, his pants undone, but pulled back up, a look of wonder on his face. "You're pregnant?" It appeared to Carla, that something very near a smile was about to emerge on Pete's face, but then, out of nowhere, he looked to be troubled by a thought. The hint of that smile disappeared, and he said, "By who?"

"I don't know," Carla said, then, only after the fact, asked herself why she hadn't lied instead of telling the truth.

Pete staggered back, as if he'd been clubbed over the head by the reality of his wife's words. He shut his eyes tight, grimaced, then threw a hand over his face. His voice was muffled, but Carla still heard when he yelled, "You let him do this to you!" Again he staggered on his feet. "We're married, and you let him do this to you!" When he pulled his hand back down, there were tears in his eyes.

"I didn't say it was his," Carla said.

"I'm going to take care of this," Pete said, more to himself than to Carla. He whipped his head about the room, as if looking for something. When he spotted his keys, he raced to them, grabbing them from the bookshelf, and again said, "I'm going to take care of this, once and for all."

He threw open the door and ran out.

Carla stumbled after him, falling to her knees just outside the doorway.

She saw Pete jump into his car, back recklessly out of the driveway, then speed off.

70

A moment later, Wayne said, "Hello," after picking up his phone.

"Leave!" It was Carla. She was frantic.

"What's wrong?"

"Just leave, Wayne. Pete's on his way over there."

"Calm down. He's not going to do anything. Everything is going to be all right."

"No, it's not. I don't know what's wrong with him. He tried to rape me, Wayne."

"What!"

"I said, he tried to rape me! Please, just get out of there before he comes."

"No! It's time I handle this situation now. I'm tired of this shit. I'm tired!"

Carla started crying. "Then I'm coming over."

"No! You stay right there. I'll call you when all this is over."

71

Pete was so enraged that he could barely keep the speeding car on the road. He smeared tears from his face with the back of a hand, as he whipped the car around the corner, almost losing control, racing down Wayne's block.

He rolled one of the tires up on the curb when he parked, left the keys in the ignition, kicked the door open, and stomped across the lawn toward Wayne's house.

He could not think. His mind was too crowded with hate, with sounds of his wife crying in fear of him, moaning in ecstasy with Wayne. Snippets of her body intertwined with Wayne's, her mouth wrenched open, begging him to "Fuck me! Fuck me, Wayne!" As he neared the house, Pete tried to shake the thoughts, tried to quiet the racket between his ears, but he could not rid himself of it, could not clear the red haze that colored everything he saw. It colored the stairs he climbed, the sight of the front door opening, of Wayne standing behind it.

Pete moved even faster up the stairs now, feeling more of a purpose.

He saw Wayne push open the glass outer door, hold it open for him.

Wayne's mouth moved. "We need to talk about this, Pete." That was what Pete thought Wayne said, but he could not read the words through the red haze, could barely hear a thing over the screaming in his mind. Besides, Pete wasn't there to talk.

Jumping up on the last step, Pete raced at Wayne, grabbed him around the collar, and with all his weight, bulldozed him into the house.

Pete felt Wayne grasping his arms, trying to push them away, beat them off. But Pete would not let go.

Wayne fell backward, tripping, stumbling over his own feet.

He was saying things again, trying to talk to Pete, but still the racket would not let Pete hear him.

Then Pete felt his feet tangle with Wayne's, felt Wayne falling, saw his eyes bulge wide, saw his mouth open as though he was yelling.

And just before both men fell, Pete on top of Wayne, the screaming in his mind went quiet and the red fog cleared, allowing Pete to hear two sounds: One was Wayne desperately yelling out his best friend's name, and the other was the back of Wayne's head hitting the brick corner border, just in front of the fireplace.

The second sound was that of a crack—like a coconut being struck with a hammer.

72

Just a minute away, Carla told herself as she sped toward Wayne's house.

He told her to stay put, but she couldn't. She knew something was wrong, desperately wrong. She just knew it.

Carla wiped at the tears that clouded her vision, that wouldn't stop coming. She kept telling herself that she should've found some way to stop Pete from going over there. She should've followed him, or tried harder to convince Wayne to leave.

But she hadn't, and now she feared that when she arrived she'd find that something terrible had happened.

73

Both bodies, Pete's and Wayne's, lay still.

Pete waited to feel movement from his friend, waited to feel him fight to get up, but there was no movement at all.

Then all Pete desperately wanted to know was that Wayne was still alive. And Pete waited again to feel the slightest rise of his chest, the faintest beat of Wayne's heart against his own, the warm breath from his mouth on the side of Pete's face. But there was not that either.

Pete raised his head, looked down at Wayne, saw that his eyes were closed, and then saw the narrow trail of blood spilling out from under his friend's head.

Pete jumped off him, pushed back away from him, wide eyed, fearful, his head now totally clear, realizing the horrible thing he had done.

"Wayne," Pete called out. "Wayne!"

No answer.

Pete quickly moved back over him, stuck two fingers into his neck to feel for a pulse. There wasn't one.

He placed his ear over Wayne's nose and mouth, looking for some sign of life, but still found nothing.

"Dammit!" Pete cursed.

But he was a doctor. He knew what to do. He could save him. He had to.

Pete tilted Wayne's head back gently to open his airway. He kneeled over him, held his nose closed, covered Wayne's mouth with his own, and breathed two full breaths into Wayne's body.

He watched as his chest inflated, then deflated. Pete then rose up, clamped his hands together, pressed the butt of one of them against Wayne's chest and started compressions.

Pete could not let him die.

74

Carla pulled up behind Pete's car. She could tell by the way it was parked, as though he had crashed into the curb, that things had gotten horribly out of hand.

She threw open her door, running as fast as she could toward the house.

75

"Come on, dammit, Wayne! Come on!" Pete yelled, still mashing down on Wayne's chest, sweat falling from his face.

He quickly lowered himself again, gave him two more breaths. He listened to see if Wayne was breathing on his own, but Wayne still wasn't.

"Please!" Pete yelled, and the thought of losing his best friend became harder and harder to fight. His head was starting to fill again, but this time with memories of him and Wayne, of when they were ten, footracing in the street. When they were seventeen, taking Wayne's brand-new car out for a spin, and not six months ago, when they laughed at a baseball game, sharing a couple of beers.

Wayne just told him how much he loved Pete, how much Pete would miss him if they weren't partners anymore, and now Pete knew he was right. And it seemed now that Wayne was going to die. And it would've been because Pete had killed him.

Pete was about to give Wayne more compressions when he heard a deafening scream behind him.

He turned his head. Carla was there, just inside the house, hysterical.

"Call an ambulance," Pete yelled.

"You killed him!"

"Carla, call 911!" Pete said, starting compressions again. "If you want him to live, call an ambulance!"

Pete heard his wife making the phone call, heard her give the address, and a moment later, Carla appeared on the other side of Wayne.

"I called them," she said, her face wet with tears. "They said they're right around the corner."

She looked down at Wayne, started to sob. "Don't let him die, Pete. Don't let him die."

Just then Wayne let out a cough.

"Hold it!" Pete said, removing his hands. "Come on, buddy. You can do it."

Wayne coughed a few more times, then gasped heavily, breathed in a great gulp of air.

"That's it, Wayne!" Pete yelled.

"Thank God," Carla said.

Carla and Pete both kneeled over Wayne, waiting for him to show some sign that he was okay.

He did by barely opening his eyes, looking up at both of them, and saying in a groggy voice, "Look, it's my two favorite people."

"Now, that's what I'm talking about!" Pete said.

Carla lowered herself to Wayne, kissed all over his face, on his lips. "Everything is going to be all right. We called the paramedics, and they should be here any second."

And just then a siren could be heard blaring, getting increasingly louder.

"I'm sorry about all this," he said, his words coming slow, his voice barely above a whisper.

"It's not your fault," Carla said.

And then all of a sudden, Wayne's eyes fell closed, his head falling to the side.

Shock appeared on Carla's face. She shook Wayne by the shoulder. "No!" she said. "Wake up!"

"Wayne?" Pete said.

Carla grabbed him by his shirt, shook him more.

Wayne's eyes opened again, barely focused.

"You will not die, you hear me," Carla cried as two paramedics rushed through the door, carrying supplies and a gurney.

But Wayne didn't look as though he was hearing Carla, looked as though his mind was going elsewhere, his eyes focused on the distance before him.

"You will not die!" Carla yelled louder. "Because I'm pregnant, and I'm carrying your child."

Wayne's eyes opened just the slightest bit wider, focusing on her now.

"That's right," Carla said, looking up at Pete, then back down to Wayne. "I'm carrying our baby, and I know it's going to be a little girl, and what are we going to name her, Wayne?"

"Ma'am, you have to move," one of the paramedics said, dropping his supplies beside Wayne, then falling to his knees.

"What are we going to name her, Wayne!" Carla said, raising her voice, moving out the way so the men could work. "Tell me that, and I'll know you're going to be all right. What are we going to name our little girl?" Carla said, tears streaming from her eyes now even more.

And just before the paramedic covered Wayne's face with an oxygen mask, he said in the softest voice, "Morning."

His eyes closed, and his head fell limp again.

"Okay, we're losing him!" The other paramedic shouted.

One of the men ripped open Wayne's shirt, the other pressing the defibrillator paddles to his bare chest.

"Clear!" he said, pressing a button that sent a powerful charge through Wayne, violently jolting his body off the floor, slamming him back down again.

Carla buried her face in Pete's shoulder. He wrapped his arm around her, held her tight.

76

Again!" shouted the emergency medical technician. The paddles were pressed to Wayne's chest for a second time.

"Clear!"

Once more Wayne was zapped, the current of electricity racing through him, making his body jerk up from the floor, his arms flail, his lifeless legs kick.

Another, dark-haired, technician pressed two fingers against Wayne's neck.

"Still no pulse."

Pete stepped forward, releasing Carla from a protective embrace. "Give me the paddles," he instructed the sandy-haired EMT.

"Sir, I cannot—"

"I'm this man's brother. And I'm a doctor. Now give me the fucking paddles."

The man held them out. Pete snatched them from his hands. To the other EMT he shouted, "Increase to 400 joules."

"Four hundred joules," echoed the EMT.

"Clear," Pete shouted, as he pressed the surface of the paddles against Wayne's chest. He administered the shock. "Pulse."

"Nothing."

"Increase to 500," Pete yelled over his shoulder.

"Five hundred joules," he heard shouted back to him.

"Clear!" Pete yelled.

Wayne's body was violently raised off the floor again, then slammed back.

"Pete, save him," Carla cried.

"Increase to 600 joules," Pete said.

"Doctor—" he heard one of the EMTs say.

"Six hundred, or do I have to do it myself?"

"Six hundred joules."

Pete prayed as he laid the paddles against his brother's chest. He looked down onto Wayne's face, his closed eyes, the skin on his cheeks starting to pale. Pete knew this was the last opportunity. If he could not revive Wayne this time, Wayne's brain would die. Pete told himself that could not happen. It would not happen.

"Clear," he shouted, looking up at Carla, her eyes wide, tears and mascara streaming down her face. Her hands were pressed together in desperate prayer.

Pete shocked his brother for the final time.

"Pulse," he ordered, holding his breath, turning to the dark-haired EMT.

The man looked up at Pete, shaking his head. "I'm sorry. No pulse."

Carla dropped her face into her hands, began rocking on her knees. "No! No! No!"

Pete stared at her. He hated her at that moment. For all that lay before him. He looked at the dark-haired EMT again. The man looked away from him, at the floor. He looked toward the other man, who turned away as well.

This wasn't real, Pete told himself. It couldn't be. Wayne wasn't beneath him, lying dead. It wasn't Wayne, Pete kept telling himself, afraid to look down.

"Doctor," Pete heard an EMT say, his voice meek.

"What?" Pete turned to him, anger on his face.

"Are you going to pronounce him?"

Pete wanted to lunge at the man, snag him by the front of his shirt, beat him for what he had just said. But he did nothing, just continued kneeling there, blank-faced, the paddles hanging from his hands.

"You have to pronounce him," the other EMT said.

Pete glared at him, then told himself that they were right. Wayne was dead. It had to be documented. He looked down at his brother's face, the face he had known for almost all his life, the face that he would never see smile at him ever again. "Time of death . . ." Pete said glancing at the clock on Wayne's wall, "11:32 P.M."

77

Carla sat beside Pete in Wayne's bedroom. She didn't want to be in there. Not long ago, she had lain in this bed with Wayne, and now he was dead and she didn't know who was to blame.

She had thrown a blanket over Pete's shoulders, had put an arm around him, was trying to comfort him. All he did was stare out at the wall before him, not saying a word.

"I wonder what they're doing out there?" Carla said, trying to get her husband talking, as she had been trying to do for the last half hour, while the coroner's officers worked on Wayne's body in the living room.

She heard the sound of a two-way radio, heard footsteps, and saw two police officers step into the doorway.

Carla immediately stood. "Can I help you with something?"

The policeman had a bushy mustache. He said, "Uh, yes, ma'am. We're going to have to take your husband to the station for some questioning."

"What are you talking about, questioning?"

"Questioning, ma'am," the other officer said. The name on his tag was Meyers. "We understand your husband was involved in an altercation with the deceased prior to his death. We have to ask your husband questions about that."

Carla stepped in front of the two uniformed men, spreading

her arms. "You aren't taking him anywhere until our lawyer gets here."

"You can call your lawyer, ma'am," Meyers said. "But you can't stop us from taking him to the station."

"Yes, I—"

"It's okay, Carla," Pete said, his voice soft. He was still staring at the space just in front of him. "I'll go with you, officers." He stood slowly.

The other officer stepped behind Pete, handcuffed him, and came back around, staring into his face. He said, "Hey, aren't you the guy who filed that adultery complaint a little while ago?"

"And that's the guy that we arrested lying dead there in the living room," Meyers said, as though it was all coming to him now.

Both officers looked at Carla, then at Pete. They exchanged a glance with each other, and one said, "I hope it was worth it." They led Pete out of the room.

"I'll call John," Carla yelled to her husband. "Don't say anything. I'll call John, and he'll take care of everything."

78

An hour later, Pete sat slump-shouldered in a wooden chair, his wrists still cuffed together.

Although he heard all the movement around him, phones ringing, gruff voices talking, heavy footsteps moving back and forth in front of him, he saw only one thing. Wayne's face was burned into his mind. No matter how hard Pete tried to clear his mind of that image, of the blood that spilled out from under Wayne's head, he could not.

Pete felt the presence of someone who had just sat beside him, but he did not open his eyes.

"Pete," he heard someone say.

He looked up to see the familiar brown face of his attorney, John Staton. John wore a brown suit and gold wire-framed glasses. He smiled sadly. "Carla called me. She told me everything that happened."

"Where is she?" Pete asked.

"She's out front. They wouldn't let her back here. But she's fine. Everything's going to be fine. Okay?" John said, clapping Pete on the shoulder.

Pete didn't answer, just turned his eyes to the floor.

Moments later, a large man in a gray suit asked Pete to stand and follow him.

John quickly stood beside Pete, as if to protect him. The big man looked at John.

"John Staton," he said. "I'm Dr. Barnes's attorney. I'll be accompanying him."

"This way," the suited man said.

Pete and John were led to a small square room, one wall made of mirrored glass.

"Have a seat right there, sir," the officer said to Pete, pointing to a chair behind a long metal-topped table.

Pete sat wearily where he was told.

The man undid the cuff from one of Pete's wrists, looped it through a metal bar on the table, then cuffed Pete back again.

"Is that absolutely necessary?" John asked.

"Protocol," the man said to John. Then, to Pete, "The detective investigating your case will be in shortly."

Pete didn't speak or acknowledge what the man said. He heard the door open and close. He sat staring at his hands. He couldn't stop thinking about Wayne lying dead before him.

"We have to decide how we'll address this," Pete heard John say. John walked in front of the table and stared down at Pete.

Pete shut his eyes.

"Pete," John said. "We have to—"

"I want you to leave, John. I don't need an attorney."

John pulled up a chair opposite Pete, sat down, and looked at him intently. "What are you talking about?"

"You're here trying to defend me. There is no defense for what I did. Wayne is dead because I—"

"Don't say that."

"Say what?"

"What you were about to say," John said. "You went to Wayne's house. The two of you got into a tussle, Wayne fell. He hit his head. You didn't intend that to happen, did you?"

"He was sleeping with my wife."

"So what? That means that you were intent on killing him?"

Pete lowered his head.

"Is that what it means, Pete? Did you go over there for that reason?"

"No, but—"

"Then there was no intent," John said. "A man who accidentally kills a child that, from nowhere, runs out into the street, is involved in a horrible accident, but it's just that—an accident. You no more deserve to spend time in jail than he does," John said, moving his chair closer to the table, attempting to look deeper into Pete's eyes. "You and Wayne have been friends since childhood. You were practically brothers. You know, just like I do, there was no way you meant to kill him. This is much more a tragedy than a crime. I will explain that to the police, and they will understand. That is, if you'll just let me."

"And if I say no? If I say I won't be able to live with myself if I'm not charged for what I've done?" Pete said.

"Then I'd say, maybe you need to seek out grief counseling of some sort, because you might be depressed. But I know you, and you're no murderer."

"I'll let the legal system decide that."

"Is that what you really want?" John asked, standing from his chair.

"Yeah. I think so," Pete said, sadly.

"All right, Pete. You always were the righteous type. So, I'll let you do things your way. You can roll the dice and hope they don't lock you away for the rest of your life."

John walked across the room about to walk out, but then said, "Oh, and congratulations on the pregnancy. Carla told me about that, too. I wonder just how righteous you'll feel raising your child behind bars."

For some strange reason, Pete had never thought about that repercussion.

John released the doorknob and took a step back toward Pete. "We aren't lying or doing anything illegal, because *you* didn't do anything illegal. I'll tell the investigator the story how it happened, they'll want to ask you some questions, and then they'll make a decision, but I'm sure you'll be free to go. Guilty conscience and all. Will you let me do that?"

Before Pete could answer, a tall thin man, wearing a shoulder gun holster over a white shirt and red tie, entered the room. He held a manila folder with Pete's name on it. He quickly looked over Pete, then glanced at John and said, "I'm detective McPherson. I'll be handling this case."

"Hi, Detective McPherson," John said, extending a hand, and smiling thinly. "I'm John Staton, Dr. Barnes's attorney. Would you mind if I spoke to you in private for just a moment?"

The detective glanced again at Pete, who looked away.

"No problem," Detective McPherson said.

Pete looked up, saw John give him a confident smile as he followed the detective out of the room.

Forty minutes later, the handcuffs were taken off Pete by the large gray-suited man.

Pete rubbed his wrists. "What's going on?"

Before the detective could answer, John walked through the door, smiling. He waited for the detective to leave, then dragged up a chair in front of Pete.

"There's a few questions you'll have to answer, sign some paperwork, and agree not to leave the state during the investigation, but just like I told you, they're letting you go. That's great news, hunh."

"Yeah," Pete said, no enthusiasm in his tone whatsoever. "Great."

79

It was supposed to have been quick and free of emotion, Pete thought when he entertained the idea of telling Me'Shell about what happened.

He wasn't up to it, he was too much of an emotional wreck himself, but he didn't want her to find out from anyone else.

When he knocked on her door, it was after 2 A.M. As he stood there listening to the chains being undone, Pete told himself that he would tell her the news, and then simply leave. He could not endure the tears that he expected her to cry, he could not console her, because he was not even able to console himself.

She wore a robe over a nightgown. She had cracked the door open, even though she had known it was him by looking through the peephole.

"Pete, what is it? It's after two in the morning."

"I have to talk to you. Can I come in?"

"Can't it wait till a more reasonable hour?"

"No, Me'Shell. It really can't."

Pete saw the look on her face go from sleepy to worried. She opened the door wider, and stepped back to let him in.

"What is it, Pete?"

"I think you should sit."

Pete followed Me'Shell over to her sofa, sat with her.

He didn't remember exactly how he told her the news. He knew words were coming out of his mouth, he heard his own voice speaking them, but he didn't even really know what he was saying.

She took the news hard. He knew that much by the look of utter disbelief that covered her face.

She said, "No. I don't believe you."

He remembered saying, "It's true."

She didn't cry out, but silent tears ran down her cheeks.

"How did it happen?" She asked.

Pete hesitated, then he told her it was all his fault. He confessed how he sped over there, how things got out of hand, and Pete tried to save Wayne's life, but he failed. He thought of telling Me'Shell that he had lost his control because Carla told him that Wayne may have gotten her pregnant, but he knew that news would hurt her. What good would it do other than to make him feel less guilty?

"You didn't meant to do it, did you?" Me'Shell said, placing a hand on his shoulder.

"No. I didn't."

"And you're sorry that it happened."

"So sorry."

Pete felt a tear fall from his eye. He quickly brushed it away. But he could not stop the others from flowing, when Me'Shell leaned over, took him in her arms and held him tight.

"I know you didn't mean it," she said. "But more important, he knows that, too. Wayne knows that."

He held tight to Me'Shell, thankful for her understanding, but not feeling any less guilty.

"You told him that we didn't really sleep together, didn't you? That it was just a prank," Me'Shell asked, her arms still around Pete.

Pete froze. He didn't answer, because he had not told Wayne

that. In the midst of all that was going on, the struggle, the fight to save his life, he had never thought of that. Without question, he should have told him.

Me'Shell slowly pulled away from him, her hands still on Pete's arms. "He didn't die thinking that I did something like that to him, did he?" Me'Shell asked, sounding more concerned.

"It all happened so fast. I didn't think to—"

Me'Shell slid away from Pete, wrapping her arms around herself. "I loved him, and that's the last impression that he had of me, sleeping with his best friend."

"Me'Shell, I'm sorry," Pete said, reaching out in effort to console her. She slid further away from him, into the corner of the sofa.

"It was your idea. You came to me with it," she said, smearing tears from her cheeks. "How could you forget to tell him that we really didn't do it, when you knew he was going to die?"

"Me'Shell."

"Get out."

Pete stood. "Me'Shell, please listen to me."

"He needed to know that it didn't really happen. Wayne needed to know. Now just leave!"

80

"That'll be $156.76, sir. How will you be paying?" the young man behind the hotel desk asked Pete.

Pete hadn't heard what the man said. He was too deep into his thoughts for the question to have registered.

"Sir," the man said again. "How would you like to pay for your room?"

Pete mechanically pulled his wallet from his pants pocket, slid out his credit card, and laid it on the desk.

"Thank you," the man said.

The room was large, a suite. A huge chandelier hung from the ceiling in the sitting room. Pete dragged himself into the bedroom, lifted the receiver from the phone, and set it beside its base. He walked back into the living room, and took the receiver off the hook there as well.

Pete sat on the sofa, pulled his cell phone from his pocket. There were the twenty missed calls from his wife that should have been on his phone that night, seemingly so long ago, when he had foolishly slept with the woman at the W hotel.

He had set the phone on silent while in the police station. Now Pete set it on the coffee table, not bothering to change the setting.

He wondered what his wife was doing that very moment. Probably sitting at home, crying, bawling her eyes out for Wayne. But for what reason? Because he was dead, or because she could no longer be with him?

Pete felt that twinge of hatred again that he had experienced for his wife when he had looked at her over his brother's dead body.

What would happen between the two of them now? If there ever came a day when he felt he could live a normal life again, he would have to ask himself that question. But Pete didn't think that day would ever come.

He had killed his best friend, killed him with his bare hands. Wayne was gone from this earth forever, gone from all the patients that came to see him at his practice, gone from all his friends, gone from his parents.

Pete was hit with the painful thought that he would be telling Wayne's parents—telling the couple that had become Pete's father and mother—that he had killed their son, their real son.

He shot up from the sofa, whipped his head from side to side, clamped his palms over his ears, as if trying to stop all these thoughts from bombarding him.

It didn't work. The images kept coming. The sound of Wayne hitting his head, Carla crying for Pete to save Wayne's life, Me'Shell kicking him out of her house. They would not stop. And then there were the final words Wayne spoke to Pete. "I'm sorry about all this," he said, looking up from the ground, bleeding from his skull.

Wayne apologized to Pete, even though Pete had come to his house bent on revenge and had ended up killing him.

It was too much. Pete could not do it anymore, could not live with this anymore. He rushed over to the closet, slid both double doors back. He saw the thick white bathrobe, saw the tie that hung at its waist. He pulled the tie from its loops.

He hurried across the room to the desk, grabbed the desk chair, and dragged it to the center of the room, just below the chandelier.

Pete looked up, and was thankful for the high ceilings.

He climbed on top of the chair, hoping that the light fixture would be strong enough to support his weight. With the bathrobe tie in one hand, he reached up, grabbed two sides of the lamp, testing it. He swung momentarily from the lamp, his feet dangling some two feet above the carpet. The lamp supported his weight, at least for the short time he hung from it. He hoped it would hold long enough for him to do what needed to be done.

It was the right thing, Pete told himself, as he went about fashioning a noose with the bathrobe tie. As doubts crept through his mind, he pushed them out. This had to be done.

He carefully fastened one end of the tie around the base of the lamp. The other end, the noose end, hung down.

He pulled the noose open and slide it over his head and down around his neck.

He could feel the hot tears slide down his face, but he told himself this would be quick. There would be a few moments of struggle, and then it would all be over.

Pete reached above the knot, and slid it down, tightening it against the base of his skull.

He spread his feet to either side of the chair. He would rock it, topple it over, and then gravity would finish the job.

Suddenly, something caught Pete's eye. It was the light on his cell phone, over on the coffee table. The screen lit up, and the red light on its corner blinked. He was getting a call.

At three in the morning, he knew it could only be his wife.

Pete continued watching the phone until the screen went dark, and the blinking stopped. It was time now. He had to do it now, or he might lose his nerve.

He allowed himself to think one last time of Wayne. He knew his brother was probably watching him, possibly sitting on the sofa, looking up at him, wishing that he could convince Pete not to do this. He had always wanted Pete to do what he said—but there was nothing Wayne could do now, and Pete smiled just a little, finding the slightest bit of humor in finally being able to have his way.

Pete prepared himself again to do what he would do, when he was startled by music that blasted suddenly from the clock radio. It came on for what seemed no reason at all. Pete thought of climbing down, turning it off, knowing it would eventually draw attention to the room, maybe make staff come in to investigate. But he would be dead by then. Besides, the volume on the song wasn't that loud, Pete thought. Then he realized it was the song that was his and Wayne's favorite as sophomores in high school. They had pushed their old recorder up to the radio, recorded it, and played it over and over again.

Pete could have made more of this than the coincidence he knew it was, but he didn't. The song went off, and another one came on.

Pete would now have his way.

But then a knocking came at the door.

Pete whipped around, listening as though the knocking could have been just his imagination.

It came again.

Just do it, Pete thought. Tip the chair, and get it over with. But he would be heard by whoever was knocking at the door. He had to answer it.

Pete pulled his head from the noose, climbed down off the chair, and peered through the peephole.

A man, blond, wearing the hotel's blue and red suit, stood outside.

Pete opened the door.

"Is there a problem?" Pete said.

"You forgot your credit card downstairs, sir," the smiling man said. "They asked me to bring it up to you."

"Oh. Thank you," Pete said, taking the card from the man's hand.

The man did not respond, just stared at Pete with piercing gray eyes, a simple smile on his face. His presence made Pete feel both calm and unsettled at the same time.

"Okay, then," Pete said, moving to close the door.

The man smiled wider and said, "If you have any other questions, don't hesitate to call the desk and ask for Wayne."

Pete held the door. "What did you say your name was?"

"Wayne."

Pete's heart began to pound in his chest, and he felt unsteady on his feet.

"Is everything okay, sir?"

"Yes. Everything is fine. Good night," Pete said.

"Good night, sir. And remember," the man said. "Life's worth living."

"Excuse me?"

"I said, life's worth living. Goodnight, Dr. Barnes."

The man turned and walked away.

Pete watched him all the way down the hall, till he turned and disappeared around a corner.

Pete felt dizzy and uncertain, as though he was being watched.

The man's name was Wayne . . . it could happen. The radio played because it must have been set to go off. But what the man had said: why would he say that? Why in the world would he speak of the value of life just when Pete was about to take his own? Then, as Pete closed the door, he noticed a sign on the back of it advertising the hotel's spa services. He read the last sentence aloud: "Indulge yourself when at the Peninsula Hotel, because—*Life Is Worth Living*."

81

Carla had not seen her husband in three days. She had called him more times than she could remember, all of her calls going directly to voicemail. When she called now, she could not even leave a message because the mailbox was full.

Carla went to Pete's orthopedic practice several times, but his receptionist told her that he had not been in, and she didn't know where he was.

"The offices are actually closed, Mrs. Barnes. We're just in to reschedule patients."

Carla didn't know what was going on. She didn't know if Pete was dead or alive, still in Chicago or not.

She tried to keep him updated, and thankfully she was able to leave information regarding Wayne's funeral on Pete's voicemail before it had filled up.

She told him the time and the place, and that she needed to see him there. Everyone did.

The nights after Wayne's death, Carla cried herself to sleep.

She felt it was selfish of Pete to not be there to comfort her, not be there to allow her to comfort him, to allow them to grieve together.

She knew Pete blamed himself for his brother's death, and although Carla fought with exactly where to place the blame, she tried her best not to fault Pete entirely.

The night of Wayne's death, Carla had called him, warned him that Pete was on his way over there. If Wayne had just left like she had asked him to, then he would still be alive.

Each night now before lying down in her bed, Carla said a prayer for Wayne. How she had missed him.

The night of Wayne's death, the night Carla had gone back to get her bag and had told Pete that she was pregnant to stop him from raping her, she still did not know for sure who she had wanted to be with. She still had a decision to make then. But now Wayne was dead.

There was only Pete now.

Carla hoped he would show for the funeral, and told herself that if she saw her husband there, she would tell him that she still loved him despite what happened. She would tell him that she didn't blame him for Wayne's death.

Carla knew he would be happy to hear that. She knew it was the reason he was probably staying away, feeling that she would not accept him back after what he had done.

But she would ease his mind, once and for all.

82

For the remainder of the time that Pete was at the hotel, he had not wanted to kill himself anymore. He didn't know if everything that had happened that night was all just strange coincidence, or if Wayne was somehow working magic from above.

The following day, he made a point of going downstairs to thank Wayne No. 2 for delivering his credit card to him.

But Pete was told no one named Wayne worked there.

"Medium-height guy," Pete said, describing him. "Blond hair, weird gray eyes. I guess he works the midnight shift or something."

"I'm sorry, sir. But I'm the manager, and we have no Wayne that works here, midnight, or any other shift, for that matter."

"Oh, okay," Pete said, smiling, and headed back to his room, not believing the manager.

The night before the funeral, Pete lay in bed, staring up at the ceiling, his hands crossed under his head.

"I hope you don't mind me coming to see you off tomorrow before the actual funeral. I want to go to the funeral, but it'll be too much for everyone, your friends, mom and dad, knowing that I'm the reason you aren't here anymore. And more than anything, I think it'll be too much for me as well. I just don't belong there. But I want you to know that I am deeply sorry for all that has happened. I love you, brother."

Pete clicked off the light, and allowed sleep to quickly take him.

The next morning Pete checked out of the hotel, and drove to his practice. There was something from Wayne's office he needed to get. Afterward, he would have to drive home to dress for the funeral and pick up a few things. He told himself that if Carla was there, then they would have the talk that he had been needing to have with her over the last three days.

The funeral was at 4 P.M.

He waited at home for Carla till some time after one.

Pete wanted to get there well before anyone else arrived. He wanted to have time to sit with Wayne, talk to him, say a proper farewell to him.

When Pete arrived at the funeral home, he was ushered back to the room where Wayne's body was placed for viewing.

"Will there be anything else you need?" the graying man in the black suit asked Pete before stepping out.

"No, sir. Thank you."

Pete was left just inside the wide doorway. Wayne lay on the other end of a large room filled with empty chairs. Pete walked slowly down the aisle in the center of the room. He stopped just in front of the casket, looking down into it, at his brother.

Wayne lay there looking peaceful, his hands resting on his chest. He did not look dead, but like he had just been sleeping, resting, the way Pete had seen him so many times when they were children. Pete smiled, allowing himself to remember all the good times they had shared. He had made a great effort over the last three days to rid himself of all the pain and confusion they had suffered during the last weeks of Wayne's life. Pete reached into the casket and brushed a piece of lint from the lapel of Wayne's suit coat.

"Everything has to be perfect for your last big day here on earth, you know what I mean."

Pete smiled again, but only to hide the tears he told himself he would not let come.

"I'm not going to do this, man. I'm not going to cry," Pete said aloud, laughing. "Why should I? So you can call me a sissy?" He smoothed what could have turned into a tear from under his eye, shook a finger at Wayne. "Not a chance. Oh, and I like all the trouble you went through at the hotel. I never could get my way with you, and still can't even after you're gone. Everything has to be done your way, or no way at all. That's right, good ol' Wayne," Pete said, his voice starting to fill with emotion.

He took the first seat in the row next to the casket and dropped his face in his hands, unable to mask his pain any longer.

"Goddammit, Wayne. Forgive me for what I've done to you. You allowed me in when I had no one. You take me into your family, and I do this."

Pete stood, walked back to the casket again, lowered a trembling hand, and placed it upon Wayne's chest.

"I gotta go, Wayne. But know I'll never forget you."

Pete leaned over, kissed his brother lightly on the forehead.

When he turned, he was shocked to see Carla standing twenty feet behind him, wearing a black dress, shoes, and gloves.

With both his palms he smeared the wet tears from his face.

Carla quickly closed the space between them, throwing herself into him, wrapping her arms around him. "I've been so worried. I didn't know where you were. I have some things I need to tell you."

Pete stood there, his arms to his sides, showing no emotion. "We can talk, but not in here."

"I don't blame you," Carla said, the two of them now in a small, private room, the double doors closed. "What happened was unfortunate, but—"

"Unfortunate!" Pete said.

"It was horrible, unspeakable. Don't act like I'm not feeling pain, too. Don't act like I didn't love Wayne as much as you did," Carla said.

"I know how much you loved him. It's not like you were trying to keep it a secret."

"Pete, we've been through all this before. It's the reason Wayne is being buried today. Why continue to dwell on it? I think it's time we start concerning ourselves with the present, and the future."

"Okay," Pete said, pulling away from the wall he was leaning against. "Fine. Let's talk about that."

Carla smiled a little. "Like I was trying to tell you, I'm not mad at you for what happened. I'm going to miss Wayne as much if not more than you will, but I think we should focus on you and me, make it work between us, otherwise all of this, Wayne's death, everything will be in vain. Do you think he would've wanted that?"

Pete shook his head at what Carla was saying. "I can't even consider what you're saying. You're the reason why Wayne is dead."

"What! And you aren't?"

"Yes. I am. When you were neglecting me, I should've been man enough to tell you to treat me right, or get out of my house. When I told you I had cheated on you, you should've left me. And when you had the nerve to tell me that you wanted permission to sleep with another man, I should've told you to go to hell. But I didn't, and now my brother is dead."

"Pete," Carla said, taking a step toward him. "You're being too—"

"Don't say I'm being too hard on myself. After what I've done, I'll never be the same. I can't look at Wayne's death as an opportunity, as if now that he's out of the way, we can be together. It was wrong of me when I told you about his infidelity. It was wrong of me to have pursued you, to have married you, and it would be wrong for me to be with you again."

Carla seemed saddened, swallowed hard then said, "And your baby. What about your child, Pete?"

"When I first asked you whose child it was, you didn't know. Now you say it's mine," Pete said, walking closer to Carla. "Maybe you ought to think a little longer—there might be a few other men who could be the father."

Carla slapped Pete across the face. It was loud, it stung, and it wrenched his face to one side, but when he turned back to her his expression was calm. "I'm leaving now," he said. "I went by the house earlier and got some of my clothes. I'll send for the rest of my things over the next couple of weeks. I won't be sleeping there anymore."

"Where will you be sleeping?" Carla said.

"Not on the street, not on the dining room table, and definitely not in the guest bedroom, but somewhere. You don't need to know that." Pete moved toward the door.

"Pete. Don't go!" Carla said, rushing to him, pressing herself against him, fresh tears running from her eyes. "I'm sorry for what happened, I'm sorry that Wayne died, and if I had known something like this would've ever happened, I wouldn't have forced you to allow me to sleep with someone else."

"But you did force me," Pete said, taking his wife's arms, pushing her away, managing to free himself. He stepped again to the door.

"Please," Carla said, standing in the middle of the room, her arms wrapped around her trembling body. "What would you have done? It was three times, Pete. Three times. You knew why I left Wayne, why I left Steve before him, but you cheated just like they did, after promising me you wouldn't. I just wanted to make sure it wouldn't happen again. Everything I did was done to get you back. But the child I'm carrying *is* yours," Carla said, rubbing her hand over her belly. "Pete, don't leave me."

Pete stood at the door. She was right. He had broken his promise to her, he had done exactly the same thing he had chastised Wayne for doing. Now Pete's brother was dead, and Pete could not help but think that if he had never betrayed his wife, none of the tragic events would have occurred.

He looked at her. She was in extreme grief. He was not the only one destroyed by what happened. They could share each other's pain. Maybe make sense of it together. Something told Pete to run to her, take her in his arms, and tell her that everything would be okay. He did still love her. He could try to make peace somehow with all that had happened, and the two of them could be together. That had been all he ever wanted. But could he be okay with that now?

During this entire ordeal, Pete had been waiting for his wife to choose if she would stay with him. Now as Pete walked back toward Carla, he realized the decision to make was his.

Pete held open his arms to his wife. She fell into them, wrapping herself tight around him, sinking her face into his shoulder. Pete felt her trembling body start to calm.

If there was ever any question at any other time as to whether she wanted him, there was no more. With certainty, Pete knew all Carla wanted at that moment was him, and to have her back, to try to put things back the way they had been, all he had to do was tell her he would be there for her.

"Carla, I love you," Pete said.

Carla raised her tear-stained face, smiled the slightest bit, and said, "I love you, too."

Pete frowned, thinking of the words he was about to speak, and then he said, "But too much has happened between us. Things can never be the same. We can never be the same. To be honest, I don't ever want us to be." He pulled away from Carla, looking her over as if trying to save her image in his brain. Then he said, "Goodbye, Carla."

She stumbled backward, shock on her face, as if she had been physically assaulted.

"Leave me, and you'll never see your child," Pete heard his wife say as he turned away. "I swear."

Pete turned back. "Don't ever threaten me like that again," he said. "Regardless of whether or not that is my child, or my nephew, I will be a steady presence in its life. I'll admit, over the time we've been married, I haven't been the man I should've been, but test me, Carla, and I will come back with an attorney and take that child from you. Try me."

Pete held his stare on Carla, waiting for a response. When she didn't give one, he stepped through the door and was gone.

In the entrance hall he spotted the graying man who had escorted him earlier, and said, "Can I go back to see my friend? There was something else I needed to say to him."

"Go right ahead, sir."

Pete quickly entered the viewing room. No one had yet arrived for Wayne's funeral, and Pete took the opportunity to say one last thing to his friend. Standing over the casket again, he pulled something from his suit jacket pocket.

"I know I shouldn't have been so hard on her, but I just wanted it to be known that my child will know its father, or your child will know its uncle. Either way, that child is going to get a lot of love. I'll make sure of that."

Pete looked down at the object in his hands, a photograph. He gently placed it in the corner of the casket, near Wayne's head.

"Happy travels, and God bless, Wayne," Pete said, leaving the picture that showed his brother, himself, and old Mr. Ruben, all smiling, arm in arm, on the opening day of their clinic—an image to forever keep Wayne company.

About the Author

RM Johnson is the author of seven novels, including bestsellers *The Harris Family* and *The Million Dollar Divorce*. He holds an MFA in creative writing from Chicago State University and is a native of Chicago, where he currently resides.